A NOVEL

# ALL THE HIDDEN PIECES

D1367060

## JILLIAN THOMADSEN

Cover Design: Cover Me Darling
Interior Formatting: Athena Interior Book Design

# CHAPTER ONE

*September 7, 2017*

There was nothing particularly unusual about the morning the Carpenter family disappeared. Greta woke up early, cooked breakfast for the family and sat at the table in jeans and a sweatshirt while she drank coffee and read emails on her phone. Olivia emerged first – her fine blonde hair matted against her head, her Minnie Mouse pajamas billowing out from her tiny frame.

"Is Daddy awake?" Olivia asked as she claimed a seat at the table.

Greta shook her head but Tuck soon proved her wrong. "I'm awake," a deep voice grunted from behind the doorway and then Tuck stumbled into the kitchen to pour himself a cup of coffee. He was a tall man, almost six foot five and husky like a linebacker. Greta could feel the kitchen floor shudder beneath his tread as he grabbed a plate of eggs and then sat down with them.

Breakfast lasted about ten minutes – its usual length of time. Tuck wolfed down his food and hastened out the door to work. Greta and Olivia lingered a short while longer but there were errands to run, appointments to keep. Greta was just about to clear the table and start the day when the phone rang.

\*\*\*

It was a short phone call, and Greta said very little. When she hung up the receiver, she was surprised to see that she was trembling.

Greta took a beat, leaned against the counter and steadied herself. Her skin felt cold and prickly and her breath felt shorter. Her instinct was to lie down and rest, take a few minutes and regain composure. But she knew she had to do exactly the opposite. They had to move and they had to do it right away.

First she called Tuck. "You need to come home," she said. He started to protest but she explained the phone call she had received. Then she raised her voice. "Now! We need to go. We need to *move now!*" He agreed and they ended the call.

"Mommy, what's wrong?" Olivia asked.

Greta walked to the other side of the table and pulled Olivia into a tight hug. The four-year old smelled like baby shampoo and milk, and she squirmed and giggled in response to Greta's gesture.

"We need to go, okay?" Greta said. "We need to leave right away." Although Greta's body was shaking, her voice was still steady. She stood up and sighed as she took in backyard view for the last time.

Outside the sun shined down in a cloudless sky. It was cold for early September but the sun cast bright diamonds and triangles across the lawn. Greta had looked at the same maple and spruce trees, the same telephone wires and hummingbird feeder for almost two decades. It seemed impossible to say good-bye to something so familiar.

Tuck appeared at the back door again and Greta let him in. He looked sweaty and impatient. "I never made it to the office. I'll need to send them an email to let them know."

"Sounds good."

Olivia hopped over to Tuck and he bent down and lifted her into his arms. "Are we ready to roll?" he asked Greta. "Or do we have to wait for John?"

John was Greta's eighteen-year old son from her first marriage. Somehow—and seemingly overnight—he'd matured from a gawky little kid into an adult. He had pecan-brown hair that used to hang loosely around his shoulders, now fashioned into a trim taper cut. He had grown several inches in the past few years, and Greta marveled that she now had to crane her head when she spoke to him.

"No, we don't have to wait," Greta answered. "We can leave right away."

Tuck put Olivia back on the floor and rushed downstairs – presumably to grab an empty suitcase, but Greta didn't ask.

Olivia ran her index finger along the stitching of her mother's jeans and asked, "Where are we going?"

"We're going on a trip," Greta answered in a heavy voice. "And we need to get moving. I'm going to pack a bag," She lifted her foot and stepped over Olivia in the hallway, then walked into her master bedroom.

The bedroom looked so cozy and comforting, it was impossible for Greta to think that she could be standing in it for the last time. All of these realities had been thrown at her so quickly – they were too large and staggering to digest. This morning she had thrown some eggs into a pan while mentally drawing up her grocery shopping list and now she was removing her clothes from her dresser, playing a real-life game of *What do I pack if I might not be coming back for a long time?*

Tuck came into the room, held up an empty suitcase, and shoved her clothes inside, along with some of his. "Time to leave, okay?" he asked.

She nodded but didn't say a word. Her face was ashen, drained of color. She followed him out of the bedroom and through the hallway, pausing to scoop up Olivia, who was apparently still clad in Minnie Mouse. *No time to change that now.*

Greta took one last sweeping look at the house. Then they all left.

# CHAPTER TWO

*September 14, 2017*

Detective Roberta Hobbs rang the doorbell at 12 Avery Place. She pressed her ear to the door to try to discern any type of noise: a dog's bark, a child's toy, or the patter of small feet against a hardwood floor. But there was no sign of activity from inside the house.

Hobbs' partner, Detective Martinez, pointed to the driveway where a mint-green Honda Civic was parked. It looked old and worn, a bit of rust around the right rear tire and some dry mud caked to the side. "There's a car parked right there in the driveway," Martinez said.

Hobbs had noticed it too, and she nodded her head in response and wrote a few things down on her notepad. Det. Hobbs was 41 years old and had been on the force for sixteen years. Many described her as hardened although smart and diligent. She was a stunning woman – dark-eyed and dark-haired – and she had a long history of fending off advances from men in the department. Her standard response was that she didn't think it was appropriate to date within the workplace, but to those few who paid close attention, Hobbs didn't seem to date anyone at all. She liked to say she was married to the job – dedicated to putting the bad guys behind bars – and her workplace commitment left little time for personal concerns.

On this particular day, Det. Hobbs was hoping for a simple answer to a nagging question: What had happened to Tuck Carpenter? The call from his law office first came into dispatch on September 12. Tuck was a paralegal, famous in his office for taking very few sick or vacation days. Four business days went by before his colleagues contacted the police to report his disappearance.

That was Tuesday. The law firm office sat tight for another two days while they waited to hear back from the police. Any number of scenarios was possible. Perhaps Tuck had just taken a vacation and forgot to key it into the shared calendar. Perhaps he'd decided to quit, and in a fit of hostility and irrationality – both traits that belied his character – he hadn't taken the time to let them know of his decision.

But Tuck wasn't answering his cell phone or his email. By Thursday it had been one full week since Tuck first failed to appear at work. On her lunch break, a legal secretary at the law office drove to the Vetta Park Police Station and officially filed a missing person's report.

This is how Det. Hobbs ended up on Tuck 's front porch, ringing the doorbell and shining her flashlight into the front foyer to see if anything seemed amiss.

"I'm going to look around back," Det. Martinez said. He disappeared and then unlocked the front door from the inside a few minutes later. "I was able to open a door to the basement," he told her once they were both inside.

Hobbs stepped into the foyer and they both donned a pair of latex gloves. The house looked cluttered and dirty. The stench of fetid eggs permeated the air, causing them both to cough and cover their faces.

They started in the rancid area, which was the kitchen. Week-old garbage was seeping out of the bin. The remains of an egg breakfast were left in a saucepan on the burner. Hobbs opened the refrigerator and was surprised to find it packed – full of milk cartons whose sell-by dates had recently expired, Styrofoam containers, decaying fruit and a few vacuum-sealed packets of uncooked chicken.

Hobbs closed the refrigerator door and went down the hall. She cast her flashlight along the interior of a bathroom – nothing unusual. Then she let herself into the master bedroom. The room was tiny – the stale air casting a musty smell. Almost every surface was covered with clothes. Hobbs ran her flashlight over the clothes, the bedspread and a paper-covered desk. Then the shine alighted on a framed family portrait on the back edge of the dresser. Hobbs walked over and studied it more carefully. There was a tall man, a beautiful blonde woman with delicate features, a pig-tailed little girl and an older teenage boy. Hobbs had glanced through their records and knew who they were: Tuck Carpenter, age 45, Greta Carpenter, age 38, Olivia Carpenter, age 4, and John Brock, age 18.

Hobbs wanted to place the photograph back on its shelf and resume her search but something prevented her. It was the appearance of Greta Carpenter, or more precisely, the way the matriarch's eyes focused on the camera lens, her heart-shaped mandible that summoned a vague memory.

Hobbs couldn't remember context or place but she'd seen the eyes and the face before. It wasn't just that Greta resembled a 1970s picture art heroine; there was something about the face that had beseeched her in the past. Maybe in a broken down shell of a car on the side of the road, inside someone's private residence, or maybe beyond the hermetically sealed window in the front area of the police station. Hobbs couldn't recall exactly what had happened but she knew there was a history. Greta Carpenter had needed help.

"Something up?" a voice asked.

Hobbs spun around and saw Martinez a few steps away. She had been too distracted to hear his approach, his heavy footsteps on the carpet.

"No," Hobbs said. "Not really. Maybe." She pointed to the photograph. "Does Greta Carpenter look familiar to you? I think we may have met with her before – maybe on a call or at the station."

Martinez studied the photograph, then placed it on top of the dresser. "Never seen her before in my life, and trust me, someone who looks *as fine as that*? I would remember!"

Hobbs was about to say something but a voice echoed from the front of the house.

"Excuse me? Excuse me? Hello?" It was an older woman's shrill. Roberta tossed her latex gloves on the bed, fingered the edge of her holstered revolver, and walked down the hallway.

In the foyer, a white-haired lady in her late sixties or early seventies cradled a dog. When she saw the detectives, she clutched the animal closer to her flower-dotted housedress, sucked in a few breaths and said, "Is everything alright? I saw the car in the street out front and I thought the family was back. I wanted to make sure everything was okay. Is everything alright?"

Hobbs glanced at Martinez and back at the woman. "Hi. I'm Detective Roberta Hobbs and I'm with the Vetta Park Police Department. This is my partner, Detective Ray Martinez." She spoke with a soft tone, her most disarming cadence – a technique most used with small children and rattled eyewitnesses.

The woman nodded and tried to meet Hobbs at the edge of the hallway but the detective shook her head and pointed towards the front door.

"We haven't finished up inside here so let's talk outside," Hobbs said. Before the woman had a chance to respond, Hobbs placed one hand on the woman's upper back and coaxed her towards the door.

"Is everything okay?" the woman repeated once they were on the front porch. "What happened to them? Where'd they go?"

Outside, they huddled closely together under the superficial protection of a rooftop eave as small droplets of rain trickled onto the pavement. The dog let out a *yap* and looked around.

"We're trying to get to the bottom of it all," Hobbs said. "Can I ask who you are and how you know the family?"

The woman brought the dog closer to her face and stroked the animal's fur. "My name is Mary Miller and I live next door. I've lived here for fourteen years."

Hobbs removed her notepad and started writing. "Have you seen anyone from the family lately?"

"No, not any of them…not for several days. Did they go away? Did anything happen?"

"That's what we're trying to get to, Ms. Miller. Did you see or hear anything unusual on September 7? Exactly a week ago, Thursday?"

Mary Miller scratched the top of her dog's head and squinted into the distance. She looked like she was trapped in her thoughts, trying to divine a significant memory from the noise of leaf blowers and dog barks. After a few moments, she shook her head. "I'm sorry but I just don't remember anything unusual about that day."

"Were you at home all day?"

"Yes, I'm retired."

"Do you usually see their comings and goings?"

Mary nodded. "I see them almost every day. I see the baby – the little girl I mean – playing in the backyard. I see the husband leave for work every morning and come back in the evening. His car is gone and John's car has been parked in the driveway for days. I've never seen it parked for so long. Usually he's here and there, this way and that. I mean maybe for one or two days, sure. But never for this length of time. Oh, I hope everyone's okay."

Hobbs placed her palm on the older woman's shoulder. "Ms. Miller, have you been in the Carpenter house before?"

"Yes, a few times."

"When was the last time?"

"I came over shortly after Olivia was born to give her a present. I knitted a baby blanket for her – pink and yellow."

"Did anything seem strange while you were there? Anything out of the ordinary?"

Mary shook her head. "No, I don't believe so."

"Did they seem messy to you? Like overfilled garbage or dishes not done?"

Mary stiffened. "No, not at all. They were very neat, organized people. Even after the baby was born."

Hobbs, nodded, scribbled a little bit more on her pad and decided to try a different route. "What can you tell me about John?" Hobbs asked.

The rain droplets abated and Mary Miller looked up at the sky, again as though she were searching. She seemed to be choosing her words carefully, rehearsing the lines in her head before she said them aloud. "Well I suppose I have complained to you all about John in the past because the music from the cars could be too loud, late at night. Always in the middle of the night. Rabble-rousers. You know, inconsiderate young teenagers, up to no good. That's all I can really say."

Hobbs nodded and felt inside her pocket for her business card. "Well thank you very much for your time, Ms. Miller, and if you think of anything else…"

Hobbs handed Mary the card and gave a wan smile. This was her standard sendoff — a quick but courteous divorce from conversation that she had perfected over the years. She took a step back and opened the screen door, but Mary took a step forward in concert, preserving the distance of space in between them. "Wait, don't go just yet. You haven't answered my questions yet. Is everything all right? Where did they go? Do I need to be concerned?"

"No need to be concerned just yet. We're still getting to the bottom of everything," Hobbs answered before letting herself back into the house. Once inside, she thought about the conversation and realized she probably could have put the older woman more at ease. There was no sign of forced entry, no sign that the family hadn't left willingly — albeit quickly — and Mary Miller would probably spend the rest of the day rousing friends and neighbors as well as herself. She would share the tale of her surprise conversation with law enforcement, scour websites or yellow pages for alarm systems and maybe weigh the option of adding a larger and more ferocious dog to the family.

Hobbs trotted up the steps and met Martinez in the hallway. He had taken off his gloves and was rubbing the tips of his fingers. "Well, I think we're just about done here," he said.

"Anything?" she asked him.

"Nope," he said. "Nothing unusual and no indications of foul play. Did you learn anything from the neighbor?"

Hobbs frowned. "Not really. She used the term rabble-rousers to describe John's friends. And she described the family as neat and organized. That's about it."

Martinez walked past the kitchen and made a show out of pretending to faint from the stench. "Neat and organized, huh?

They're in for quite a treat when they get back. I've been in homes with *dead bodies* that smelled better than this!"

Hobbs didn't say anything. She had been paired with Martinez for so long, she knew he had a way of reaching conclusions without the compulsory discussion, the careful weighing of evidence and poring over details. And even though Hobbs wanted to say: W*e don't know for sure that they'll come back*, instead she froze – one finger placed against her lips and the rest of her muscles immobile.

"Hobbs?" Martinez asked. "What is it?"

"Shhh."

Martinez stared at her for a few seconds and then repeated: "What is it?"

"Shhh...I heard something..." Hobbs whispered. She pivoted very carefully on her toes and crept into the living room, prudently avoiding the sounds of footsteps on tile.

Then they both heard it. A brief buzzing sound, so fleeting and quiet, she couldn't be certain exactly what it was or where it was coming from.

Martinez went into the dining room and started looking through shelves, rummaging through a box of unopened mail. Hobbs thought about mentioning the need for latex gloves but decided against it. She walked closer to the living room couch and stared. Then she saw a narrow sliver of white and black beneath a magazine on the side table, the plastic carefully concealed by a striped pattern of a perfume ad.

Hobbs reached forward, felt under the magazine and saw that the object was charging. She flicked the wire and snapped up the device. "It's a cell phone!" she called out. Then she saw the message lit up on the front panel, a display of words that made her stomach churn and her breathing hasten. "Um, you need to come here and take a look at this," she said.

Martinez walked over and stood behind her. After a few seconds he mumbled, "Shit," in a soft voice.

And Hobbs knew that in that instant, the entire case had changed. They wouldn't be heading back to the precinct, filling out some paperwork and moving on to the next thing. They would need to push forward to find out exactly what happened, to loop in Captain Weaver and maybe some other officers from the Vetta Park P.D. What was once a question that could be left on its own to unravel was now a problem that had to be solved – the sooner the better.

In her hands, the cell phone glowed, the words splayed across the screen with doughty indifference.

Someone from the local area code had texted: Dude, where the hell are you?? Is ur family ok? U kept saying a bad thing was gonna happen, did it happen??

***

Hobbs and Martinez spent the next thirty minutes in the front seats of Martinez's car. Hobbs tried not to think about how quiet the neighborhood was, how Mary Miller's shades were parted just slightly enough for the older woman to peer at them from her windows facing the street.

While Martinez reviewed their notes, Hobbs ran the phone number that had sent the text through their in-car computer. A short while later, she had a name, age and occupation for the text sender: Mitchell Davis, 35 years old, Vetta Park resident and service manager at Avery Auto Body.

Hobbs remembered the auto shop when they'd first driven onto Avery Street that morning. The building itself was not terribly memorable: It was a one-story block of cement surrounded by open chassis and hunched mechanics. But the sign announcing the shop was a limestone monolith that jutted out of the ground and towered over nearby buildings.

The detectives drove the short distance and parked in front of the auto shop. One of the mechanics spotted them and quickly trotted over. He motioned for Martinez to lower his window. "We're all full today, sorry!" the mechanic barked – his breath a piquant whiff of stale tobacco.

Hobbs leaned across her seat. "We're here to talk with Mitchell Davis," she said. She thought about pulling out her badge but the mechanic immediately softened, took a few steps back and pointed at the building. "He's in the office."

The detectives walked inside the shop and found it just as small as it looked from the outside. There was a pantry to the left, a waiting area to the right and an office right ahead of them. Inside the office, a dark-haired man had been sitting behind a desk, but he stood as soon as the detectives started down the hallway.

There was a sign affixed to the man's door: *Mitchell Davis*. While she walked, Hobbs focused on the large black lettering rather than participate in a staring contest through the glass.

As soon as she and Martinez entered, Davis reached out his right hand. "You're with the police, aren't you?" he asked nervously.

Hobbs shook his hand and took a seat opposite him. Martinez did the same.

"That's correct," Hobbs said. She and Martinez flashed credentials and gave their names but Davis didn't appear to notice or care. He was flustered, one hand running through the thinning shock of hair on his head while the other tapped on his desk. "I knew it; *I knew it!*" he said. "This is about John Brock. I *knew* I should have done something! Dammit!"

"Can you please have a seat and talk to us?" Martinez asked.

Davis huffed and sat down promptly.

"Are you Mitchell Davis?" Hobbs asked.

"Yes, that's me," Davis said. "What happened?"

"We're trying to figure everything out," Martinez said. His words were slow, mechanized, deliberately spooled to assuage the tension in the room. "Can you tell us how you know John?"

"He's a mechanic here, part-time. I manage all the mechanics out there." Davis brought his fingertips up to his lips and started chewing. He didn't even seem aware he was doing this but Hobbs watched as the pink skin around his cuticles became raw.

"Has John shown up in the past week?" Martinez asked.

Davis brought his fingers down and shook his head. "No sir."

"Did he tell you he was taking some time off?"

"No sir. He just stopped showing up for work. Friday morning, I had to call someone else in. And he's not picking up his phone or anything."

"Has John ever done that before?" Hobbs asked.

"No, sir. Not ever. Can you tell me what happened?"

Martinez ignored the question. "Did he give any indication lately that something was wrong?"

Davis's face reddened and he swallowed nervously. "Oh yeah, before he left...something was up." He started to embellish but his voice became wobbly, so he covered his mouth with his fist for a few seconds and then tried again. "I can't tell you when it first started but not too long ago and for no apparent reason, John started moping around, sulking, barely talking to anybody. I mean, John was not what you would call a *talkative* guy anyway. He was pretty quiet. But about ten days ago, a few of my guys pulled me aside and said: 'You gotta talk to him. We're worried he's gonna blow his brains out or get into one of these cars, start the ignition and close the gate.'"

Davis laughed but it didn't seem like a mirthful gesture – more like a reflex.

"Did you notice a change in his behavior too?" Hobbs asked.

"A little bit maybe. But the other mechanics spend a lot more time with him than I do. I brought him in here and asked him what was goin' on. School trouble? Girl trouble? He said his family was in trouble, said something really bad was about to happen."

"Those were his exact words?" Martinez asked.

"Yeah, I mean, it's hard to remember *exactly*. But yeah, I think those were his words."

"Did he tell you specifically what?"

Davis shook his head. "No, ma'am. I asked but he wouldn't tell me anything more. Then I asked if he needed some time off, he said no and I sent him back out onto the floor. I think that was my longest conversation with him in two years. John never talked about his personal life."

"I see," Hobbs said. She glanced down at her notes. "Anything else you can tell us about him? Anything that stands out?"

"No, not really," Davis said.

"Do you mind if we talk to some of the mechanics out here?"

"Sure. I mean no, I don't mind."

Hobbs and Martinez stood up and she handed him a card. "Thanks for talking to us. If you think of anything else, my phone number's on there."

The detectives were nearly out of the office, just through the doorframe that led to the service area, when Davis jumped up from the desk and called out to them. "Hey! There is one more thing. I don't know if it's relevant or not…"

Hobbs and Martinez stepped back inside and looked at him.

Davis walked over and faced Hobbs. "Right when we hired him, one of the guys said he was bad news."

"One of the guys said that about John?" Hobbs clarified.

"Yeah, one of the mechanics. But I mean…John's been fine. I've had no issues with him."

"Which mechanic?" Martinez asked.

Davis shook his head. "Can't remember. It was years ago and we turn over guys all the time. Probably doesn't even work here anymore. It's just a comment that came back into my mind last week."

"What did he mean by *bad news*?" Hobbs pressed.

Davis shrugged. "I don't know. He didn't say and I didn't ask."

Hobbs shook her head. It was this type of information that drove her mad – illusory clues that revealed nothing. She tried not to seem too incredulous, too pejorative when she responded to him.

"Mr. Davis, you heard that one of your new employees might be…might be…*bad news* and you didn't ask any follow up questions or make any motion to find out what that meant?"

David shrugged again. "I'm not a cop, Detective," he said. "And I'm not hiring Boy Scouts; I'm hiring auto mechanics. If I see someone doing something wrong, I fire them. But as long as they do their job, that's all I care about."

"I see," Hobbs said. "Well, thank you for your time."

She and Martinez stepped out of Davis's office and into the large pen where the mechanics were working. One by one, the mechanics spoke to the detectives and one by one, the detectives learned absolutely nothing new about John or the Carpenter family's disappearance.

None of the mechanics could provide specifics about John's recent bout with melancholy, except to confirm its existence. One mechanic had worked at Avery Auto Shop for over a decade and remembered telling Davis that John was bad news. But he couldn't remember why he had said such a thing, or who exactly had fed him that tidbit or what it really meant. And besides, the mechanic pointed out, John had kept his head down, said very little and worked hard for two years. There was nothing amiss, nothing out of the ordinary that could be said about the teenager…not until now.

# CHAPTER THREE

*September 14, 2017*

Hobbs and Martinez sat next to each other in chocolate colored vinyl chairs and waited for the Captain to arrive. Hobbs stared at the textured nameplate facing her, which read CPT. JOSEPH WEAVER in bold lettering. She looked at the neat square piles of paperwork laid across his desk, a few framed photographs of beaming children, and a large leather chair.

A voice behind her said, "Sorry I'm late," and then Weaver briskly strode in and sat down. An older man of about sixty-five, he had wisps of white hair above the ears and on top of his head and deep frown lines across his forehead.

Weaver threw a heap of papers across his already crowded desk. "So what did you find in the Avery Place house?" he asked.

Martinez cleared his throat and read from his notepad. "No sign of forced entry, nothing disturbed, no sign of a burglary. There are two cars registered to the family. One has been parked at the house for seven days; the other hasn't been seen in seven days."

"Have any family members called, saying they haven't been able to get in touch?"

Hobbs glanced at Martinez and then at the Captain. "No sir."

"So the family is gone, along with their car, there's no sign of forced entry, nothing disturbed in the house, and no anxious family members...have I got that right?"

Hobbs nodded.

"Tell me again why we're talking about this?"

She sighed. "Sir, we thought the same thing at first, but then we spoke to John Brock's boss. He told us that John had been very upset lately and said something bad was going to happen to the family. Then they all disappeared."

Weaver frowned and sat back in his chair. "Huh."

"There's more," Hobbs added. "Tuck Carpenter's law office reported him missing. They said he had meetings and conferences scheduled, and he would never just not show up for them. He's been at that same law practice for *twenty years*. And there were still eggs on the stove in the kitchen. The trash was overflowing. It smelled pretty bad in there."

"So they left in a hurry," Weaver said.

"Yes," Hobbs agreed. "But why?"

The room was silent for a few moments and then Weaver said, "It's this advance knowledge that something bad was going to happen to them right before the disappearance that has me thinking about foul play. Why don't you get a subpoena for the family's credit card and bank accounts? Find out if and where they're spending their money. Look into the phone records too. See if we can track them down from pings. I assume you've called their cell phones to try to get hold of them?"

Hobbs cleared her throat. "Yes Sir. John Brock left his phone inside the house but I called and left messages for Tuck and Greta. No word back."

Weaver reclined in his seat, stretched his arms behind his head and grunted. "Okay. See what you can find. Anything else?"

Hobbs nodded. "There's also Greta's ex-husband, John's biological father, Griffin Brock. We'd like to call him in and see if he knows anything."

"By all accounts, yes, bring him in here," Weaver said. "Anything else?"

Hobbs nodded but instead of looking at him, she looked out the window of his office. Vetta Park was a small municipality in Eastern Missouri, just twenty miles or so south of St. Louis. On clear days, such as this, she could see the Arch from his office – burnished and looming, like a beacon signifying the big city.

"Detective?" Weaver prompted.

Hobbs brought her gaze back to Weaver. "One other thing, Captain. The eighteen-year old, John Brock. I have a funny feeling about him. I don't know if it's because the neighbor said his friends were inconsiderate or the mechanic who said he heard John was bad news. I can't put my finger on it. Also I couldn't find anything about him online. No social media or online presence, and I just—"

Hobbs swallowed hard, tasting the metallic ripple of a lump that had formed in her throat. "I just think something's off."

# CHAPTER FOUR

*May 6, 2004*

The sun shined down on Edwardsville Elementary School's Kindergarten picnic. It was a beating sun – not ferocious but not obscured by a single cloud in the sky. The five and six year olds ran around the playground carelessly while parents worried themselves with sunscreen and hats.

In one corner of the grassy area – far from the other kids – John Brock busied himself with a self-instructed task. He was to count all the flower petals on top of the rusty wire gate that separated the schoolyard from residential housing. It was an impossible task; the schoolyard stretched for almost half a mile end to end. John usually got up to two or three hundred before losing count, quietly chastising himself, and starting the pursuit from the beginning.

"Johnny, don't you want to play with the other kids?" Greta asked. John squinted as he turned to face her. At twenty-five years old, Greta looked flawless. Wherever she went, she captured the gaze of admirers – usually until they saw the brown-haired tot pattering next to her or the plain gold band on her finger.

"No Mommy, I don't," John responded. "I'm busy here." He then glared at her and resumed his count from the beginning. "One, two, three…"

Greta reached into her bag and pulled out an envelope. "I know it's a day early, Johnny, but I got you a birthday card."

John abandoned his count for a moment and looked suspiciously at the red envelope, which Greta had adorned with hearts and stickers. "Is there money inside?" John asked.

"Open it up and see," Greta said.

John leaped forward, took the envelope and tore it open – paying no mind to the scraps of ripped paper that fell onto the grass. When the card was free, he opened it, turned it upside down and shook it. "Awww there's no money!" he protested.

"Read it," Greta urged, smiling at him.

"It says *I love you*," John said with a scowl.

"It doesn't just say that," Greta said. "Read the rest." She stayed smiling at him as she waited. This wasn't a fool's errand; John's teachers routinely send home notes about how well the class was progressing. Greta knew they had all surpassed the standards for phonetic reading of two and three letter words. John's main problem was that he needed to slow down…he tended to race through words as though they were quaffs of liquid, satisfying a thirst. It was always the same books – the ones with clever rhymes and anthropomorphized animals…the books she used to read to him religiously that he now read to her and in the classroom. Now, she stood next to him patiently as she waited to hear the remaining two words of the little note she'd written inside the card.

John turned the card upside down, studied it for a moment, and then threw it into the grass along with the discarded shreds of red envelope. "I can't," he said hopelessly.

"What do you mean *you can't?*" Greta asked. She picked up the card and crouched next to him beside the fence. She pointed to the word *to*. "What's that word?" Greta asked.

John refused to look at the card. "I don't know."

"What letters are here?" Greta asked.

John shrugged but looked at her index finger. "T."

"And what sound does 't' make?"

"Ta-ta-ta."

"Right. And what's that letter?" She moved her index finger one centimeter over.

"That's an O."

"Right, and what sound does that make?"

His eyes searching, John gave her a blank look. "Aaah?" He conjectured. When he was able to read the response in her face, he gave a few other stabs. "Ih? Uh?"

"No, Johnny, it makes the sound *oh* or *ah*. Although in this case, *ooh*," Greta said. She tried to mask her surprise, her mental revision of all the notes sent home in his backpack, trumpeting the class's literary achievements.

"So what does this word say?" Greta pressed.

John stared down at the card and took a deep sigh. "It says *oooooh…*"

"Johnny, the *t* comes before the *o*, so it should start with *tttt…*"

John ripped the card from her hands and threw it down. "I hate this stupid card!" he yelled, just loud enough to attract the attention of some parents at the periphery of the playground. He then ran several yards away from her and resumed his exercise of counting flora – tiny red berries dangling from the branches of a tree.

Greta picked up the shreds of the envelope and threw them into her bag, then opened up the card again and stared at the note she'd written. *I love you to death!*

*To death*...She hadn't hesitated when writing the end of the sentence but now it seemed inappropriate, or even worse, a harbinger of some kind. Perhaps it was fitting for John not to finish the sentence; doing so would have undoubtedly brought about queries or nighttime anxieties. Greta exhaled sharply and tried to console herself. Maybe a different, more child-friendly set of words would have had a different result.

But no, that wasn't really the problem. Greta knew the truth. It was a certainty that had been lingering in the back of her mind for a while, a query that John had just answered. Even if *death* was a word too advanced, too forbidden, too daunting for her kindergartener, he should have been able to sound out the word *to*.

Looking down at that short, seemingly innocuous sentence, Greta realized how John had been able to race through books so impeccably. He could adopt the right cadence, the right inflections, all the right words – while having no idea how to actually read. His memory was strong and sharp, and it could do its job after hearing words only one time.

Greta walked a few yards and found John's kindergarten teacher, Miss Alice, administering a Band-aid to one of the kids on the playground. Alice was a young woman – perhaps just out of college or maybe closer to Greta's age. She had dark hair, a slight build and a sweet smile.

"Hi Greta," Alice said warmly, once the wounded child had recovered and returned to the playground.

Greta returned the greeting and then surprised herself with a litany of worries about John. She mentioned his difficulty getting along with other children, his inability to follow complex directions, his reluctance to write any letters, his lack of knowledge about vowel sounds and his most recent difficulty sounding out the word *to*. Most of these concerns Greta had never discussed with anyone – not even John's father. They occupied a place in her mind along with terrorism, kidnappers and dangerous weather. Concerns that could run unrestricted if they weren't checked, concerns that weren't likely to be fully realized, that were products of an overactive imagination. Only talking to Miss Alice did Greta realize how strong her worries about John really were, and she was surprised by her fortitude even as she pressed his teacher.

Miss Alice responded with reassurance, summing up all of Greta's fears into one word: *developmental*. All of John's issues were perfectly age appropriate and he would grow out of them.

Greta left the conversation both optimistic and deflated. She hoped that everything Miss Alice said was true…but she couldn't shake the notion that the teacher just wanted to enjoy her end-of-year picnic and be done with it all.

Greta, on the other hand, would have to sit back and trust that things would work themselves out over time. Meanwhile…her child whose report card said he could read was unable to figure out a two-letter word.

# CHAPTER
# FIVE

*September 15, 2017*

Griffin Brock was a commanding presence. Six-feet six inches tall, wide shoulders, and a bristle of gelled black hair only starting to recede. He stood at the counter of the Vetta Park Police Station as though he belonged there – seeming completely unfazed by the bustle of police activity, the handcuffed transient sitting on a metal chair, the buzz of police radios that officers wore on their hips as they brushed by him.

Detective Hobbs walked over and claimed him. "Mr. Griffin Brock?" she asked. Griffin was the only person in the waiting area wearing a suit – the only one with expensive leather shoes and a clean shave. In the mid-September heat, when the waiting room's ancient AC unit was sputtering and stammering, Griffin Brock was the only one not breaking a sweat.

"Did you find the station okay?" Hobbs asked conversationally, as she led him down a hallway and into a conference room. Everything about the room was bare: white walls, white table with wood-colored folding chairs and an uncovered white light bulb dangling inches from the ceiling.

"I got here fine," he answered curtly as he assumed a seat. He moved as though he'd been through the motions before – or at least seen enough of it on TV that he didn't need to be coached through the gestures. When Hobbs took a seat across from him, he sighed, looked pointedly at his watch and then leaned back in his chair.

"Are you aware of why we asked you to come in?" Hobbs asked.

"You told me over the phone," he said in an irritated voice. "My ex-wife and her family took off."

"Do you know anything about their disappearance?" Hobbs asked.

"No, I do not. If I knew anything, I would've said something over the phone. You think I want to be brought in here in the middle of the day on a Friday? I had to rearrange meetings, reschedule conference calls. I've already told you everything I know." Griffin folded his arms across his chest and glared at her.

"Are you concerned about your ex-wife?" Hobbs asked.

"Concerned how?"

"Are you concerned about her safety? And concerned about the safety of John, your son?" Hobbs lingered on the words *your son* for a few extra beats, hoping to shake some paternal obligation from his seeping self-importance.

"No I'm not concerned, Detective. Greta always had a flair for the dramatic. I'm not at all surprised that they just took off this way. It would have been courteous for them to let someone know they were taking a trip but I don't think *courtesy* is a characteristic Greta is familiar with."

"I see," Hobbs said, peering down at her notes. Griffin was obviously irritated but she tried to gauge whether he was merely annoyed with his ex-wife or if there was a more pernicious rage lingering underneath. She decided to start from the beginning of their story.

"How did you meet Greta?" Hobbs asked.

"She was my waitress at this diner I used to go to. I was an undergraduate at Wash U in St. Louis. She was the most beautiful girl I'd ever seen, and one day when she was serving me toast, I asked her out."

"Was she a student there too?"

"No. She never finished high school."

"How would you describe your marriage?"

"We had fights, like any couple. We had a lot of fights – especially as Johnny got older."

"What were the fights about?"

Griffin glowered at her but answered her question. "Money…and Johnny. Like I said, Greta could be very dramatic at times. She always thought something was wrong with the kid when he was just fine. Drove me crazy."

"Were your fights ever violent?" Hobbs asked. She and Martinez had pored through the police records earlier in the day and there was no record on file of domestic assault…but Hobbs was as certain as ever that she'd interacted with Greta in the past and maybe an unreported crime had something to do with it.

Griffin clasped his hands together and looked straight at at her. "No," he said. "It wasn't violent."

"What do you do for a living Mr. Brock?"

"I work in real estate."

"Are you a developer?"

"No, Detective. I buy and sell land to developers."

"I see. And what did Greta do during the time that you were married?"

"Not very much. She stayed at home and watched Spanish soap operas for all I know."

Hobbs looked down at her notes while she thought of her next question. Griffin clearly didn't think very highly of his ex-wife. She was prone to dramatics, unreasonable and lethargic. Even her absence had roused him from his busy workday and compelled him to sit in a small room and answer uncomfortable questions about his past.

But was this normal acrimony among exes or was there something deeper? Hobbs still felt no closer to discerning whether Griffin had anything to do with their disappearance. She tried another approach.

"Can you think of anyone who may have wanted to harm your ex-wife or her family, Mr. Brock?"

Griffin answered quickly. "No, Detective…but I wasn't too close to them. I didn't talk to them very much."

Hobbs scribbled on her pad, taking notice of the fact that Griffin was now speaking in the past tense. "Not John?" she asked.

"No, I didn't talk to him much either."

"Do you know who your son associates with?" Hobbs asked. She thought about Mary Miller, the concerned neighbor. *Inconsiderate young teenagers, up to no good.*

"No," Griffin answered. "Greta didn't keep me in the loop very much."

"When's the last time you saw them?"

"Last month."

Hobbs stopped writing and looked up at him. Her heart skipped more furiously inside of her chest, as it always did when she felt she was onto something. "Last month? That recently?" she asked.

"Yes, I stopped by the house to let them know that my mother had had a stroke. And that my wife was expecting."

"Oh I see. I'm sorry to hear that…about your mother. How's she doing?"

"She died. The funeral is Monday, in Winnetka."

"I'm so sorry for your loss."

"Thank you," Griffin said. His response was emotionless, a dry mutter. Perhaps it was because Hobbs had grown accustomed to seeing witnesses and suspects open up under questioning. If they didn't end up weeping by the end of it, they typically appeared moved, sentient. Griffin seemed as reticent as the room itself. Even the topic of his mother's death wasn't enough to affect his stance.

"Were Greta or John close with your mother?" Hobbs asked.

"No."

"How about your wife? Did she have the baby?"

Griffin nodded and responded in the same robotic locution. "Yes, she had a boy last week. Marshall Owen Brock. We named him after my mother."

"Congratulations," Hobbs said. "A lot of life changes in a short time."

"Yes, that's right," Griffin said. The room was silent for a moment and then he added, "Detective, I don't know what happened to Greta or John...or Tuck or the other little girl. I want you to know that I had nothing to do with it. I'm in a good place right now. My wife just had a baby and now I'm a father to a young boy. I would never do anything to jeopardize that."

Hobbs nodded and smiled at him. "Thanks for coming in, Mr. Brock. I appreciate your time during what I know was a busy day."

She stood up and Griffin did the same. They shook hands and then she led him through the hallway and out of the building. Throughout their brief good-bye, she was calm and polite, smiling pleasantly while she encouraged him to call if he thought of anything else of interest.

But once Hobbs was free of him and back at her desk, she sunk into her chair and ran a loop of his final few comments over and over in her mind. All she could think were words she hadn't thought to say at the time: *You already* are *the father to a young boy.*

# CHAPTER SIX

*September 15, 2017*

An hour after saying good-bye to Griffin, Detective Hobbs found Captain Weaver in the kitchenette. The Captain looked especially tired – hunched over the coffeemaker as though it was about to perform a trick, with sunken cheeks and bags beneath his eyes.

"Everything okay?" Hobbs asked him.

"My daughter in law and her kids moved in with us while their house is being renovated," Weaver explained. "Nothing that a few jolts of caffeine won't fix."

Hobbs waited patiently for the coffee machine to oblige, and the two of them headed into Captain Weaver's office. There they found Detective Martinez seated on one of the vinyl chairs, waiting for them.

"You watched the interview with Griffin Brock through the glass?" Hobbs asked Martinez as she sat down next to him.

Martinez nodded.

Captain Weaver assumed his place behind the desk and took a giant sip of his coffee. He swallowed and looked expectantly at his two senior detectives. "Well, it's been a day and still no word from the family. Fill me in on the interview."

Hobbs rummaged through a few pages on her notepad. "Griffin seemed very unfazed by the experience," she said. "Aside from learning that his mother recently passed away, we didn't learn much else."

"When's the funeral?" Weaver asked.

"Monday, in a Chicago suburb," Hobbs said.

"Get an officer to go and take a look around, talk to people," Weaver ordered. "You never know."

Both detectives nodded and the room was silent. Weaver sighed and looked outside his window. It was an especially windy day for Vetta Park – gusts pushing the branches of a nearby tree against the windowpane.

Hobbs thought about her small apartment a few miles south. It was on the third floor of a structurally dubious apartment complex that seemed to be made out of sticks. Every time there was a windstorm, her walls shook and her appliances rattled. At least the police station was solid. Erected so it could withstand a tornado, the building neither swayed nor nudged every time the wind squalled.

"You know what bothers me…" Weaver said, still looking vacantly at the tree branches. He didn't wait for a response. "Where the hell are all the concerned neighbors? Where are the candlelight vigils? Where are the family members passing out posters, yelling at us that we better do our jobs right? Where's the anger over this family, who hasn't been seen in *eight days*?"

Detectives Martinez and Hobbs were quiet as they considered this. Since Tuck's legal secretary had first filed a missing person's report, no one else had come forward. It was as though the Carpenter family lived in a self-contained vacuum.

"Well…" Martinez said with a sigh. "Greta Carpenter stayed home with the little girl all day. The girl wasn't old enough for public school and the mom didn't work. John Brock dropped out of high school at some point and spent his time at Avery Auto Body, whose employees have already spoken with us. And then there's Tuck Carpenter, whose colleagues were the ones to file the initial report. I'm not sure there's anyone else, you know, out there."

"What about their extended family?" Weaver asked.

"Greta has a mother, living somewhere in southwestern Missouri. We're still trying to track her down. Tuck's parents are both deceased but he does have a brother, Richard Carpenter, who lives in Orlando."

"Have you talked to him yet?"

"I called and left a message but no one's gotten back to me yet."

Weaver shifted so he was facing Hobbs. "What did the phone records say?"

Hobbs blinked and stammered. "I…it's only been one day since we requested…"

Weaver pushed a button on his desk phone. "Get Lt. Adams in here," he ordered, then looked up at the detectives. "We were able to get an emergency court order for the phone records. I asked Adams to look after it."

Lt. Adams was burly, with spiky brown hair and a partially shaved beard that stretched from jaw to jaw. Mid-twenties and intensely loyal, Lt. Adams was Captain Weaver's favored son – his go-to errand man whenever he wanted to get a job done quickly or quietly.

After his beckoning, Lt. Adams appeared in the doorway with a few sheets of paper.

"What have you got on the Carpenter phone records?" Weaver asked.

"We haven't received all the cell phone records yet, but I just finished looking through the calls to their house phone. At seven forty-six on the morning of September 7, a call was made to the Carpenter house."

"Was someone there to pick up the call?" Weaver asked.

"Yes, someone picked up the call. They spoke for just under three minutes."

A few seconds passed with no one saying a word. Everyone seemed to comprehend the gravity of this new bit of evidence. The police finally had a timeline, a starting point. The Carpenters had received a telephone call…and almost forty minutes later, Tuck had failed to show up to work on time.

"Who was the call from?" Weaver demanded as he placed his coffee mug to his lips.

"It was a burner phone," Adams said. "We don't know who bought it or from where. It's completely untraceable."

Captain Weaver placed his mug back on his desk. His face looked a shade paler, the bags underlining his eyes more pronounced. His voice seemed more forceful as he gave his next instruction. "Whatever this is, whoever is behind it, someone knows something and they're not speaking up. I'm going to do two things. First, I'm going to issue an APB for this family. If they're still driving, maybe an officer will spot them on the road. And secondly, I want to get the community involved. Let's set up a press conference for later this afternoon to officially announce the investigation into the disappearance of the Carpenter family. If no one will raise a stink about these four people, at least we can."

*** 

The press conference was held at five o'clock that evening. It was a local affair – covered by a few St. Louis TV stations, and one reporter from a Vetta Park online journal that had a few hundred subscribers.

Captain Weaver chose the time so the event would get mentioned in the local six o'clock news. He knew that no channel would interrupt their regularly scheduled programming, but at least he could offer a clip or a sound bite that would warrant mention in a later broadcast.

The event was held outside. Weaver stood behind a brown podium that was set up in front of the police station. Flanked by trees and concrete benches, he spoke passionately about the missing Carpenter family and urged anyone with any information to call the station. A huge family photograph was perched on a nearby table – same as the one in the family's bedroom – and Hobbs wasn't able to look away from the smiles that swayed in the breeze. What was once so innocent now seemed cryptic. The Carpenter family had looked so pure when she held them in her hand…but there was something disturbing about seeing those life-size faces flick back and forth. Hobbs wondered what secrets those smiles were concealing – whether they knew what the future had in store or whether they were taken by surprise.

Weaver stepped away from the podium and then it was Adams' turn. He described the family members, using all the details and characteristics at his disposal. It didn't amount to much. Olivia Carpenter liked Minnie Mouse and frequently wore her hair in pigtails. Tuck Carpenter was a St. Louis Cardinals fan who watched almost all the games, according to his colleagues. Greta was a devoted mom. And John Brock was eighteen years old and worked part-time as a mechanic. None of them had been seen since September 7, and the police suspected foul play.

The entire episode lasted less than ten minutes. When he finished describing the family members in the photograph, Weaver rested his hands neatly on the sides of the podium and offered to take any questions. The journalists exchanged glances with each other and looked at their notepads but no one asked a thing.

***

The phone call came in at 5:40pm – just a few minutes after all the journalists packed up their cameras and went back to their trucks.

Lt. Adams was the one to receive it. He put the receiver down and yelled out, "Hobbs, I have Richard Carpenter on line 1 for you!"

Hobbs darted to her desk, inhaled sharply and picked up the line. "Mr. Carpenter?"

"Yeap, that's me. Is this Officer Hobbs?" The voice on the other end was gruff, a smoker's rasp.

"Yes, I'm Detective Hobbs. Thanks for returning my call, Mr. Carpenter. I wanted to talk to you about your brother, Tuck. Have you spoken to him in the past week?"

Richard cleared his throat and Hobbs could hear the shouts and shrieks of small children in the background. One voice in particular was shrill and insistent. *Daddy! Daddy! Daddy!*

"Hush now, I'm on the phone!" Richard barked. Then, more calmly into the receiver: "No, I ain't spoken to him. Is he alright?"

"Mr. Carpenter, no one has heard from him or his family in eight days. Do you have any idea where they could be or who they could be with?" It was this part of the job that Hobbs detested – giving this type of news to family. She always tried to project her most businesslike demeanor – professional, official, deep, clear voice and unemotional. But these moments made her question why she'd gone into the profession in the first place.

It was quiet on the other end of the line.

"Mr. Carpenter?" Hobbs asked, her voice softening.

"I'm here, I'm here," Richard said quietly. "I sent the kids…to go and play…in the other room." He spoke slowly, each word carefully measured.

Hobbs tried again. "Do you know—?"

"Naw – I don't know where they went, who they're with. I don't know who they talk to. We only chat about a few times a year – birthdays and Christmas. I last spoke to Tuck in June and he didn't say much."

"Mr. Carpenter, anything that you could tell us about their lives would be a huge help to the case. Can you think about *anything* that might have been discussed during that conversation?"

"Hmm. We talked mostly about the summer weather, and the bugs they were seeing. He said he was thinking about re-siding part of their house. He'd gone to a Cardinals game that week. That was Greta's birthday present to him. Is any of this helpful to you?"

"Yes, all of this is helpful to me. Please go on," Hobbs said. On her notepad, where there should have been names, leads and timeframes, Hobbs had scribbled tiny dots into the margins. She waited for something more useful.

"Uhhh … I guess…the only other thing I can think of is that Tuck said Greta was taking time to teach the kid to read. Or that she had finished doing that. That's all I can think of."

Hobbs continued drawing dots on the faint blue lines of the page. "They were teaching Olivia to read themselves or they were sending her to a preschool program?"

"Not Olivia. John."

Hobbs stopped scribbling and took a beat before asking, "Greta had just finished teaching John to read?"

"Yeah. That's what he said."

"The eighteen-year old?"

"Yeah, I think so."

"Mr. Carpenter—" Hobbs was about to plow forward with her next question but she caught the edge in her voice and took a pause. This wasn't a suspect. This was a missing family member's relative.

"Mr. Carpenter, did you know that your nephew was learning to read at age eighteen?"

"He wasn't my nephew, Officer. He was Greta's boy. And yes, Tuck had mentioned that John had a lot of difficulties in school but I didn't ask too many questions. It's not my place."

"I see," Hobbs said, her pen frozen in her hand.

"Do you need me to come up there, maybe help out for a day? See what I can do?" Richard asked.

Hobbs' head snapped up. "Are you close with anyone here who knew the family?" she asked.

"Naw. And I don't know what help I'd be anyway. Besides, I've got my kids down here and my wife works, and we can't really pull them out of school…you know?"

So the question had been an empty gesture. Hobbs was quiet for a moment and Richard broke the silence by saying, "Officer? I need to get back to my family. Can you keep me posted on what y'all discover?"

"We will, Mr. Carpenter. Take care."

Hobbs hung up the phone and looked down at her notes. Along with the dots, and shapes and random scribbles spread across the page, she had written: *John???*

# CHAPTER SEVEN

*February 4, 2005*

John wasn't breathing right. His breaths were quick and staccato – short up-and-down gasps that pulled on his belly. Greta first noticed it when she was giving him a bath but she thought she might be imagining it.

Later that night, when it was time to tuck John into bed, Greta pulled Griffin aside. "Does Johnny seem alright to you?" she asked her husband. "His breathing is strange."

Griffin had been sitting at the dining room table, working on a project. Greta knew he worked in real estate but never mired herself in his details. He was gone a lot – scoping out land, talking to developers, selling to investors. She didn't know exactly what he did during his trips but she knew they made him anxious. The days before a trip meant late nights at the office and long conference calls from their tiny study even when he was home.

Sometimes she thought Griffin was gone even when he was still in Vetta Park. She would tuck Johnny into bed, and tell him stories of his father's fanciful adventures in other cities, then tuck herself into bed alone a few hours later. In the middle of the night, he'd come home – keys dropped loudly onto the kitchen counter, shoes stomped against their wooden floors…and then he'd make his way into their bedroom. Awake and frustrated, Greta would pretend to be asleep until he changed his clothes, stretched out next to her and turned out the lights.

She had so much to ask him, so much she wanted to know. The gaps in their marriage seemed to widen each year until they were no longer gaps but canyons – deep gorges of silence with a riverbed of anger flowing through them.

By 2005, she had been in the marriage seven years and felt she knew Griffin no better than when they'd first met. When he'd first walked into her diner years before, at least there was the hope of getting to know him better, of opening up to him. But now he seemed primarily motivated to get out of their conversations as quickly as possible. He seemed always searching for the nearest exit.

So when she saw him at the dining room table that evening in February, pounding at his keyboard and staring at the monitor with deep concentration, she knew that broaching the topic of John's health would be as futile as discussing the state of their marriage – the state of anything for that matter. But she asked him anyway.

"He's been making a strange noise when he breathes," she continued. "Do you think I should take him in?"

"You're always hovering over him, Greta," Griffin said. "I'm sure the kid's fine."

She let the matter drop, but later that night they could hear a seal's bark emanating from John's room. Greta sprinted into his bedroom and found him feverish and shaky, with inhalations that seemed forced.

"I'm taking John to the hospital!" Greta yelled. She wasn't sure if Griffin heard but she pulled John out of bed anyway, rushed him into his car seat and sped to Children's Hospital in St. Louis. It was a thirty-minute drive but the cold air helped soothe his respiration. By the time they arrived in the reception area of the Emergency Room, John sounded better. His breaths were less forced and more even, although still barky.

The hospital took him back right away and it didn't take long for a young resident to diagnose him with croup. While they waited for two breathing treatments and a dose of steroids to calm his breathing, Greta sat with him in his hospital bed and told him stories.

"One day you'll meet your grandmother," she murmured to him. "Her name is Johanna, which means *God is gracious*. You were named after her, and you kind of look like her too. Did you know that?"

John smiled and closed his eyes, but didn't say anything. He was long asleep by the time the ER nurse came back into the room and told them they could go.

"Watch his breathing and bring him back if he has any difficulty," the nurse advised. She then gave Greta the discharge papers and waved them out of the room.

Greta carried John back into the car and buckled him into his booster seat. It was nearly 2 a.m. when she got back on the road.

\*\*\*

Greta drove quickly through the main highway that connected St. Louis to Vetta Park, and then onto more familiar streets. The nocturnal silence was sporadically broken by a distant siren – and

Greta took note of how eerie it was to be the one of the only cars on the road. The night itself was damp, with a light mist settling over the streetlamps.

When she was closer to her house, Greta noticed a pickup truck behind her, its headlights blindingly bright as it trailed a few hundred yards back. She got to a stoplight and continued through the intersection. The green shined down on her car for an instant as she made her way through. A few seconds later, Greta peered through her rear view mirror at John. He was peacefully sleeping in the back seat, his chest rising and falling with even breaths.

In an instant, a yellow sports car gunned through the same intersection from the cross-street and slammed into the pickup truck that had been trailing her. Greta saw it all in her rear-view mirror. First the accident itself – that happened so quickly it was over in a second – then the shrieking sound of iron, aluminum and steel crushed together at a voracious speed.

Greta hollered and pulled a U-turn in the middle of the road. The traffic light was still green as she headed back to the blazing collision.

John woke up in a panic from his backseat slumber. "What is it, Mommy? What happened?" he yelled.

"It's okay, Johnny," Greta said in a trembling voice. "Some people are in trouble and we'll see if we can help."

She drove closer to the mangled cars in the middle of the intersection and parked on the road's shoulder. The yellow sports car was pinned beneath the pick-up – its front barely visible – although from closer inspection, Greta could see that it was a Ferrari. She stepped out of her car onto the street and started dialing on her phone.

"911," a voice said.

Greta tried to steady her voice, to calm her rising panic. The pickup driver emerged from the wreckage of his truck and surveyed the remains of the sports car beneath. He was an older man, with a blood-spotted St. Louis Cardinals cap pulled down over his head.

"911," the dispatcher repeated.

Greta cleared her throat and found her voice. "Yes, hi. I'm at the intersection of Memorial and Olympic Boulevards, in Vetta Park. There's been a terrible car accident. Can you please send someone right away?"

"Memorial and Olympic? Is anyone injured?"

"Yes, yes I think so. There was a yellow Ferrari that ran a red light. I haven't seen anyone come out of it. And there's a pickup truck driver. He's walking, but there's blood on his baseball cap." Greta pulled the phone away from her ear and yelled, "Sir? Sir? Are you okay? Do you need an ambulance?"

The man frowned at Greta and put his hand to his forehead. Just beneath the bill of the cap, Greta could see a bloody tear of skin that she hadn't noticed before. She brought her phone back to her ear. "Yes, one maybe two injuries. Maybe more. I'm not sure." Her voice was shaking, her body trembling in concert. The night air suddenly seemed extremely cold.

"What's your name?" the dispatcher asked.

"My name is Greta Brock. Can you please send some help?" she asked urgently.

"Yes, there is help coming that way. Can you tell me what happened? You said a Ferrari ran a red light at an intersection?"

Greta started to answer but then she saw some signs of life from inside the Ferrari and she all but forgot she was having a conversation. The passenger side door slowly opened and a man emerged. He was African-American, lanky, well dressed but disheveled. His shirt had blood spots and was torn in a few places and his nose was bleeding. He looked to be in his mid or late twenties.

"Are you okay?" Greta called out to him. "Do you need help?"

The man held up his left hand but didn't say anything and stumbled backward into the passenger seat. Greta wasn't sure what the gesture meant.

The police arrived a minute or two later. First Greta heard the sirens, then two Vetta Park police cruisers, a fire truck and two ambulances arrived.

It took about twenty minutes to remove the Ferrari's driver from his car, but the emergency responders were able to place him on a stretcher and get him into an ambulance. From what Greta could see, he was also in a suit, and also looked to be in his late twenties or mid-thirties. The Ferrari's passenger went in the other ambulance and the pickup truck driver declined medical attention.

With both doors of the sports car wide open, Greta was close enough to smell the stench of rum or maybe whiskey.

"Excuse me!" A deep voice barked. "Miss, can I ask you to take a few steps back while we clear the scene?"

Greta pivoted and saw a tall, muscular, non-smiling man in a police uniform standing behind her. His badge read *Hardy*.

"Is that your car over there?" Hardy asked.

Greta nodded. "My son is asleep in the back seat."

They walked over to Greta's car and verified that John was indeed, still in the back seat. Instead of sleeping, he was awake – staring at the scene of the accident with an expression of terror.

Hardy peered into the backseat and smiled at John. "How you doin' there, little guy?"

John just swallowed and blinked in response.

"He's a little overwhelmed by everything." Greta said.

"I can imagine. It's also three in the morning. What are you two doing out so late?"

"I took him to Children's Hospital – in St. Louis. He had croup."

"I see," Hardy said with a nod. "Did you witness the accident?"

"From my rear view mirror, yes. The Ferrari ran a red light and slammed right into the pick-up truck."

Hardy pulled out a pad of paper and jotted a few things down. "You sure about that?" he asked.

"Yes," Greta said. "The pickup truck was right behind me. The traffic light was green when I went through…and hadn't changed by the time he went through. I'm positive."

"I see," Hardy said again. He then asked a few questions about Greta – her name, her address, her phone number. A few minutes later, tow trucks arrived to clear the accident scene and Greta was free to drive back home.

With John finally asleep in the backseat, Greta drove the remainder of the way home in a trance. She felt stunned and horrified by what she'd witnessed. She was mildly placated by the news Officer Hardy had given her that everyone involved was going to live…but the experience itself was scarring. She wondered what long-term psychological effects John would suffer from watching the aftermath of the collision. She wondered what combination of factors – maybe alcohol, mixed with hubris – had fueled the driver of the Ferrari to plow through the red light at top speed. And mostly she was jolted by the knowledge that her involvement in the scene would have been much greater and more horrific were it not for a few seconds of time.

\*\*\*

Greta gently opened the front door to their small house on Avery Place and carried John up the stairs and into his bedroom.

He mumbled as she placed him neatly in his bed but he didn't wake up.

In the master bedroom, Griffin was lightly grunting and tossing his weight around their double bed. Greta tried to be quiet, but Griffin woke up as soon as she got under the covers.

"What the hell, Greta," he slurred in a dream-like voice. "What time is it?"

Greta glanced over and saw that his eyes remained closed and his body was still.

"It's late," Greta whispered. "Sorry – I didn't know if I should call and wake you up."

Griffin pulled the top sheet over his head and turned on his side, away from her. He muttered to the wall, "I was worried about you. I heard sirens."

Greta got onto her back and faced the ceiling. She realized that she was still shivering, and she pulled her side of the covers closer to her body. She sighed. "I know. I saw an accident."

"Mmmm. Was it bad?"

"It was bad, although the police say everyone is going to be okay. A car ran a red light and plowed right into a pickup truck."

"Dangerous," Griffin said sleepily.

"It *was* dangerous. A few seconds earlier and it would have been John and me. Anyway, I stuck around and gave an account of what I saw to the police. It was so strange. The driver at fault had a yellow Ferrari. Two men in suits were inside the car. I don't think I've ever seen a Ferrari since I've lived in Vetta Park—"

John shot out of bed. "What a minute. Wait a minute!" he yelled. Suddenly he was fully awake – words articulated and springing off the walls of their room. He slammed shut the door to their bedroom and flicked on the lights. "What did you just say?" he demanded.

Greta's face went pale. She sat up in bed and held the covers even closer in front of her – as though they were breastplates that could shield her.

"Greta…what did you *just* say?" Griffin repeated.

"I said I'd never seen a Ferrari in Vetta Park before," she whispered.

"It was a yellow Ferrari?"

"Yes," she whispered.

"Two men in suits inside?"

"Yes."

"And you spoke to the police and told them the Ferrari driver was at fault?"

Greta nodded.

"FUCK! GRETA!" he bellowed. At the same time, he picked up a VHS tape from the TV stand in front of him and launched it at the far wall. It marked the pale yellow paint before shattering into pieces on the ground.

Greta had never seen him this angry. "Griffin, please stop; you're going to wake up John!" she pleaded. Tears started furiously rolling down her cheeks. Her shivering had evolved into quaking and then sweating. It seemed both cold and hot at the same time, as if her body didn't know how to deal with the present situation and was staging a confused response.

Griffin left the doorway and sat next to her on the edge of her bed, facing the closet. She thought he might make a sudden move – whirl backwards and strike her or grab her exposed hands. Instead he clenched his hands together and said to the closet: "Tomorrow you will go to the police station and tell them you got it wrong. The other driver was at fault, *not* the Ferrari driver. You couldn't see clearly and you got confused. Do you understand me?"

Greta shook her head. "I can't lie to the police, Griffin. I know what I saw–"

Griffin stood up and towered over her. His face was so furious that he looked foreign to her – her husband wearing a mask of rage. He bent down until his face was just inches away from hers. "Tomorrow. You will go to the police station. And you will tell them you got it wrong," he repeated. "Do you understand me?"

Greta swallowed and nodded.

Griffin bent down and cupped her chin with a firm hold.

"Greta?"

"Yes?" she responded beneath the strain of his grip.

"Don't get cute. Don't try to outsmart me. Don't think you can fuck with me. Do you understand me?"

She nodded and he let go.

Griffin stood up straight again and walked calmly to the other side of the bed. He grabbed his pillow and marched out of the room, turning off the lights on his way out.

After he left the room, Greta shuddered underneath her covers for a long time. She stared up at the ceiling and blinked away tears for most of the night – drops that fell in small rolling cascades that stung her cheeks.

It wasn't just the task Griffin had set before her – the demand that she lie to the police and blame an innocent person for an offense he hadn't committed. It wasn't just the cryptic nature of this particular situation. She knew now that he was in some way involved with these men in the Ferrari and he didn't feel the need to tell her who they were, or what their particular dilemma meant for him.

It was the way he treated her – the way he yelled and broke things and grabbed her. If she was upset before that he was mysterious and unknowable, now she saw that he was threatening and forbidding. He had secrets, which he ferociously guarded, even at the expense of their relationship.

That night in February – staring at the ceiling of their bedroom and reviewing the timeline of the night's events, Greta realized she could no longer be in the marriage. She would rather parade their troubles in front of strangers in a courtroom than quietly put up with the charade any longer.

She knew what she had to do. At six or seven in the morning -- when the sun finally emerged and rays of light came through the window and bounced off the shattered pieces of plastic on their carpet, Greta came up with her plan. First she would lie to the police – as promised. Then she would tell Griffin she wanted a divorce.

# CHAPTER EIGHT

*September 17, 2017*

Detective Hobbs lay awake in bed and sighed. She glanced over at Lt. Adams and sighed again. It was eleven-thirty at night and neither of them was asleep. At least Adams wasn't trying to fight it. He was thumbing through a detective novel, vigorously turning each page. Clad only in boxer shorts, he looked like a model from a fireman's catalog – naturally tan and hairless, with muscles that clung to his frame while he read.

Hobbs and Adams had been sleeping together for three months and both were amazed that no one else had figured it out. At first there were code names and dates in nearby towns, late-night meet-ups and secret texts. It was as though they were a detective story within a detective story. But as the weeks progressed, they grew sloppier about protecting their liaison. They went out by the light of day and attended outings together in Vetta Park – once, only a few miles from the police station.

Still there were no sightings, no surprised colleagues, no leaked gossip – at least not as far as Hobbs could tell.

Hobbs was at first surprised by the interest from Adams. She was over a decade older than him – although they didn't look mismatched to the casual observer. In addition to being young, Adams often acted young. At times he seemed driven primarily by his libido, he laughed at puerile jokes and he seemed openly, irrationally optimistic about the world. The job hadn't hardened him yet, and even though Hobbs knew it eventually would, she kept her cynicism to herself.

Hobbs could not have been more different from Adams. She didn't tell dirty jokes with her colleagues, didn't implore her colleagues to tell her stories and didn't howl with laughter when they did, didn't believe in some illusory future destiny that awaited them just for being good people.

Hobbs felt most comfortable in the presence of her partner – Ray Martinez – simply because he'd known her the longest out of anyone. And even those encounters could be stilted. Late nights in the squad car, watching a doorway or an alley for hours, Detective Martinez would often implore her to tell him stories – her childhood, her parents, what college was like. Hobbs would listen to his requests but do her best to retain her laconic shell…and she heard the refrain from him and others multiple times: she was tough and unreadable, a closed book.

The closed book might have been an accurate analogy but *tough* couldn't have been further from the truth. Hobbs was quiet because her personal life was a mostly-kept secret and she wanted to keep it that way.

Hobbs also believed that the squad car talks should reflect the nature of their professional lives. Even as they were mired in boredom and searching for conversation topics, she didn't want to talk about herself; she wanted to talk about unsolved cases and overlooked leads. As they sat in the front seat and stared at a vast landscape of stillness, she passed the time by telling stories of old – and if Martinez had heard them all before, he never protested and she didn't really care. In this line of work, she needed to keep her safeguards in place.

Hobbs viewed Adams as different from most of the men who propositioned her because he was immature and blithe and still in the phase of moving from one doting female acolyte to the next. If he just wanted to add a notch to his bedpost, Hobbs was fine with that. She had no particular desire to settle down anyway.

Adams closed the book and rolled over to face her. "We should get some shuteye Roberta," he said quietly, moving closer to her.

Hobbs smiled and caressed his hair with her fingertips. She tried not to flinch when he mentioned her first name. It was that same contamination of professional into personal. He was a colleague – a subordinate, actually – but here in the bedroom, they were intimate and on the same terms. It was only right that he use her first name when they were lying next to each other and she tried to do the same.

"I know, Dean. There's just something about the case that's keeping me up." Her words lurched from her mouth unnaturally. She didn't want to talk at all, to explain why sleep wasn't coming to her despite the late hour. She just wanted to lie awake with her thoughts.

"It's okay, baby," he said, and flicked off the light next to her bedside table. In the darkness he couldn't see her flinch again. At some point she was going to have to talk to him about the pet names. *Enough with the baby and the sweetie*, she would say. And, if she was really feeling honest: *please just call me Hobbs until I can get used to someone from the precinct calling me Roberta.*

For now, she settled with staying still and silent while he tried to wrap his body around hers. Hobbs' mind was swimming with details – hidden puzzle pieces that didn't quite fit together. There had been the phone call from Tuck's brother, the home search, numerous interviews, the press conference and the APB – all of which had turned up very little. Perhaps there was some bit of minutia she had overlooked. As her mind continued to race, she tried to think of where a family of four could hide for days without being sighted. Or, if she let herself think about it, where a perpetrator could hide a family of four without any trace. Hobbs shuddered and tried to move her thoughts back into the past.

It was a long time before sleep finally came.

# CHAPTER NINE

*September 18, 2017*

Hobbs woke up suddenly, forcefully, at 3am. She gasped and tossed the duvet cover off of her side of the bed, shot straight up and breathed heavily a few times. Beads of sweat covered her forehead and the collar of her shirt.

"Roberta…are you okay?"

Hobbs looked over and saw that Adams was sitting up too – squinting and blinking. He looked half-dazed, as if he couldn't tell if he was still in a dream. He tenderly brushed her hair away from her face.

"Did you have a bad dream?" Adams asked.

Hobbs shook her head. "No, no, it was nothing like that." Her voice sounded soft, unusually quiet. She scratched her temple as she caught her breath, still reconciling the subconscious with the conscious – what was real and what was imagined.

"Can you tell me what's going on?" he pressed.

Hobbs turned and examined the shape of her knees underneath the sheets. She circled them with her hands and drew them up to her chest – a protective stance. "I remember her," Hobbs said.

"Who?"

"Greta. Carpenter. Although at that time she was Greta Brock. I know where I've seen her before. She came into the police station. She was scared."

Adams leaned over and turned on the desk light. He reached slowly, delicately, as though a sudden move might corrupt her memory.

"What was she scared of?" he asked.

Roberta shrugged. "I don't know. But I remember thinking that someone got to her. She had seen a car accident and she gave a report to the police at the scene of the incident. Then she showed up at the police station the next morning and gave a completely different story. And I remember...I remember that she seemed so scared and so shaken."

Adams was quiet for a moment while he considered this and then asked, "Did you update the police report after she came into the station?"

"Yeah, of course."

"Then why didn't it show up in our records search?"

"Because, this happened...I mean...this must have been *over a decade* ago." She grew quiet and stared out the window, preferring to see the dark shadows in her backyard than to look at his face. Discussions of the past unnerved them both – especially occurrences that happened in the far distance, when she had been a young police officer and he was no more than a teenager.

"I don't understand. The precinct didn't use computers over a decade ago?"

Roberta brought her gaze back to him. "Yes, we had computers but we still primarily wrote everything down on paper. The computer system we had then was entirely different than what we have now and even the building was different. When the paper files were moved to the current building, a lot of them were misplaced or got stored out of order. When the systems were upgraded, some of the data was lost. I'm not surprised we didn't find her in our search, but I know…Dean I *know* it was her. It was Greta."

Hobbs was staring at him, imploring him to believe her – unblinking and steadfast.

"Okay," he said with a sigh. "So, let's say it was Greta. What do we do now?"

Hobbs leaned back and rested her head against the tawny, polished bedframe. "We'll need to search the paper files and see what we can find…"

Adams recoiled. "*We?* Roberta, there are probably tens of thousands of files down there."

Hobbs nodded. "I know." She reached forward and caressed his shoulder. It was a compassionate gesture – an act she didn't typically do. But they both knew that there was going to be no *we* in the exercise she had proposed. There was only *him* – low-ranking, new to the force and young. Maybe Weaver would assign a grunt to help him through the task.

Something else they both understood: the chore would be mind-numbing and tedious. Felonies such as violent crimes had been meticulously filed and archived…but the same couldn't be said for traffic incidents. It could take days or weeks for Adams to sort through all of the paperwork in the basement until he came up with the correct file.

"Anything else you remember?" Adams asked.

"Yeah," Hobbs said softly. "There was a Ferrari involved – a yellow Ferrari."

"A yellow Ferrari," Adams repeated. "Huh. That's different. Was Greta driving it?"

"No, it was one of the cars involved in the accident," Hobbs said. "I wish I could remember more."

Adams nodded but instead of saying anything, he leaned closer to her and ran his palm up and down her arm. Hobbs neither reciprocated nor balked. She allowed him this gesture for five minutes until sleep overcame him and he sank back to his side of the bed.

Hobbs stayed awake for another hour or so. With cases like these, her mind felt like a runaway train – proceeding along tracks of uncertain relevance. The only thing that helped was to mentally review the long list of tasks she would assume the next day.

The Carpenter family's cell phone files had finally come in, and Hobbs and Martinez were going to look through them in the morning. There was also bank and credit card activity to look into, and now Adams would likely be holed up in the precinct's basement, looking through traffic files.

All of this occupied her mind with possibilities and scenarios – best and worst cases. As soon as her eyelids finally felt heavy, she was dreaming about a scared young woman, a yellow Ferrari, and a family who had abandoned their home in a terrible hurry.

*** 

Hobbs usually woke up before Adams, and this morning was no different. She was in and out of the shower and dressed before he rolled over, patted her side of the bed and sat up. "What time is it?" he asked.

"Six-thirty," she said as she stepped into her shoes. The sun was just beginning to rise, although thick storm clouds hung in the sky. It had been raining heavily in the early morning and it was going to storm again.

"It's early," he said. Then he looked at her for an extended beat, surveyed her blue pantsuit and said admiringly, "You look nice."

Hobbs smiled. "I'll see you at the office." She knew he wanted a kiss, an acknowledgement or perhaps just a return compliment but there was too much to do, too much clouding her thoughts. She grabbed a cup of coffee from the kitchen counter, affixed her badge to the belt of her slacks and then she was off.

\*\*\*

Hobbs parked her car and reached the lobby of the police precinct just before the downpour. She could hear the rain tapping on the roof as she made her way to her desk and it reminded her of puddle jumping with her brothers in grade school. She was from Kansas – part of a large family inhabiting a patch of farmland in a town with one traffic light. When it had rained, Hobbs and her brothers would grab their slickers and boots and chase each other over grass and pasture land in the deluge. Perhaps this was why she loved the rain so much, the metallic smell of a storm, the current of distant lightning.

"Um…Detective Hobbs?" a voice said.

Hobbs had been sitting at her desk and staring down at her phone, absorbing nothing in particular. The voice was young and cautious, and when Hobbs turned around, she saw one of their newly hired officers behind her – a petite red-haired woman named Rochelle.

"Yes?"

"Sorry to interrupt. I wanted to let you know that the cell phone records arrived. I put them in the conference room."

Hobbs nodded her acknowledgement and got up from her desk. In the conference room, there were a few stacks of papers – records for Tuck, Greta, Griffin and John. She took a seat and got to work.

An hour later, Ray Martinez showed up. He pulled up a chair next to her and pointed to the largest of the stacks of paper. "Hey partner. Are those the cell phone and text records?"

Hobbs smiled. "Yes. Those are Griffin Brock's."

"Have you gone through them yet?"

"No I haven't. Still sorting through Greta's. Knock yourself out."

Martinez smiled back and pulled the top paper from the pile. They didn't say another word to each other until the late morning.

\*\*\*

The rain had completely abated by the time of their meeting with the Captain, and everything outside his office window looked like it was gleaming – the green tops of trees just starting to brown, the reflective glint from other buildings in their one-block radius of downtown Vetta Park. Even the Arch – visible only if she squinted and mentally connected silver patches – looked as though it was shining after a fresh wash.

"What have you got for me?" Weaver asked. He shifted in his seat and clasped his hands together.

Hobbs brought her gaze away from the window. She glanced at Martinez and then down at her notepad. The page that she'd set aside for all of her notes was nearly empty.

"We didn't find much," she said. "Greta's cell phone has been turned off or discarded. We can't track it. She hasn't sent out any text messages or calls since they left. The few texts on her phone from before their departure aren't meaningful. No indication that the family was in trouble or about to leave."

"What about Tuck's cell phone?"

"Well, yesterday a forensics team went through the house very carefully and did a second sweep. They found Tuck's phone underneath the bed. So obviously, no texts have come from him since the family left."

Weaver sat forward. "So Greta is presumably the only one who has a cell phone with her?"

"Correct."

Weaver paused and looked up at the ceiling, deliberating. Whenever they got a piece of news or evidence that didn't quite seem right, Weaver would take a deep breath and look skyward, exposing the fuzzy white stubble on his upper neck while he thought.

After she'd taken the call from forensics, Hobbs had done nearly the same thing – head held aloft, torso frozen while she thought. It was one thing to have John's cell phone thoughtlessly left behind, but now Tuck's as well? It was as though whoever was on the other end of the burner phone had instructed them to leave their devices behind – and the absence of Greta's phone in the house made Hobbs wonder whether the woman had tacitly snuck hers along. At some future point in their searching, perhaps the Detectives would receive a ping from Greta's phone – like a honing device that painted a rhumb from Vetta Park to their whereabouts.

"What about incoming texts to their cell phones?" Weaver asked. "Surely some messages have come their way."

Martinez fielded the question this time. "Well…a few texts have come in – all to John. Those might be the best we have to go on."

"Hmmm." Weaver scratched his head and sat back in his chair. "Before we get to John, talk to me about the ex-husband. Griffin Brock. Anything interesting there?"

"We learned that Griffin is a grade-A asshole," Martinez said. "Maybe we knew that already. There were no texts to, from, or about the Carpenter family – or John. Just a lot of flirtatious messages to various phone numbers. Maybe they were all to his pregnant wife but I doubt it. And there were a lot of disparaging and off-color texts too. The guy seems like a piece of work."

"I see," Weaver said. He thought about this for a few moments and then said, "Alright…so talk to me about John Brock."

Hobbs cleared her throat. "John Brock. No outgoing texts from before he left. But he did receive three texts from a guy named Tai Gausman. A few weeks ago, Tai asked John to meet up to go to a rock concert. And then, after getting no response, he asked again on September 7 – the date of the disappearance, and then asked John where he was on September 12. Since then, he's apparently given up."

"Track down Tai and go knock on his door."

"I've already located his address, Captain. It's five miles south of here. Martinez and I were going to visit him after this meeting."

"Take Adams with you instead," Weaver instructed.

Hearing Adams's name made Hobbs shudder. It was a reflex – one she hoped would go unnoticed. The thought of her on an assignment with Adams bothered her. The demarcation of professional from personal would be erased; the appearance of propriety would be tougher to maintain.

She decided to protest – lightly. "Captain, I asked Adams to take a look at the traffic files downstairs. I think Greta filed a report with the station about a traffic accident maybe ten years ago – and then she may have changed her mind about what she said the next day. Adams is looking into the files as we speak."

"Roberta, it isn't your responsibility to ferry out assignments. Rochelle can dig through the files. Lt. Adams is a good interviewer and young people have a strong rapport with him."

Weaver's voice was unusually stern and his eyes were narrowed and fixed at Hobbs as he spoke. The issue was not up for debate. Hobbs nodded her assent and Martinez concluded.

"Nothing else of interest turned up," he said. "That's all we've got."

"Meaning you've got jack shit," Weaver clarified. "And we had a few guys search the home again and they found jack shit too. Not one shred of evidence."

Weaver smacked his desk with his fist. "We've got no bank or credit card activity since they left. The officer who went to Marcia Brock's funeral saw no sign or mention of the family. The cell phone records are useless. No reliable tip has come through our tip line. I mean, what…did the earth open up and swallow them up?"

Hobbs shrugged even though she knew the question was meant to be rhetorical.

Weaver continued. "And now you say that Greta Brock provided a statement about a traffic accident a decade ago and then changed her story?"

Hobbs nodded.

"Are you serious with this? What, did this float down to you in a dream?"

Hobbs pressed her lips together and said nothing.

Weaver sighed heavily. "In my twenty years, I don't think a case has ever provided so little to go on."

"I know, Captain," Hobbs said.

"Good luck with Tai," Weaver said. "I hope you guys find something."

***

Tai Gausman was spraying water at his pickup truck when the Vetta Park police showed up. Lanky and gruff-looking, he wore a green-checked, flannel shirt and loose jeans that hung from his frame.

Hobbs and Adams showed up in her unmarked car, but Tai seemed to recognize law enforcement when he saw it. He turned off his hose – although he tightened his grip on it – and stiffened as he watched them approach.

"Are you Tai Gausman?" Hobbs asked. She had seen a mug shot of him from a previous narcotics arrest and he looked about the same.

"Yeah, that's me," Tai said. "What's up?"

"My name is Detective Hobbs and this is Lieutenant Adams. We're here to talk to you about John Brock."

Tai gave them a half-smile. He walked towards the front of his one-story ranch house and pointed at two plastic chairs arranged on the concrete just in front of his front door. "Do y'all want to have a seat?" he asked. "My ma's inside so we should stay out here."

"We can stand right here. It's fine," Adams said.

Tai smiled vaguely again – as though he were indulging in an inside joke with himself – and dropped into one of the seats. "I guess I'll sit down if none of y'all will," he said.

"Tai, when is the last time you saw John Brock?" Hobbs asked.

"Is he in some kinda trouble?" Tai asked, squinting up at her.

Hobbs shook her head. "We're not sure. That's why we're hoping you can help us out."

"Uh," Tai said – a grunted acknowledgement. He bowed forward in his chair, carefully fingering the laces of his sneakers with his head bent. This motion provided Hobbs with a view of his lower back. There were two tattoos – one a black cross, the other a black cat. There were also several red pimples poking through his skin. Hobbs swallowed and looked away.

"I can't really help you out," Tai said, pulling himself up and sitting back in the chair. "I ain't seen him in a few years."

"Did you call or text him recently?" Adams asked.

"Yeah, Legends of Death was playing at the Ampitheater. They're a band. I thought he'd want to go but I didn't hear back from him. Not too surprised."

"How did you meet John?"

"We were in study hall and then we both dropped out of Vetta High at the same time – tenth grade I guess."

"Why'd you drop out?"

"There wasn't much for us, you know. The teachers just thought we was dumbasses or something."

Hobbs took out her notepad and scribbled a few notes. "Was John able to read and write?" she asked, recalling her conversation with Richard Carpenter, John's distant step-uncle.

"He could read but not much. Although he wasn't dumb or nothin'."

Hobbs stopped scrawling, looked up and asked, "Why did you stop hanging out with John?"

"It wasn't me, it was him. I heard he got his ass kicked by a bunch of guys and then he avoided me after that even though I didn't have nothin' to do with it. At one point, I thought he moved away, but then I drove by his house and saw his car...so he's still there. Or least, he *was*."

"You're saying he was beat up by a bunch of guys?" Adams asked.

"Yessir."

"Who? And why?"

"I don't have a freaking clue, officer. Maybe he pissed off the wrong kind of people. Maybe he looked at someone the wrong way. It don't take much, does it?" Tai shifted forward, snatched a tiny circular object from his back pocket, and placed a wad of chewing tobacco in his left cheek.

Hobbs took a step back. "Do you know approximately when this incident happened?"

Tai excused himself, jogged inside his house and emerged with a yellow plastic cup. He spat into the cup and cleared his throat. "Sorry. Say what?"

"When John was attacked. Can you let us know approximately when that happened?"

Tai thought as his jaw rocked slightly. A few moments later he said, "I guess 2015…maybe spring?" He spat again.

"And was he hospitalized?" Hobbs pressed.

Tai shrugged. "I dunno. Like I said, he stopped hangin' out with me and then someone told me he got his ass kicked in. I didn't see it happen, so I can't tell you no more about it. Sorry."

A petite older woman jogged through the front of the house, slammed the front door behind her and positioned herself in between Tai and the police. She had long, gray-flecked greasy hair and pockmarked skin. She eyed Hobbs and Adams and then kicked one of Tai's chair legs. "What's goin' on?" she demanded.

"Jesus, Mom. They was just asking me about John Brock!" Tai looked into his cup and then spat.

The woman kicked his chair leg again and then turned to face Adams. "Y'all ain't allowed to talk to him unless he's got his lawyer!" she yelled at Adams, her head angled back, her chin jutted forward. She was angry, but she looked diminutive next to

Adams, and her chin – even extended to its fullest -- reached no higher than his neck.

"I'm sorry ma'am," Adams said. "We were just leaving." He waved to Tai – who was by then fully engrossed in his ritual of chewing, examining and spitting, and who failed to return the gesture.

In the car, Adams drove while Hobbs summarized what they learned. John Brock was a high school dropout, who was attacked at the age of sixteen for – most likely – pissing off the wrong kind of guys.

Hobbs felt a sense of apprehension but also a dose of relief as they made their way back to the station. At long last, their mystery had a path forward.

# CHAPTER TEN

*January 25, 2009*

Greta waited patiently in the school counselor's office of Edwardsville Elementary. After ten minutes passed, a young woman hurried into the room with a stack of papers in her hand. "I'm so sorry I'm late," the woman said. When she held out her hand to shake Greta's, silver and gold bracelets jangled on her arm. "My name is Brooke Tremble," the counselor said. "Thanks so much for meeting with me, Mrs. Brock."

"It's Ms.," Greta clarified – perhaps a bit too hastily. "My husband and I – John's dad – are going through a divorce."

"Oh, I'm so sorry to hear that," Brooke said. "I know that can't be easy."

"We've been separated for four years, so we're all used to it by now," Greta said. She thought about the first time she knew with absolute certainty that she would be ending their marriage – the night she'd witnessed the car accident. What she had thought would be a quick break ended up being a slow churn. She hadn't wanted to confront Griffin with a divorce, and surprisingly, she didn't have to. The marriage could decay on its own accord through attrition.

For months after the car accident, Greta barely spoke to Griffin. She couldn't shake the anger she felt about his quiet inner life – the secrets about his associates and work activities that he kept from her. She knew there were secrets about other women too – smells of perfume and lavender lotion that lingered on his clothes when she was doing the laundry.

The best way to avoid a confrontation was to disassociate from him, to view him as the occasional co-parent who shared a bed with her but satisfied his craving for intimacy elsewhere.

So Greta avoided Griffin and he acted like he didn't notice. Initially, on the occasions they ate meals together and were forced to interact, they talked about John – always about John. Most of their earlier conversations followed the same cycle. She would express her worries about John and he would brush them aside, accuse Greta of excessive mothering and the conversation would end. After a few months of this, Greta learned they could quite civilly interact with each other as long as the topic was the weather, traffic or the St. Louis Cardinals. Such an untenable situation lasted for four years. They were separated while still living in the same house – living a life that could have been fodder for dramatic or comedic cinema except that they evaded instead of fought with each other.

One evening in the summer of 2008, Griffin came home and announced that he wanted to make it official. In quick succession, he hired a lawyer, moved out of their Avery Place home, and agreed to see John one weekend every other month.

This was a workable arrangement, and Greta was at first buoyed by the new set of circumstances. The eggshells she had so painstakenly tottered across for years were finally gone. She could decorate the house as she wished – speak as openly as she wanted about anything – even if she was just addressing the walls or a child who was too young to understand her. Everything seemed like it was moving in a positive direction – her life was *finally* moving forward – until two developments shattered her sanguine shell.

First came the realization that Griffin wasn't going to provide any child support. For him, moving on was both an emotional and a physical state, and he didn't want a schedule of monthly payments tethering him to his former life. Greta responded by taking out a loan in her own name and then retaining the counsel of Lucroy, Broxton & Hill. After four years of polite hostility, Brock vs. Brock was shaping up to be a battle.

The other shoe to drop was the phone call from the school. At age nine, and despite various well-intentioned interventions, John Brock was still unable to read and write. The school psychologist tested John for learning disabilities and then phoned Greta to come in and discuss the results. This is how Greta found herself in Brooke Tremble's tiny office on a cold day in January – shivering slightly in her seat at the conference table and waiting to hear the results.

\*\*\*

"John is quite a smart boy." Brooke said. She addressed Greta while sorting through her stack of papers and pitching a few of them in front of Greta.

"None of us were surprised that his IQ was above average," Brooke continued, with a smile. "So you should be happy about that."

Greta nodded. "I'm not surprised."

Brooke's smile quickly faded and she gave Greta a look of concern. "However, with the academic testing, we saw that he was unable to decode letters – assigning sounds to assemble words. He wasn't able to read a simple first-grade text. Usually he would take the first letter of a word and wildly guess what it said. He had great difficulty with selecting rhyming words, he wasn't able to follow multi-step directions and he skipped some words altogether. In his writing prompt, he mixed up and reversed letters, avoided punctuation, spacing and capitalization, and almost everything he wrote was indecipherable – not only by the testing administrator but by John himself. He can't read his own writing."

"I know this," Greta said. She took a few quick breaths, trying to calm the swell of anger brewing inside of her. "I know all of this. I've raised this before. I raised this in kindergarten – with Miss Alice. I've raised it every year since! All the school has told me was to be patient and that it was developmental. Be patient, be patient, we're working on it. That's what you all said!"

"And that's what we did—"

"Well then why…why is he still…" Greta swallowed hard and threw her hands up in the air. "Why can't he…why is he still illiterate? He's nine years old!"

Brooke placed her hand gently on Greta's shoulder. "Greta, I promise you, it's going to be okay." Her voice was calm and trained – a well-seasoned responder to parental hysteria. She continued. "John has learning disabilities – in reading, writing and spelling. He's going to get services and an IEP – that stands for *Individualized Educational Plan.* He'll get specialized instruction, accommodations and modifications to the fourth grade lesson plan. It will all work out. Don't worry."

Greta shook off Brooke's hand and stood up from the table. She was angry and didn't want to be comforted. The school was telling her to believe in its ability to get to John, to be patient and relax. It was no different than what she'd been told for the previous five years. Meanwhile, other fourth graders were putting together science fair projects and reading chapter books, developing models of the solar system and testing soil. John was barely able to function at a first grade level, despite his high IQ. Somehow the boat of elementary school education had left the dock, with John standing humble and alone at the shore.

"I hope you're right," Greta said weakly to Brooke. "I sure hope you're right."

\*\*\*

Lucroy, Broxton & Hill had a very uninspiring waiting room. There were two black leather couches, two oval-shaped glass coffee tables, a smattering of niche-hobby magazines and a mounted television that broadcast the local news.

Greta had been waiting no more than two minutes when a man in a blue-button down shirt and khakis greeted her. "Are you Greta Brock?" he asked.

He was tall – neck-craning tall, with a broad chest and curly brown hair that threatened to flop over his eyes. When she nodded in response to his question, he smiled. "My name is Tuck Carpenter and I'm the paralegal assigned to your divorce proceedings. Can you come with me?"

She followed him down a hallway and into one of the conference rooms. They sat across from each other and made idle chatter while waiting for her lawyer to arrive. Greta learned that he lived in the small downtown section of Vetta Park, that he was unattached except for a Labrador retriever who chewed up his furniture and that he dreamed of traveling the world one day.

Tuck was candid and funny – and during their conversation, he frequently threw his head back and laughed fully – an authentic, deep-voiced chuckle.

Greta laughed too, and not just because of the jaunty nature of the topic at hand. For the first time in years, she could envision the future and all of its promises, everything she had spent her girlhood waiting for. She saw a speedy conclusion to the divorce proceedings, the ability to focus solely on John and his needs. And if she looked hard enough or even allowed herself, she saw herself dating attractive, available, kindhearted men – men who looked directly at her instead of at numbers smattered across rows and columns. Everything that had once seemed crushing or impossible now seemed manageable.

That is, until her lawyer showed up and dropped the anvil.

"Griffin's suing for full custody of John," her lawyer said as soon as he arrived and closed the door behind him. His name was Lance Garcia and he was a partner in the firm. He spoke and moved quickly, as if propelled by a motor. When he delivered bad news, he usually stared at the person he was speaking with and pressed his lips together. This time he pressed them into a line so thin they nearly disappeared.

Greta shook her head. "That's impossible! Why would he do that? He barely sees John. He's been such an absent father. He doesn't even know all that John has been going through. He can't have full custody! That's crazy! The judge will see that, right?"

Lance stood up straight and crossed his arms but didn't say anything.

"Why would he do that?" Greta repeated. "He can't *actually want* full custody of John!"

"He's doing it to get back at you and to run up your legal bills," Lance said. "I see it all the time."

"Well he's got no case, right?" Greta insisted. "I mean, he never sees John so obviously he would have no case."

"It's too soon to tell what kind of a case Griffin has," Lance answered. "He might claim to be a more suitable parent due to financial reasons. He might claim to be more stable. If there's anything unseemly in your past, such as mental illness or drug use, he might try to use that against you. There are several tactics he could try to take. So our job is to figure out what *we* claim to convince the Family Court judge that he's a negligent parent."

"The fact that he's a *negligent parent* makes him a negligent parent!" Greta said. She turned around to face the window so as not to display her emotions. A tear fell and she tilted her head back to staunch the cascade. She had been so silly to think that this could be easy – that her divorce could be processed without a battle. And why wouldn't she have foreseen that Griffin would try to take away John – the one person in the world who meant more to her than anyone else? The only person she had left in her world.

Lance cleared his throat. "Ms. Brock…Greta…we promise you that we'll do everything in our power to ensure you get custody of John. Our legal team is among the best in the greater St. Louis metro area. We'll do whatever we have to do."

Greta stared out the window for a few more moments. The threat of tears had passed but she still felt a pit in her stomach. Lance's tone of voice reminded her of Brook Tremble – both professionals trying to comfort her without any way of knowing what would happen. They gave her assurances, platitudes, sound bites that had been rehearsed on countless others before her. For the sake of her sanity, she chose to believe them, even though she knew how real life could play out.

A minute passed and then Greta turned around and faced the two men. "Okay," she said. "Let's go to court."

# CHAPTER ELEVEN

*May 5, 2009*

It was ten o'clock at night and John was still awake. When Greta went to check on him, she found him curled into a fetal pose on top of his sheets. He was trying to read a book, lips moving in a soft whisper as he ran his index finger along one of the lines.

Greta smiled at him, taking notice of his thick brown hair, recently grown out because he thought long hair was a sign of maturity. A few strands stemmed away from his head – like branches of a tree – and Greta had to resist the urge to reach forward and flatten them down. He was ten years old now – and always battling for sovereignty over his appearance. Whatever he wore out the door in the morning, whatever he looked like when he went to bed at night – as long as he was weather-appropriate and hygienic, Greta had to let it go.

"What're you doing?" Greta asked, joining him on the bed.

John's head popped up and he inched closer to the wall. "Reading," he said. "It's my homework. I have to have this book finished by tomorrow."

He closed the book for a moment and Greta saw the title. *Jacob Gray Wants a Dog.* A banner across the front of the book announced in thick black letters: *I Can Read! Step 1, For Emergent Readers, Grades Pre-K – K.*

"Can you read it to me?" Greta asked.

John shrugged and re-opened the book. He took a deep breath and placed his finger under the first word.

John read slowly. "I...do...I...do...want...him. I...will...take...cay-...cay-...care...of...him."

He glanced up expectantly to see Greta's face and she beamed. "Great job!" she acclaimed.

John continued. "I...will...give...him...food...to...eat."

Greta smiled again, trying to quell the growing unease she felt as she heard him read words strung together for children half his age. It wasn't just his slow pace but the fact that he was now four months into his IEP and clearly relying on his old tactics, reciting one-syllable words he had previously memorized at a glacial pace.

When John finished the book, Greta smiled, heaped praise on him for the effort, and then took the book in her hands. She pointed to the word on the cover's banner: *Emergent.*

"Can you tell me what that says?" Greta asked. She knew it wasn't a word he had seen before, but it was a word that could be sounded out. There weren't any silent letters or deviations from known rules. The hard *'g'* might be a struggle but everything else was guessable.

John looked at the word just off the edge of her fingernail and then looked back at her. "I can't read that," he said.

"Just try it," Greta urged.

John pushed her finger aside and stared at the word. "It says…" he brought the book up to his face and stared harder. "Muh…Muh…mutt."

"Well, what's the first sound?" Greta asked.

John looked at her curiously.

"The first sound is *'em'*, right? E. M," Greta continued. "Em…em…emergent. Do you see?"

Despite her intentions to buoy his schooling, to nudge him forward, Greta could hear herself and knew how she sounded: pushy instead of patient, judgmental instead of unfailingly supportive. She wasn't surprised when John threw *Jacob Gray Wants a Dog* on the floor and thrust his covers over his head.

The book landed with a clatter on the hardwood and Greta responded by placing it gently on his backpack and rolling his desk chair to the side of the bed. She would respect his desire for space and sit a few feet away from him.

"It's alright, John. You'll get this down. I can tell you're working hard and that's what matters."

"No I won't." John's voice was muffled from underneath the covers. Then he pulled them back and sat up. "Bryce Lipnowski says I'm stupid. Today he called me 'brainless Johnny Broccoli' and the whole class laughed."

"What?" Greta was furious. "I can't believe he said that! Tomorrow I'm going to call his mother."

"You can't call his mother, Mom."

"Why not?"

"Because it's *embarrassing*. If you call, I'll wish I hadn't said anything to you. And also, it's not just him. It's the whole class. They call me John Broccoli instead of Brock because they say my brain is the size of broccoli."

A million thoughts flooded Greta's mind. Her first instinct was to teach him how to fight back, to call out the weaknesses of his classmates. Surely Bryce Lipnowski and his classmates had flaws – and John could learn to counter-punch with a caustic jab that could take the heat off of him and onto them.

But she hesitated because it wasn't *him*. John was sweet and curious, imaginative and kindhearted. She had never heard him tease another kid and she didn't want him to start because she'd encouraged him to. It wasn't his personality to make fun of someone else and that made his vulnerability all the more crushing.

"You know, Johnny, a lot of successful people struggled when they were younger. Visionaries, leaders, CEOs, politicians, artists…so many of them were just like you. They learned how to cope with their issues and how to think outside the box…and that's why they're so successful today."

John didn't say anything so she continued.

"And John, you are *so smart*. Don't listen to those kids in the class. They have no idea what they're talking about. You have a lot of potential and you're going to do great in life, I have no doubt."

John flopped down on his bed, his head crashing on the pillow like a paperweight. He gave no indication that her words had sunk in or that he'd even heard them. Instead he leaned over, produced a frog-shaped stuffed animal from the area between the mattress and the wall and flung it on the floor. "I'm too old for that," he declared.

"Did you hear what I said, John?" Greta pressed.

John moaned and writhed a few times in his bed. "Can't we *change the subject?*" he asked.

"Okay…sure," Greta said. "Do you remember our plans for the weekend?"

John appeared to like the new subject. His face lit up. "Yeah! Mr. Tuck is going to help me with baseball practice!"

"That's right. And then you have a game on Saturday."

He nodded and traced the line of red lettering on his St. Louis Cardinal-branded sheets. Then he looked up and asked, "Who drives the yellow car?"

Greta frowned and leaned forward. "What do you mean, John? Which yellow car?"

"The yellow car that got into an accident. When I was six years old. Who drives it?"

Greta was completely taken aback. "You remember that?" she asked.

He nodded. "Yeah, I wasn't sleeping in the back seat. I remember it. Who drives it?"

"Well…I don't know, John. I haven't thought about that accident in years."

It was a lie – well delivered without the faintest pause. Greta had thought a lot about that accident in the years since – who the two men were and how they related to Griffin. But for the sake of mollifying John and leaving the past in the past, she acted like the accident was nothing. Just a blip in that crazy February night when he'd come down with croup and had to be rushed to Children's Hospital.

"Are you ready for bed now, John?" Greta asked. It was late and *she* was ready for bed, eager to tuck him in, help herself to a half-glass of red wine and then call it a night. A lot had been discussed – from the mean kids at school to the yellow Ferrari. She wasn't sure if it was a stalling tactic or if he felt the need to purge his thoughts on this night, for some particular reason.

She stood up from the chair, tousled his hair and planted a kiss on his forehead. "Good-night, sweet boy."

"Mom, why do we spend so much time with Mr. Tuck?" John asked when she was perched over him. "He comes by like every weekend and plays baseball with me. Why does he do that and not Dad?"

Greta sighed, resumed her position in the rolling desk chair and thought about how to answer John. Whether stalling or genuine, his question deserved an answer.

Since first meeting Tuck at Lucroy, Broxton & Hill, Greta had become romantically involved with him. She never intended to start a relationship before her divorce was finalized but it was one of those non-prescribed things that sort of happened.

In early March, Tuck had stopped by with some paperwork on a rare evening when John was with his father. She had offered Tuck a glass of wine and they talked for hours. It was clear they both wanted more than friendship but they were unsure how to proceed, or even whether they should. Greta was concerned about jumping into anything too soon and Tuck had doubts about dating one of his firm's clients.

Just before he walked out the door, they made promises to each other. They would take things slowly and with caution. They would start with a friendship and see if anything blossomed from there when the time was right.

Then Tuck leaned forward to give her a hug and they began passionately, fervently kissing – tossing aside everything they had just proclaimed. For Greta, it was the culmination of years of pent-up distance – a marriage started when she was too young, then years of being ignored by her husband.

The kissing continued for ten minutes but then Greta prodded him towards the door. It was too much, she insisted. She needed some time.

But it only took a few days for Greta to realize this was something she really wanted. Soon there were other nights – nights Tuck stopped by after John was asleep, evenings he encouraged her to get a babysitter and meet up with him for dinner. Before long, they were seriously dating and he was integrated into her life with John – all in the span of two months.

Greta was caught up in the deliriousness of it all – a love affair, a positive role model for her son, and a partner to talk to. She hadn't stopped to think about how the hasty addition to their family structure was affecting John. At least, not until he asked.

"We spend time with Tuck because he likes spending time with us," Greta answered. "Your dad does too but he's very busy with his job. He sees us every chance he gets. Is it confusing for you?"

John nodded. "Yeah, sometimes it's like I have two dads."

"Well you should consider yourself very lucky. I wish I had even one parent. My dad died a long time ago and my mom—" Greta caught herself and stood up to leave the room. She could feel her face flush at the last memory of her mother. "Good night, John."

"Wait!" John called out. "You didn't finish what you were saying. What about your mom?"

Greta was halfway to the door but she stopped. The room was still mostly dark and she faced the closet to ensure John wouldn't be able to see her face…although he could still hear the fluctuation in her voice.

"My mom was a lovely woman…is a lovely woman," Greta said. "Did you know that you were named after her?"

"Yeah. You told me that already. You said that one day I'd meet her."

Tears formed in the corners of Greta's eyes. "I said that, huh? Well I hope so."

"What happened?" John asked. "Where is she?"

"It's too late to talk about it right now," Greta answered. "But one day I'll explain it." She tiptoed out of John's room and made her way to the wine cabinet. She needed just a half a glass to take the edge off of the night.

She sat outside, on the concrete slate of steps that led from her backdoor to the backyard. Next door, she could hear the neighbor's dog scuttling through the grass and yapping at birds.

She took a sip of the wine and looked up at the sky. It was a pitch black night with a smattering of stars – no clouds or light pollution. She took another sip and could feel her muscles relax. Greta was never much of a drinker, but sometimes a glass helped when she needed to divert her thoughts, to keep from thinking about her mistakes.

By the time the drink was finished, a slight breeze was gusting into a draft, and she felt too cold to stay outside. Opening up the screen door, she paused for a moment to glance at the sky again and thought about something. She wasn't making a wish exactly, but wordlessly expressing a few hopes.

She hoped that the kids in class would quit teasing John – or at least that their stinging words would have no affect on his self-esteem.

She hoped that Tuck would remain a fixture in their lives – not only for her sake but for John's too. He had become so attached to Tuck already that she worried about what would happen if he departed as quickly as he'd arrived.

And lastly, she hoped the right words would come to her the next time John asked about his grandmother Johanna. Oddly enough, he never did again.

# CHAPTER TWELVE

*October 15, 2009*

The Edwardsville County Family courtroom was showing its age. Dimly lit, with saggy wood paneling and a broken bench in the back, it was in much need of repair.

Griffin's mother, Marcia Brock, was seated in front of the broken bench in one of the few spots available for spectators. She looked regal as always – gray rooted brown hair coiffed neatly into a bun, a silk scarf, wool suit and expensive shoes. She always wore just a touch of makeup and bright red lipstick, painted across thin lips. Her face always bore the same mask – a frown marking disapproval – critical. At least, that's how it seemed to Greta.

Aside from her soon to be ex-mother-in-law, Greta didn't recognize anyone else in that area of the courtroom. She sat on the witness stand and looked past everyone – past Griffin and his lawyers, past her own lawyer, Lance Garcia – and stared at the clock in the very back of the room. The air felt thick and stifling and she willed time to hurry up while one of Griffin's lawyers questioned her.

The first several questions were easy – softballs lobbed with a graceful underhand. But after he'd gotten the banalities out of the way, Griffin's lawyer -- a stiff man with white hair and a graying moustache — changed his tune. He started pacing briskly and glowering at her while she answered. His questions seemed more like demands than queries.

"When did you meet Griffin Brock?" the lawyer asked.

"I met him about twelve years ago," Greta answered softly.

"Can you please be more precise? And speak up?"

"I met him in 1997," Greta said, in a louder voice. "I was eighteen years old."

"And were you single at the time that you met Mr. Brock?" the lawyer pressed.

Greta could feel where this line of questioning was headed and she shuddered. She stared at Lance. His head was down and he was sorting through papers on the table. "Yes sir," Greta said. "Well I was living in someone's apartment – in a man's apartment – but yes, I was single."

"You were *living* with someone but you claim you were *single?*" The lawyer repeated her words as though an arrangement was preposterous. He half-smirked and then asked, "So let's back up and talk about this *other man* who provided you with an apartment. How long after meeting him did you move into the apartment he provided?"

"I moved in about two weeks after I first met him," Greta answered. She could sense a shift in the courtroom, as subtle as the movement of air, but still palpable. The heat of everyone's judgment washed over her. "But I can explain..." she started to say.

"And just out of curiosity, how long did you know Mr. Griffin Brock before moving in with *him?*"

"Again, it was a few weeks."

"So, you meet a guy, you move in with him. Then, two years later, you meet my client, decide you like him, and a few weeks later, you move from the one guy's apartment to the residence owned by my client. Is that correct?"

"Well…I…" Greta placed her palm on her cheeks. They felt like they were on fire.

"You're a fast mover, Ms. Brock."

Greta shook her head. "I'm telling you, the first guy, it wasn't that type of relationship. And as for Griffin, I thought I was in love…"

Griffin's lawyer was pacing through the courtroom. He seemed unstoppable. "Let's talk about this first guy – the one who gave you the apartment to live in. Can you tell us about him?"

"You want his name?"

"Yes, Ms. Brock. Please tell us his name."

"His name was…is…Steven Vance. And again, I wasn't living with him – exactly. He just provided me with an apartment and he only stayed there occasionally. Very occasionally."

Greta looked around as though she expected a shocked response from the courtroom – a gasp, a murmur – some type of minor eruption. Steven Vance was a well-known figure in the small municipalities that skirted St. Louis. He was equally loved and loathed – depending on whether he was dodging the law or performing a favor. He was a big looming man – rounded shoulders, tall broad frame – the kind of guy who took charge of every room he walked into.

Vance owned two hotels and a nightclub – all on the western bank of the Mississippi River. The hotels were small and luxurious – heavily advertised along the I-55 corridor from Chicago as a place one could find solitude, escape at the hands of massage therapists and yoga instructors.

By contrast, the nightclub was loud and raucous. *The Thirst*, a two-story glass structure with dim lighting and a wraparound bar was seen by many as a stain on the quaint and quiet riverbed town where it was located. It drew its clientele from a college town across the river in Illinois, and the students were faithful patrons despite the thirty-minute drive.

Young revelers started lining up at six-thirty p.m. on Fridays, waiting for the doors to open at seven. At two a.m., they piled out on the streets, inebriated, stumbling and slurring. They noisily staggered into car services and drove off only to appear again before the red velvet rope that evening, ready to repeat the ritual.

If the townspeople were faintly irked by the noise and commotion of The Thirst, they complained very quietly. One reason for the calm dissent was economic. The Thirst provided tax revenues for the city, and it employed at least thirty townspeople as dancers, bartenders, waiters and bouncers.

But another reason – the more pressing reason – was that everyone knew Steven Vance was behind the enterprise, and no one wanted to provoke him. In the past, those who took him on had been publicly criticized, condemned and embarrassed. Steven Vance knew no boundaries when it came to shaming his critics, and nothing was off limits. He protected his ventures with the ferocity of a mother cub, and the people living in the municipalities south of St. Louis learned to accept – and sometimes revere – him.

Vance loved the limelight and embraced publicity. He wrote editorials in the local news, appeared on local television, sponsored local charities and chaired benefits. By the time Greta met him in 1995, he was already larger than life and untouchable.

So she was shocked when he walked into her diner that hot morning in August, sat down in her section, and ordered a coffee and roast beef sandwich. She recognized him instantly and her hands trembled as she poured the dark blend into his cup. When she finished, he put his right hand over her left wrist and said, "Hey, it's okay."

She had at first expected him to be gruff, and possibly flirtatious or charming. But she was surprised that he was none of the above. He was avuncular and kind. He left his business card along with the tip, and told her to call if she was ever in any trouble. She called him that evening.

"How would you characterize your relationship with Mr. Vance?" the lawyer asked.

"He was like a father to me," Greta answered. "When I met him, I was living in a homeless shelter for teens. He gave me a place to stay."

"How old were you?"

"I was sixteen."

"And Mr. Vance? How old was he?"

Greta coughed. "I think he was around thirty-five or forty years old at the time."

The lawyer's voice boomed. "A sixteen year old girl! Living with a forty year old man!"

"But, I'll repeat it for the third time. It wasn't that kind of a relationship. He was like a father to me. And he didn't live with me full-time. I think he had a number of homes, and he only visited me every so often, to see if I needed anything."

"Were you in school?"

Greta shook her head. "No, I dropped out after ninth grade."

The lawyer snickered, and got closer to Greta. She could see droplets of sweat forming above his moustache. "So, let me see if I get this straight. You are a high school dropout and former teen runaway who was living in a homeless shelter. In 1995, at the age of sixteen, you met and then moved in with the town's most notorious…ahem, businessman…?"

"I've already explained my living situation to you. And I don't know what you mean by *notorious*---"

"You don't know what I mean by notorious? Let's put aside the questionable businesses associated with Mr. Vance, and focus on this person who you say was like a father to you. Are you aware of any other endeavors Mr. Vance was involved with when you were living with him? Anything besides clubs and hotels?"

Greta looked helplessly at her lawyer, at Griffin, at the judge. She answered in a small voice. "He...he sold drugs."

It was a matter of public record. In 1998, Steven Vance was arrested for drug distribution and trafficking. His arrest occurred one year after she had left Vance's cushy penthouse apartment overlooking the river, piled her belongings into a friend's van and moved into Avery Place with Griffin.

Greta had known about Vance's drug operation the whole time she lived at his apartment. She heard his instructions to associates when he was on the phone in the kitchen. She saw the boxes neatly lined with little baggies of plastic coated pills and white powder. At times, he moved the whole setup into the apartment. She would hang out in the back bedroom, while streams of people and their apparatuses came through. She could put her ear to the door and hear how it all went down. The Thirst was a venue for pushing narcotics, coke and weed. Greta was never a part of it, but she knew about it.

In 1998, she was settled into her new life with Griffin, pregnant with John, when she heard about Vance's arrest on the radio. The disc jockeys giddily speculated that a jilted ex-girlfriend had taken Vance down. Greta had never said a word to anyone about what she'd seen and heard in his apartment but she was certain at that moment that police would be banging on her door. She expected to be hauled into an interrogation room and questioned about her former life.

To her surprise, Steven Vance accepted a plea deal, performed a marginal amount of community service, went back to his former life and no one in law enforcement ever said a word to her about it. Not until eleven years after his arrest, when she sat stirring and sweating in a witness box in family court, with Griffin's lawyer perched over her, pointing an accusing finger.

"You lived with the town's biggest *drug dealer*!" he exclaimed.

"I know it seems that way to you," Greta said. "But to me, he was family. The only family I had. He got me off the streets and into an apartment."

"Ms. Brock, you say he was the only family you had, but at the age of sixteen, where were your parents?"

Greta looked down at her hands. She thought of Marcia Brock in the back of the courtroom, twisting her scarf and casting judgment. Marcia, who lived in a brick and stone mansion in one of the wealthiest counties in Illinois – a woman who had known privilege her entire life. Marcia had made no secret of her disapproval about her son's marriage, and now – as Greta's past was laid bare in the courtroom for all to critique -- came Marcia's vindication.

"My father died of lung cancer when I was small," Greta said.

"And your mother?"

"My mother…" Greta sat back and tried to stem her tears. "My mother…um…I ran away from home when I was sixteen. We were arguing a lot and she told me that if I left, I could never come back…so I guess I never went back."

By now her tears were falling – thick droplets that moistened the wooden perch in front of her. Someone produced a tissue box and Greta wiped her eyes and blew her nose.

"Ms. Brock…" the lawyer continued, "when you moved into the apartment provided by Mr. Vance, at the age of sixteen, did you work?"

"Yes, I worked at a diner in St. Louis. I had the morning shift. I was a waitress. That's how I met Griffin, actually."

"And in the afternoons?"

"Excuse me?"

"What did you do in the afternoons, Ms. Brock? While you were living in the apartment provided by Mr. Vance?"

Greta wasn't prepared for this and she froze. She took another tissue and spread it apart into a rectangle, fingering the softness while she thought of how to respond.

"Were you doing drugs, Ms. Brock?"

"What? No!"

"But you were aware of Steven Vance's drug operation?"

"Aware of it? Yes I was aware of it. I was never involved with it though."

"Did you work in his hotels or nightclub?"

"No, no, I just went back to the apartment."

"Well what did you *do*, during all of those hours to yourself in the apartment, Ms. Brock? You had no one around you, you weren't in school and you weren't working. And you yourself claim that Steven Vance wasn't even there most of the time. What were you *doing?*"

"Um…I was…" Greta looked at the judge but didn't complete her sentence.

At last, Lance Garcia came alive. He sprung from his seat and said, "Your Honor, I don't see how revisiting the daily life of Ms. Brock twelve years ago is at all relevant."

"It's *entirely* relevant," Griffin's lawyer countered. "Mrs. Brock is requesting full custody of a *child*. It's important for us to know about her character, to fully understand what types of things John would be exposed to in her presence."

The judge nodded. "I'll allow it."

Lance rounded his seat and took a few steps closer to the judge. "But Your Honor, this was *twelve years*—"

"I said I'll allow it!" the judge bellowed. His voice seemed deep and angry, and it filled the room.

Griffin's lawyer smelled the victory. He smiled at the judge and then at Greta. He walked slowly towards the witness stand, like a predator taking great aims not to perturb his prey before the kill. "Ms. Brock, for how long were you living at the apartment provided by Steven Vance?"

"Two years. 1995 to 1997."

"So, I'll repeat my earlier question. For *two full years*, Mrs. Brock, in the afternoons, what were you doing?"

Greta looked up at the judge and gave him a pleading look. But whereas last time he seemed stoic, this time he looked aggravated at her hesitation, annoyed at the time it took for her to simply open her mouth and reveal secrets she'd sworn she'd never tell a soul.

"Ms. Brock…" the judge said. "Please answer the question."

# CHAPTER THIRTEEN

*September 19, 2017*

Tuesday morning, they were all seated around a conference table – Weaver, Martinez, Adams and Hobbs. Adams had the hospital report in his hands and was crumpling it slightly while he read aloud. Hobbs didn't understand why he didn't just distribute copies and let everyone read silently but she was too tired to argue. Adams had been the one to meet with the records department of Edwardsville General, to express the urgency of the situation. And Adams was the one who got the call from the hospital once the office had located the medical file for John Brock. It didn't require a warrant or a court order. It just required Adams to state quite plainly that John was considered a missing person and this file was critical to discovering what had happened to him.

Adams cleared his throat and read. "November 1, 2015. Edwardsville Emergency Department Record Medical Chart. Name: John Michael Brock. Age: 16. Accident? Box initially checked *No*, then crossed off and someone checked *Yes*. Chief Complaint and Onset: Bruised ribs, swollen jaw. Patient complains of chest pain and headache. Breathing rapid and shallow with pain on inspiration. Physical Findings: Vital signs revealed BP 100/60, temp: 98.3. Tender chest wall over left pectoral muscle. Left sign is markedly swollen, with bruising. Closed fracture of other specified part of fourth rib. Cerebral contusions...."

Adams continued but Hobbs was no longer listening. The list of injuries seemed impossibly long, the medical terminology unsettling – as though the injuries were less severe when described with an erudite vocabulary. There had been no accompanying police report – at least none that the grunts at the police station had been able to scrounge up. Hobbs could imagine the rookies' frustration...sorting through file after file of unsequenced paperwork, looking for any spark of recognition under the dim track lighting and stuffy air of the precinct basement.

As for Adams, Hobbs had thought he'd be one of those grunts, but now he was at the table with the rest of them. He'd apparently earned the respect of Captain Weaver – and Hobbs didn't know whether that made her proud or uneasy...or maybe both.

Weaver interrupted Adams with a raised hand. "Can you read from the police report, not just the medical report? At least then we'll have a chance of understanding half of what you're saying."

Adams looked up from the table and shook his head. "There is no accompanying police report."

The room was quiet for a moment. Every so often, they came across a case like this – usually a domestic violence victim, red-purple eyes swelling out of her sockets, scratches and bruises across the flesh, with an outlandish tale of personal responsibility that the hospital staff chose to take at face value.

"How did John say the accident happened?" Weaver asked.

Adams thumbed to the next page. "He said he had a skateboarding accident."

"Huh," Weaver said drily. "Well...anyone want to take a wager on whether John Brock ever owned a skateboard?"

They were all quiet again. Hobbs stared down at her notepad and felt as though she were hanging her head – an accomplice to the news of a prejudicial system.

Adams eventually broke the silence by coughing. "Hey, there's just one more thing I wanted to read about John's injuries. The report says that he had a superficial stab wound in his neck. John said that he fell on something...but someone wrote in the file that it's the type of injury usually caused by small sharp edge such as a box cutter or pocketknife. According to this, the puncture penetrated the scalene muscles and missed the internal jugular vein by about one millimeter. Any closer and John would've bled to death."

Martinez and Weaver gasped while Hobbs jumped up and left the room. She stood outside, closed her eyes and caught her breath. Her pulse was racing and the contents of her stomach felt liquid. She could hear Adams say from inside the room, "What? What does that mean?"

And she could hear Martinez respond in an even voice, "It's a professional hit, a calling card..."

Hobbs couldn't stay and hear any more. She had never been a regular smoker but she needed a cigarette – something to soothe her nerves. She could feel her pulse coursing through her, a current of emotion and stress. Summoning the strength to walk outside, she caught site of Rochelle – the station's newest officer – just in front of the door. Small, red-haired, and ever-eager,

Rochelle frowned when she saw Hobbs. "Detective…is everything okay?"

Hobbs gave Rochelle a nod and walked outside. The fresh air felt tremendous, as though it was breathing new life into her. She leaned against the concrete post and inhaled deeply. Rochelle joined her.

"Is everything okay?" the rookie repeated. "Do you need anything?"

"Just…do you happen to have a cigarette?" Hobbs asked. She was surprised at how weak and tinny her voice sounded.

"No, sorry, I don't smoke. I could run to the corner gas station and buy you a pack…"

"No, it's fine. Don't worry about it."

Ray Martinez joined them outside. "Hey Rochelle, can you give us a minute?" he asked. Rochelle nodded at him and went back inside.

"You okay?" Martinez asked her.

Hobbs looked at him and smiled. He was just a few inches taller than she was, but built like a wrestler – a dense mass of muscle. He had closely cropped dark hair, light brown skin and the faintest hint of an accent. He reached for her but she shied away. "I'm okay. I'm okay."

"The Captain was asking me what happened in there. I wasn't sure what to say."

She and Ray Martinez had been partners for so long, she couldn't remember what he knew about her and what information she had shielded from him. He looked at her so knowingly right then that she was certain she must have said something to him at some point.

"Well, I can't be on this case anymore, Ray. You understand, right? I just can't be on it."

"Roberta…"

At that moment Rochelle reappeared with a cigarette and a lighter. "Found one," Rochelle said. She lit the cigarette for Hobbs and then went back into the building.

"You smoke?" Martinez asked.

"No," Hobbs said, just as she took a long deep drag and felt it hit her lungs.

"Well, you can't be off this case. There's no one else who can take your place. And Weaver will want to know why and then you'll have to explain it all to him. And I'm not even sure I understand the full story myself."

Hobbs took another inhale and felt her whole body slacken. "This case is too close to home for me. Do you hear me? I can't do it. Adams can do it. He's young but Weaver loves him."

Then, as if he'd been summoned, Adams appeared. He looked younger than usual, Hobbs thought. His beard a bit more shaved than usual, his hair a bit longer on the top.

"I'm going to go," Martinez said, and he patted Hobbs on the shoulder before he walked inside.

Hobbs puffed a few more times and almost laughed. *They're dealing with me in shifts*, she thought. *Like I'm a mental patient.*

"Roberta, is everything alright? Why'd you run out? What happened?" Adams asked.

"Nothing," Hobbs said.

"Why don't you tell me what's going on? After you left, Captain Weaver said that this was the calling card of a professional and that there was really only one guy in Vetta Park who could be behind it. He said the guy's name was...I think...Steven Vance. And I want to know why—"

Hobbs didn't give him a chance to finish his question. She finished the cigarette, stamped it under her heel a few times, and walked back inside the building.

# CHAPTER FOURTEEN

*October 15, 2009*

Everyone was waiting for Greta. She could feel the tension in the courtroom and then the air conditioning whirred on, the forced air splitting the silence.

It had been an uncharacteristically warm day – both outside and in the courtroom. Greta glanced at Marcia Brock, sitting in her chair, using a bookmark to fan herself. Marcia typically looked smug but at that moment she looked distant – unsmiling, unsatisfied, almost bored – as though waiting for a show to begin.

"We're all ready, Ms. Brock," the judge prodded and Greta smiled in response. It was an involuntary reflex – the friendly smile to get out of an uncomfortable situation.

"I know," Greta said softly and she looked down at her hands. There was no way to frame her words so they shielded what she had to say, no way to spin it so she looked better.

"I was learning to read…and write…in that timeframe," Greta finally said. She knew that she was speaking too haltingly, too quietly, and that she was going to be asked to raise her voice. It was as though they wanted her to stand up and loudly proclaim her childhood illiteracy – a lifelong secret now bellowed, preacher-style, to the waiting masses.

"You say you were learning to read and write during those afternoons to yourself?" Griffin's lawyer repeated.

"Yes," Greta said. "It took me two years but I was able to teach myself."

The courtroom was silent again and the lawyer actually looked mildly surprised. Greta figured he had been in the market for a different kind of bombshell – prostitution, opioid addiction, illegal trafficking or maybe religious radicalism. Still, while illiteracy wasn't an issue with the law, Greta still found it embarrassing to confess it to the courtroom, and she knew that Griffin's lawyer would find a way to exploit her situation to his advantage.

"Tell us again how far you got in school before dropping out?" the lawyer asked.

"I completed ninth grade."

"Please tell the court…how on earth did you make it to ninth grade without learning how to read and write?" He seemed incensed – although Greta wasn't sure whether his irritation was directed at her or the school system.

"It was pretty easy when I was younger. I had a good memory so I could memorize those little books after I'd heard them a few times. I learned and memorized some sight words too. It wasn't until I was…"

Greta stopped mid-sentence and looked down. Not until she was ten years old – John's age – did she realize something was terribly, wretchedly *wrong*. In fourth grade, the class went ahead with different subjects – the thirteen colonies, the solar system, fractions and European paintings – and it was suddenly impossible keep pace with everyone else. The other kids somehow had a base knowledge that had eluded her. She struggled with everything.

Late nights involved tantrums at the dining room table and fights with her mother. *Try harder! Do more!* She didn't know how to explain why she couldn't learn. In the meantime, the years passed and she got further and further behind – still physically present in the classroom but with a mind that absorbed nothing. She felt like a ghost merely going through the motions – a stupid, illiterate ghost.

By ninth grade – high school – Greta was officially lost in the cracks. With few friends and no literacy – a schedule of study halls and below average classes that bored her and were primarily focused on containing the behaviors of her classmates – she dropped out.

Her mother was furious, but Greta learned to stick it out in the tiny house they shared in Southwest Missouri for two more years. She lied about her age and got a waitressing job to fill her time. Then, once she turned sixteen, she packed her suitcase after a particularly bad argument. Tears streaming down her face, a few crumpled fifty-dollar bills in her pocket, she turned away from that house, boarded a bus to St. Louis, and never looked back.

"Ms. Brock, you've told the courtroom that you used to be a waitress at a diner near the Wash U campus in St. Louis, is that correct?" Griffin's lawyer asked.

"Yes sir."

"Well, how were you able to wait tables if you couldn't read or write?" he asked. His voice cracked as it inflected – an expression of bewilderment.

"All of the food and drink items on the menu had numbers. So I just memorized which numbers went along with which items customers ordered and wrote the numbers down for the kitchen staff."

"I see. So are you...were you...dyslexic?"

Greta shrugged. "I don't know. I've never been officially diagnosed with anything. I mean, I've never been tested for anything." Greta felt angry every time she thought of the elementary school she'd attended in rural Missouri – a flat, orange-brick structure that boasted useless platitudes on its marquee: *Strive for Success* and *Effort = Achievement*.

At least John had a chance. He'd been tested and diagnosed; he was being singled out, he was getting personal instruction and he had an IEP. At least he had the chance to learn that she never had.

"And what worked for you as a teenager that didn't work for you beforehand? Why were you finally able to teach yourself?"

"I guess effort, patience and the wherewithal to sit down and learn, for hours every day. I didn't have the focus when I was in school...but by the time I was sixteen, seventeen years old, I was really motivated. I could sit at a desk for hours and repeat drills until I got it. I wouldn't let myself get up until I'd written a bunch of sentences that were completely legible. It helped that I didn't have anyone hovering over my shoulder, telling me what an idiot I was, telling me I needed to try harder or work faster. It was just me and that took the pressure off...so I finally learned."

"Hmm, I see." The lawyer finished questioning her – even gave her a smile as she stood up from the witness stand – but when it came time to wrap up the case before the judge, he was unsparing. He mentioned her childhood illiteracy as though it were a disease she'd brought upon herself. He brought up her status as a runaway teen and her life with the notorious Steven Vance.

Then he presented a portrait of his own client, Griffin Brock. Griffin had graduated from Washington University in St. Louis with honors, had worked steadily in real estate for years. Griffin was solid and reliable, with the financial means to provide for John in a way that Greta couldn't or wouldn't.

Greta listened to the lawyer and tried not to think too deeply about it. The man was just doing his job, presenting her in the worst possible light on behalf of his client. The argument was technically true, but this layering of statistics and salaries and degrees earned missed the deep conversations, the affections and attachment – which in her view was the very nucleus of parenting. When Griffin's lawyer sat down, Greta prayed that Lance Garcia could persuade the judge to see what was most important.

Lance stood up and put forth a decent effort, although not impassioned as Greta would have liked. He stated quite plainly – blinking in the courtroom's yellow-orange lights – that Greta was a good mother, reliable and loving, and that Griffin parented from afar.

Greta wanted to jump up from the bunch, to echo his words with a thousand Amens, to cite specifics – dates and times when Griffin had been physically or emotionally unavailable to John. But instead she stayed silent and watched her lawyer reason on her behalf.

When Lance stepped down, the judge thanked both parties, mentioned a conference he was going to attend in another city, and said he would need to take a few days to make a decision. He then stood up and left the courtroom.

Almost immediately, a crescendo of murmurs swelled up as people chatted to each other while leaving the courtroom. Greta's case wasn't the only one heard that day, and the smattering of visitors in the back reflected the diversity of the docket.

Greta waited for everyone to clear out and then told her lawyer she needed some water. She didn't make it to the water fountain though. There was a bench along the way that called out to her, and as she sunk into the uncomfortable wooden frame, she could feel her whole body release. She felt as though she'd spent the last few hours in the courtroom tensed up – a tightly coiled wad of skin and muscle.

With the emancipation of her body came the reveries of her mind, to places she didn't even want to explore. She could lose custody of John. She might lose custody. Was she likely to lose custody? It was impossible to know. Now she had to wait a few days for the judge to leave town, come back and make a decision. Now she had to act as if the most momentous decision in her life wasn't both outside her control and swaying against her.

***

A few hours later, Greta and Tuck were sitting together on the bleachers at John's soccer practice. The warm weather had given way to a cool breeze, and the couple huddled close together while they watched John chase down balls at the other end of a grassy field. It had been a muted, dismal evening while they searched for topics that didn't involve the custody hearing.

It was an impossible task. "We're losing the case," Greta said after a long period of silence, her words materializing from the air.

Tuck responded quickly. "Greta, we're not losing…"

"Tuck, make no mistake. We are losing. Griffin looks like a Boy Scout and I look like an illiterate former runaway who hangs out with drug dealers."

"I'm sure the judge will see…" Tuck started, but his voice trailed off.

Greta thought about the judge. Who knew what he was able to see? She looked ahead into the outfield and saw the sinewy silhouette of her son, a baseball cap pulled down over the top of his face, catching bugs in the cool air while he waited for a soccer ball to come his way. Her breath caught in her throat.

"I can't let Griffin have full custody over John," she said. "Griffin has no idea how to care for John; he never even sees him. I'd sooner run away with John – to Mexico maybe. Or South America."

Tuck frowned and shook his head. "Greta, now you're just talking crazy."

"I'm not talking crazy, Tuck. I can't lose him. I could do it, you know? I know people who could help me do it." She didn't explicitly say it but he knew which *people* she was referring to: Steven Vance. Steven Vance could help her vanish with John.

"I'm not going to entertain this," Tuck said. He stood up and moved to the other side of the stands.

Greta stayed on the bleachers for the rest of the practice, watching John. Occasionally she looked over at Tuck, who was perched against a silver fence, looking at the players instead of in her direction.

For the first time in their romance, Greta felt a pang of anger towards Tuck. He could remain analytical because John wasn't his child. And just as Greta had promised herself that she'd never adopt an us-vs.-them attitude about she and John facing down the world, she had to admit that she sometimes felt that way.

Even after years of self-discipline and self-education, Greta still occasionally struggled. There were words that interposed themselves in her mind, words that couldn't completely form no matter how long she stared at them. No one in her life could understand that but John. And no one could better explain it to him than her. The words united and untied were still tricking her to this day, reserved and reversed.

And there were two words that she knew would always evade the both of them – two simple, one-syllable kindergarten-level words that brought her back to exercises she used to repeat over and over at her little desk in Steven Vance's apartment, to no avail.

*I was.*

*I saw.*

*I saw.*

*I was.*

*I was.*

*I saw.*

\*\*\*

Greta knew she had precious little time before the court reconvened. The next day was October 16, a Friday. It was still warm for autumn – the sun shining down in a cloudless sky, the air still thick with the last vestiges of summer.

Greta dropped John off at school and drove thirty minutes into downtown St. Louis. She found the building without difficulty – a tall glass tower with reflective windows. The lobby was modern and elegant. There was a coffee bodega, a koi pond and a quiet waterfall. Greta leaned over and looked at the fish. They clustered in front of her, bobbing and gaping, as if begging for food.

A security officer walked over. "Can I help you?" he asked.

"Yes," Greta said with a smile. "I'm here to meet with Colt Bundy."

The officer looked confused so she added, "He works for St. Louis Investigations."

"Ah right." The offer nodded. "Floor ten."

Greta took the elevator up and met a young man in the reception area. He was a few inches shorter than her – dark eyes, tan skin and facial scruff. He smiled broadly when she got off the elevator.

"Greta Brock?" he asked.

"Yes." She shook his hand.

"I'm Colt Bundy. St. Louis Investigations. Please follow me."

She followed him down a hallway and into a corner office. The office had potted plants at each end, mounted brown cabinets, a long brown desk, two brown leather sofas placed perpendicular to each other and a coffee table.

Colt took a seat on one of the couches and Greta sat down on the other.

"Can I get you anything?" Colt asked.

"No, I'm fine. Thank you."

Colt leaned forward and rested his forearms on his legs. "So you mentioned you're in the middle of a custody dispute…"

"That's right. And I need your help. The case isn't really going my way. But I think I have something on my ex-husband that might help me out. I just need your help."

"What can I do for you?"

"Four years ago, in 2005, there was a car accident in Vetta Park, Missouri. I remember it very clearly because I witnessed it. I remember the exact night too, February 4. It must have been three or four in the morning. A Ferrari with two men inside ran a red light and hit a guy in a pickup truck. The men were wearing suits. I need to know who those men were. And I need this information in the next few days – Monday or Tuesday at the latest. My case resumes in court next Thursday."

Colt had been scribbling on a yellow-lined notepad. When Greta paused, he looked up at her and frowned. "I have an incredibly busy docket right now. With the holidays coming up, I have so many requests for surveillance on people who suspect their spouses are cheating…you have no idea."

Greta swallowed. "I just need their names and that's it. I'll agree to whatever payment terms you require to accelerate this. Just the names."

Colt smiled. "I have a friend at the Vetta Park police station. Let me see if this is as easy as a simple phone call, okay? I can't promise anymore than a phone call within the next few days."

"Thank you," Greta said. She shook his hand again, left the building and headed home.

As she drove, she silently prayed that Colt's contact at the Vetta park police station would come through for them. She even mentally envisioned it – a phone call from a longtime friend, a discrete trip to the records department, the procuring of a yellow manila envelope, then a return phone call to Colt Bundy's direct line. Finally, a call to her with the answers to a mystery she had wondered about for four long years.

# CHAPTER FIFTEEN

*September 20, 2017*

Captain Weaver looked stressed. There were wrinkles angling across his face that Hobbs hadn't noticed before, oblique circles casting shadows under his eyes. When he updated Hobbs on the failed efforts of the APB, he seemed not mad as much as surprised. "They can't be on the road anymore," Weaver said. "No surveillance video or roadside cruiser has spotted them anywhere."

Hobbs nodded at Weaver but didn't say anything. She wanted to be anywhere in the world except for at work that day, and it didn't help that temperatures outside were hovering in the low 70s with a slight breeze rustling through the fall foliage.

Hobbs had spent the morning wishing she could call in sick, and occasionally her wishes surged through her like an unsettling queasiness. Was there such a thing as Munchausen syndrome by desire? It would have been so easy just to make that one-minute call, to open the windows around her apartment and sit on the couch with a book for the day. No one in the office would have thought too much about it.

But she wasn't the type of person to hide from confrontation, to allow others to assume situations she needed to lead. She got dressed as usual and affixed her badge to her belt, drove to the office and parked in her usual spot, and tried to feign a confident gait as she made her way to the precinct.

Inside Weaver's office, they had their morning catch-up – which lately was no more than a litany of futile efforts. Once that part was over with, Adams appeared in the doorway. "Captain – oh hey, Hobbs – uh, Steven Vance is here. He's in room one."

"Thanks," Weaver said. Adams retreated from the doorway and then Weaver pressed his lips together and looked at Roberta. "You ready?" he asked.

Hobbs swallowed hard and felt a hot wave of anxiety wash over her, like she had suddenly been dipped in a sauna. Her stomach rolled and she felt sweaty. She bent over in her chair and rested her head just beneath her knees. She could feel the rush of blood.

"Hobbs? Roberta?"

Hobbs tried to take a few deep breaths and then come up slowly. When she was sitting up again, she saw deep frown lines on Weaver's face, a look of concern.

"I'm okay," Hobbs said in an unsteady voice. "I just don't feel one hundred percent today. Can I sit this one out? Maybe Martinez can do the questioning himself?"

"Sure," Weaver said. "You can watch from the glass. Unless you need to go home."

"No. I'll be okay."

He didn't ask her to elaborate on her condition and she was appreciative for that. When she walked through the hallway, she saw Martinez just outside the interrogation room. He gave her a quick nod and then walked inside the room.

"Steven, thanks for coming in today," Martinez said.

Steven Vance looked up at Martinez and grinned warmly. "And thank you so much for inviting me. You know I love to spend my Wednesday mornings with you guys."

Hobbs hadn't seen Steven Vance in five years. He hadn't lost his penchant for sarcasm. But the years had slightly greyed his hair, placed a few more wrinkles on his forehead, given him scattered sunspots on his face and arms. He was thicker too than she remembered – bulkier and more muscular but also heavier. When Martinez sat down at the table, Vance appeared to loom over him. His voice was scratchy and deep...exactly how she remembered.

"I'm sure you know why you're here," Martinez said.

"Of course I do," he said with a smirk. "You guys are looking into buying my resort in Kiawah Island. Well, like I told the chick over the phone, give me eighty percent of the asking price up-front, and then we can negotiate the rest."

Martinez stood up and kicked the leg of Vance's chair. To Hobbs' surprise, it moved an inch – although Vance didn't seem fazed.

"You want to be here all day?" Martinez asked.

Vance laughed. "Relax, okay? Jesus, simmer down." He pulled a pack of cigarettes from the pocket of his shirt, took one out and dangled it in between his lips. "Got a light? The cute redhead at the front took mine away. I think she likes me."

"Do you see an ashtray in here, fuck stick?" Martinez asked.

Vance made a display of searching the table for an ashtray and then said, "No, the last guy must have taken it with him. Can I get a light *and* an ashtray, in that case? And a soda?"

Martinez smacked the cigarette away from Vance's lips and Vance responded by getting up. He stood about a foot taller than Martinez.

"I should get in there," a voice next to Hobbs said. She looked over and saw Adams next to her. She wasn't sure when he'd arrived or what Weaver had mentioned about her brief episode in his office. At some point, they were going to figure out that she got physically ill every time Steven Vance's name was mentioned – that she preferred to leave the room rather than entertain a conversation in which he was named. Maybe they already had put the pieces together.

"Steven Vance looks like a gladiator next to Martinez," Adams added. "I mean, it's no contest. I should get in there, right?"

Hobbs looked at the two men – still standing confrontationally a few feet apart but neither behaving violently. Hobbs barely knew Vance anymore but she remembered that he was feckless – always preferring to send his deputies out to do his dirty work rather than partake himself.

And Martinez wasn't especially huge or intimidating but he was a veteran. He'd dealt with every miscreant Vetta Park had to offer – from violent repeat offenders to drunk bar patrons. She knew he could hold his own against Vance.

Sure enough, Vance settled down, eased into his seat and looked straight ahead. Martinez continued the questioning. "Are you familiar with the Carpenter family?" he asked.

"This is about their disappearance, right? I mean, I watch the news. Wait – you think I had something to do with this? Are you guys the worst police force ever? Honestly, if you worked for me, I'd fire you."

"Well, good thing I don't work for you." Martinez sat in a seat at the edge of the table, next to Vance. Despite the insult, he gave the mogul a disarming look and asked, "What kind of soda do you want?"

Vance looked briefly surprised and then said, "Coke."

Martinez stood up, walked over to the door and said something to someone stationed outside. Thirty seconds later, someone handed him a Coke can. He took the can, closed the door and reassumed his seat.

"Steven, if you ask me for a chilled glass or a straw or whatever, I'm going to take this token of good measure and fling it across the room. No one is saying you had something to do with their disappearance. I'm just asking you some questions. Okay?"

"Sure," Vance said. He cracked open the top, took a few sips and leaned back. "But I don't think I can help you."

"Did you know Greta Carpenter?"

"Oh well yeah, I *knew* her…twenty years ago…when she was Greta Wagner. Cutest girl you ever saw. I helped her out; you know that, right? She was a little pixie thing, blonde hair, blue eyes. Looked like the type of girl who should've been surfing a beach. And she was living in a homeless shelter! I found her an apartment, got her cleaned up."

"Were you ever involved with her?"

"Involved how? She was like a daughter to me. Are you asking me…do you mean *were we intimate*?"

Martinez stared straight at Vance.

"Christ, detective. She was a kid. Fifteen or sixteen and I'm a businessman with a reputation to protect. Once she turned eighteen I tried to hire her to work at my club. I'm sure you know I own The Thirst. Dancing or waitressing or even being a shot girl…she would have made some great tips. But instead she found some loser, moved in with him and got pregnant. And that's it."

"So once Greta moved out, you never saw her after that?"

Vance made a motion – a cross between a twitch and a shrug. His eyes flitted across the room and then rested on the top of his soda can. He hunched forward slightly, ran his fingers through the top of his hair.

"You've got him," Hobbs whispered.

For five or ten seconds, it was completely silent in the interview room. Hobbs thought that Martinez should repeat the question – maybe louder and more forcefully, a signal that indicated they knew this was leading somewhere. But Martinez just remained still, staring at Vance with an unforgiving look.

"Yeah, I saw her," Vance finally said. "She came to see me."

"When?"

"Uh, I guess it was about two years ago."

"She came to see you at home?" Martinez pressed.

"No, in my office. I have an office in the back of The Thirst."

"Why did she come to see you?"

Again Vance was silent. He rubbed his eyes, massaged the bridge of his nose. To Hobbs, he appeared to be searching for the right words or phrasing – a way to spin his way out of a mess instead of into one.

"Detective, I do not know," Vance said. "I wasn't expecting the visit. I was surprised by it. She looked...she looked kind of crazy."

"Crazy? What do you mean by crazy?"

"I don't know. I don't know how to describe it. I mean, I knew her when she was a teenager. She was young and...and...full of life. And then twenty years or so went by and when she came to see me, she was the complete opposite of what I remembered. Crazy-looking. She looked tired and *nuts*, if I'm being honest. She said someone had hurt her son and she thought it was me."

"Was it you?" Martinez asked.

"No! No, of course not. I don't know where she got that idea. I tried to tell her but she wouldn't listen to me. Maybe I did some shady stuff years and years ago, back when she knew me...but I got out of that line of work in the late nineties. You know...after the plea deal. And Greta, unfortunately...there was no reasoning with her."

Martinez nodded and looked down at his file of notes. He seemed to accept what Vance was saying about his professional life but Hobbs knew better. She had heard it all before – his lies, his pleas of legitimacy, his smooth earnestness. Steven Vance was – and always had been – a very convincing liar. So many people bought it because he had practiced and perfected the act. His lies were smooth, sugar-coated mendacities. Hobbs had once swallowed his deception but no more.

She was just thinking about how she needed to get in there and press him on his line of work – to overcome her apprehensions about seeing him again and burst into the room wielding pointed accusations – when he added some more color to his previous statements.

Without any particular prodding, Vance said, "Do you know that Greta threatened me when she came to see me?"

Martinez looked up from his file of papers but said nothing.

Vance continued. "She said she'd bought a gun. And that she'd been to the firing range and knew how to use it. Those were her exact words."

"Really," Martinez said, rubbing his chin.

"I'm serious," Vance said, shaking his head. "When I tell you that Greta went crazy, *she went crazy*. That woman was out for blood."

# CHAPTER SIXTEEN

*October 19, 2009*

Greta waited by the phone for most of Monday. She busied herself with random tasks to keep her mind occupied. She was just beginning to give up hope when the phone rang. She wanted to leap for joy when she recognized Colt Bundy's voice on the other line.

"Your friend at the police station came through for you?" Greta asked.

"Yes, my friend came through," Colt said. "I have the names of the guys in the Ferrari. Do you have a pen?"

Greta found a pen and a piece of paper. "I'm ready."

"Alright..." Colt said. "The driver of the Ferrari was Will Carter, born in 1976. Illinois driver's license, issued January 1, 2005. He's a male, 5'10, 165 lbs, brown eyes. His home address as of 2005 was 104 W. Oak Street, Apartment 5A, Chicago Illinois 60610. Did you get that?"

Greta was writing furiously while he spoke. She said, "Mmhmm," but as she stared at the name and personal information of the driver, she was struck by its lack of familiarity. It was just words on a page, like a grocery list -- carrying no meaning for her. "How about the other guy – the passenger?" she asked.

"The passenger's name was Arthur Forsett. He left in an ambulance and there's no driver's license information for him. The officer noted he was in his early twenties and African-American."

"Okay," Greta said. "Is there anything else?"

"Yes, they told the officer they were here traveling for business. They said the name of the company they owned – Carter Commercial Development Company. The notes say they worked in the firm's Chicago office. That's all we have."

"Okay," Greta said. After sharing her credit card details with Colt, she hung up the phone and stared down at her scrawling, disappointed. She had waited so long to get these names, convinced that there would be an accompanying epiphany – an *a-ha* moment that explained Griffin's actions and put all the pieces together.

Instead, it just spelled out more work for her: First, a call to Tuck to beg him for a favor and then, a hastily arranged trip to Chicago.

\*\*\*

Greta approached the Chase Tower Building and looked up. The building was a large, boxy rectangle jutting towards the sky, gray-black and glassy, with a patch of greenery in front.

After giving her personal information to the lobby security, she rode a mirrored elevator to the 61st floor, stepped off and looked around.

Carter Commercial Development took up the entire floor, with the interior just as glossy as the outside. There was a reception area, with leather couches, coffee tables and a young, attractive receptionist. There were framed oil portraits of previous executives on the walls and marble tile on the ground, which accentuated the clack of heels and shoes as employees rushed past.

The receptionist greeted Greta and led her into a conference room. The room had a long wooden table flanked by black Aeron chairs. "Can I get you anything?" the receptionist asked sweetly. "Coffee? Tea? Bottled water?"

Greta took a seat and shook her head.

"Well, I'll just let Will and Arthur know you're here then," the woman said and then left the room.

Greta felt unmoored by her surroundings – the procession and formality of it all – the sense that there was a way things worked that existed outside the narrow scope of her life in Missouri. She was reminded of her childhood schooling – being different than everyone else, the sense that everyone else got what she had missed.

When she'd called late Monday afternoon and set up the meeting with Will and Arthur, no one on the phone flinched at her insistence that the meeting happen immediately. No one even asked her for specific details on the meeting.

Perhaps this was how deals got done – with firmness and an impatient voice, the offering of a name and nothing more. Perhaps the folks at Carter Commercial were nervous about offending her if they asked for more.

But, as Greta sat in the conference room and waited for them to arrive, she was disturbed by the thought that she was already in way over her head…and that the two men would quickly show her the door once they learned why she was really there.

\*\*\*

They showed up in the room in quick succession. Arthur first, and then Will. Both looked professional – dressed in business suits just like four years ago. They introduced themselves and shook her hand with the savvy of salespeople – men who wanted to charm their way into a deal.

They sat down – Arthur across from her, Will next to her – and took out notepads. When the room was quiet for a minute, Arthur asked, "What can I help you with? I'm guessing Griffin asked for this meeting?"

Greta was taken aback. "You know who I am? That I'm married to Griffin Brock?"

Arthur smiled. "Yes, of course. He's mentioned your name a few times."

"We're actually going through a divorce now."

Arthur's smile faded. "Oh, I'm sorry to hear that."

Greta sighed. "Griffin didn't send me. I'm here because I'm curious about…about an accident four years ago…in Vetta Park, Missouri – which is where we live. You were driving a yellow Ferrari and you ran a light and crashed into a pickup truck. It must have been two or three in the morning. Do you remember?"

The men glanced at each other. "I'm not sure it happened just like you describe it," Will said. "But I do remember the accident, yes."

"I remember it too because I was out driving that night," Greta continued. "I gave an account to the police and then Griffin made me change my story. I told them at first that you were at fault but then I changed my story and said you weren't."

"What is it you want from us?" Will asked. His voice sounded cross; his words were curt.

"I just want to know why Griffin did that. I want you to tell me why he insisted on protecting you."

Will shook his head. "We never asked for anything from Griffin. If he had you change your story to the police, that's on *him* and *you*."

"No one's saying you pressured him. I just want to know *why* he did it – exactly how you both are connected to him."

Will stared straight ahead and Arthur took interest in his hands. Greta started to get the feeling that this was a big waste of time. These men were businessmen, not mobsters. If anything, their association with Griffin would probably make him appear more legitimate to the judge, not less.

She had been expecting something different – two men who operated in the shadows of the economy: hitmen or loan sharks hired to scare the pickup driver. She had envisioned walking into a secretive, poorly lit back room, learning of schemes and dark plots that Griffin had somehow partaken in – maybe by providing funds, or laundering them.

This meeting had been her Hail Mary effort to go back to the courtroom with *something* to show the judge. She just wanted to paint a picture of Griffin that was closer to accurate, something aside from the flawless, doting part-time father he played in court. Instead, he just seemed like a man associated with two well-established businessmen.

"We were in town that day to look at some land that Griffin was selling," Arthur said. "A few acres of grass and brush along a busy commercial street. If Griffin told you to change your story about the traffic accident, I think he was just worried that if you pointed the finger at us in the traffic accident, we'd abandon the deal."

"Oh," Greta said. "Did the deal fall through?"

Will laughed. *"You don't know?* We went ahead with the sale and developed that land into Northman Shopping Center. It's actually made us a ton of money."

Greta sat back in her chair and considered this. Northman Shopping Center was a high-end retail mall that housed boutique clothing stores, three expensive restaurants and a jewelry store. It was technically outside Vetta Park, in an area east of her suburb that was known for affluence. Greta drove by Northman Center occasionally, and each time tried not to scoff at the clientele's air of superiority. She had no idea Griffin had any connection to Northman.

"I don't know why you thought I would know about that deal," Greta said. "Griffin didn't clue me in on anything work-related, ever."

She felt a little foolish for voicing one of her marital criticisms to these two men. If they had initially been under the impression that Griffin sent her, they had no idea what her marriage had really been like – and probably weren't too concerned with the personal details.

"Well, Arthur and I thought you were his partner this whole time," Will said. "The mysterious business partner..."

"Griffin has a business partner?" Greta asked.

"Yes, I mean – Griffin is the one who signs the paperwork and the one whose name is on all of the documents. But there's a silent partner who works with him who he talks about every once in awhile," Will said. "Based on his comments, I think this partner provides initial funding for land and the ultimate approval on the deals that go through."

"Yeah, and right now we're looking at doing a second deal with Griffin – a commercial building on Olympic and Prosser," Arthur added. "We've been a little unsure about whether to go ahead and he seems like he's really itching to close...so that's why we thought he sent you."

"No." Greta smiled and shook her head. "I had no idea about any of it."

The conversation ended a little while later, and Greta walked back to the parking lot while she thought about the meeting. Griffin – who was stoic and taciturn to the point of being almost reclusive – actually had a business partner. Someone who clearly had a role but who remained behind the scenes, someone who made decisions but stayed hidden. Greta knew the realm of possibilities was infinite but there were only a few large-scale real estate players in their town. One name in particular echoed in her head as she made the long drive back to Vetta Park: *Steven Vance.*

\*\*\*

Greta didn't drive home after her meeting with Arthur and Will. It was late when she arrived back at the St. Louis suburbs – night fog settled over the October sky, a few stars visible and not many cars on the streets. Instead of turning left off the highway exit towards Vetta Park, Greta turned right – in the direction of Griffin's new townhouse.

She hadn't been there before but she knew his address. She smiled to herself as she passed Northman Shopping Center, and two gated communities of exquisite mansions that backed up against the Mississippi River. At the end of the street was a cluster of newly developed condominiums – a large banner at the entrance marketing the *spacious and luxurious* vacant units to would-be buyers.

Greta drove up to the security booth and was relieved to find it wasn't staffed yet. She drove through and found Griffin's unit, parked her car and rang the doorbell. He answered quickly.

"Oh…hi," he said. His face fell as though he'd been expecting someone else.

"Hi," Greta said. "Can I come in?"

Griffin seemed unsure of what to say but Greta didn't wait for him to find the right way to turn down her request. She brushed past him into the foyer and looked around. The apartment was bright and airy, with exposed brick and a fireplace in the living room. The interior looked like a furniture and lighting designer had staged it. Greta saw hallways and staircases, high ceilings and a huge kitchen. Their split-level house on Avery Place was diminutive and run-down by comparison.

"What are you doing here?" Griffin asked. "Did you just come here to look around?"

"No, no," Greta said pleasantly. "I wanted to let you know about a meeting I just had. You'll never guess who I met with so I'll just come right out and tell you. My new friends, Will Carter and Arthur Forsett."

Griffin's jaw hung open – suspended for a few seconds before he tried to mask his surprise. "What? They're here?"

"No, no," Greta said again. "I went there – to Chicago. I figured it was time I paid a visit to Carter Commercial Development."

She was purposefully light and casual – perhaps sounding a bit too proud of herself. Griffin continued to stare at her as though he didn't even recognize her, and Greta understood why.

She had always been so afraid to annoy or anger him, so eager to gratify him and to prove she was a worthy wife. But that stopped here and now. Now she was in the fight of her life and she was going to do whatever it took to win. He had underestimated her and not for the first time.

"What do you want, Greta?" Griffin asked.

"You know what I want. I want John. And I want more than full custody. I want a good life for him. He's having a hard time in school but I found a tutor who specializes in kids with learning disabilities. It's not cheap; the cost is eighty dollars an hour but I think he needs it. And I want the house." She saw him recoil so she added, "Don't think you can just walk all over me, Griffin. I'm not some eighteen-year old kid, pouring people's coffee and begging for tips and waiting for the next good thing to happen to me! I have open lines of communication with your business associates. They mentioned you're about to do another deal – the Prosser and Olympic property – and I could tank it, Griffin. I could tell them things that would destroy that deal and any other deal–"

Griffin turned suddenly, grabbed a vase from a nearby shelf and smashed it across the kitchen floor. His face had become surly – a snarl stretched across his lips, his eyes wide and round. He looked inhuman, or at least, primitive – a rage unleashed. His face unchanged, he took another vase – a mirror of the first one – and smashed it on the ground with the same fury.

Greta stood back and tried to remain expressionless while she watched him. She reminded herself that he was prone to theatrics, not violence. He could be mean and underhanded, sneaky and wrathful, but he was not abusive.

Sure enough, once he'd finished with the two shattered vases, he stepped carefully over the shards of glass and walked up the stairs. He was gone for ten minutes. Greta stayed in the foyer and waited. She wondered if she misjudged him, just as he had misjudged her. Could he be polishing or arming a weapon? Thinking about his best tactical response? She stayed still and tried to listen, but all she could hear were muffled sounds that wafted downstairs every so often. It was impossible to tell if he was speaking to himself or to someone else – or if he was even talking in coherent sentences.

At last Griffin trotted down the stairs and stood a few feet away from her. He looked angry, but his rage was contained behind a clenched jaw. For a few moments, he just stood against the front hallway closet and glared at her. Eventually, he said, "Alright. I talked with my lawyer. You can have full custody of John and the Avery Place house. But that's it. Nothing else. You want some holistic, eastern medicine doctor for John, you figure out a way to pay for it…"

"It's a *tutor, not a doctor*, Griffin. The public schools are failing him…"

Griffin continued in a voice that was cool, words carefully measured. "Greta, believe me when I tell you that I do not care. The public schools in Vetta Park are *fine*. John will get a fine education. He doesn't need a tutor. He needs his mother to start imposing some discipline and get him to work harder. He's a lazy kid, Greta, because you allow him to be."

"He's not lazy! He tries really hard…"

Griffin held up his right hand and shook his head once sharply – right to left. "Greta, I don't care. Here's the deal: full custody of John and the house, I'll pay some alimony and child support and we cut all ties to each other. Otherwise we can drag each other through court and mutually ruin each other's lives. Now, what's your answer?"

"Are you still going to be in John's life?" Greta asked.

"What did I say, Greta. I said *cut all ties*. How about this? I'll see him once every few months. My secretary will call you to arrange it. Besides, he's probably better off this way, right?"

"It's not – that's not…" Greta searched for the right words but she was too caught in the moment to think of how to phrase it.

"Are you taking the deal or not?" Griffin pressed.

Greta knew she should talk with Lance Garcia but she didn't want the moment to pass. She didn't want to give Griffin time to meet with his lawyer and come up with a different arrangement, or for him to chat with Will and Arthur and learn that his connection with them was impermeable, regardless of what she told them. At this very moment, Greta had ammunition against Griffin that was valuable and she had to strike then or potentially lose full custody.

"I'll take the deal. Full custody and the house, alimony and child support and we cut all ties."

"Deal."

They shook hands tersely and then Greta left and went back to her car. During the drive home, she felt both content and hesitant about the agreement they'd reached. It was a huge relief to get full custody over John and to not have to worry about moving somewhere else – a cloud of uncertainty that washed through her – threatening to consume her, to commit her to acts of lawlessness such as running off to Mexico – now dispelled.

But there was something about Griffin's desire to be done with her that bugged her – something about the certain way he repeated *cut all ties* that made her wonder whether she was doing the right thing. At that moment, she had a ten-year old boy who wanted to spend time with his father. And Griffin's all-or-nothing attitude towards custody made her worry about downstream implications of the arrangement that she might have to confront in the years ahead.

It wasn't until she was three blocks from home that she realized she'd forgotten to press him about the identity of his business partner.

# CHAPTER SEVENTEEN

*September 20, 2017*

Martinez seemed stuck. He was caught in a carousel of interrogation questions – directionless and circular. Vance was cordial and succinct – answers too brief to weave a web that could be used to ensnare him – and mostly reiterating his lack of knowledge, rather than providing any helpful leads.

Martinez asked, "How did Greta Brock know where to find you?"

Vance: "I have no idea."

"Why do you think she was acting crazy?"

Vance: "Probably because her son had just gotten assaulted. But why that anger was aimed at me, I don't know."

"You had nothing to do with her son's assault?"

Vance: "That's right."

"Can you offer up any suggestions as to why the family is missing now?"

Vance: "I have no idea."

"Or where they went?"

Vance: "No idea."

Martinez sat back in his chair and frowned at his notes. The room was silent for a short while. Vance sipped his Coke and interlaced his fingers. He pressed them together and then released – a nervous habit.

Hobbs was still watching through the glass. It was during this moment of stillness that Hobbs realized she needed to act. This decision was less of an urge and more of a moment of clarity.

Steven Vance got away with too much. He was given too much leeway. Hobbs knew it was a delicate dance. Dig into him too much and Vance might demand a lawyer. But the Vetta Park Police Department needed to do more than repeat the same questions and accept the same answers. If Martinez wasn't going to do it, Hobbs was going to try.

She stepped away from the glass and left the room, took a few steps, inhaled sharply and opened the door to the interrogation room. The room had a tangy odor – like lemony fresh scent cleaner – and she had to take another breath to calm the churn of her stomach.

Vance had his back to her and he barely stirred when the door opened –but Martinez shot up quickly and approached her with a surprised look.

"Hi," he said. "Did you want to talk to me outside?"

"No," Hobbs answered. "I want to talk to Steven Vance in here."

Vance turned around then and recognized her. Perhaps he had recognized her voice. "Roberta?" he asked.

She felt unsteady – in the presence of a man she had tried strenuously to avoid for years. Up close, his bulk took on an exaggerated quality. He looked giant instead of tall, hulking instead of muscular. And he still had the same aroma that whiffed off of him – light deodorant, mixed with coffee. She tried not to remember.

"Hi Steven," Hobbs said flatly, her stomach still churning. She took a seat next to him and across from Martinez. She tried to appear smooth and cunning but her heart was pounding and her limbs felt weak.

For five years, she had mentally prepared for the moment they saw each other again. Then, when it seemed likely that they could coexist in the same city without running into each other, she grew comfortable with the idea of never having to face him. The St. Louis metropolitan area was large enough to accommodate two completely separate social circles. Every time his likeness or name appeared in a local charity register, she could turn the page. Every time someone casually mentioned his name, she could change the subject.

But now she was sitting next to him and in this context, she had the upper hand. She was a police detective and he was – not a suspect exactly but a suspicious person. She could decide what to ask, what type of interrogation this would be and when the questioning would end. This reversal of status was completely different from how it had been.

Hobbs was thinking of how to begin her questioning when Vance spoke up. "How have you been, Roberta? I've thought about calling you up every once in awhile."

"Steven, let's keep the topic on Greta Carpenter and the whole Carpenter family, shall we? Otherwise we'll be here all day."

Vance shrugged. "Fine by me. I've already said everything I have to say."

"Well you may have provided some answers, but we think there's more to the story that you're not telling us," Hobbs said. Her heart was still throbbing, body trembling, but her voice was smooth and calm.

"What more can I tell you?" Vance asked.

"We know you were involved in the assault of John Brock," Hobbs said. "Even though you didn't assault him directly, you still ordered it."

Hobbs had no proof backing up this claim. She didn't have an arrest for the assault, nor did she have a victim statement, a police account or any eyewitness statements. All Hobbs had to go on was the indication of a professional – the shallow wound that would have told a much different story if it weren't the mark of someone who knew what he was doing.

"I'm not telling you anything in here," Vance said. "You want to talk to me, let's go outside and have a talk. Otherwise, unless you arrest me, I believe I'm free to go."

Hobbs gave a vague nod and thought about the request. Outside there was no recording device, no one-way glass and no ability to showcase what he said in front of a courtroom at a later date. Then again, she was at an absolute dead end...and getting any kind of admission from Steven Vance remained her only hope for forward trajectory. She had no ability to keep him in the police station and he was well aware of this fact. The prospect of an outside chat wasn't ideal, but it was a lifeline that kept the case tethered to a resolution.

Hobbs stood up and scraped her chair underneath the table. "Let's go outside then."

\*\*\*

Hobbs led Vance out of the interrogation room, through the hallway and out to the back parking lot of the police station. It seemed conspiratorial and anachronistic – meeting him this way. If she closed her eyes and just took in his scent, the tread of his footfalls behind her, the singsong of robins in the distance – she could almost place herself in the previous decade, playing the role of her previous self.

But no, that was ridiculous. Now it was 2017, she was 41 years old and she knew better. She had to be smarter this time. The filament of their relationship could not be a line that stretched infinitely into the future – tattered and broken off in places but still there. Their relationship had to be over – defined by both a start and an end date, a stretch of time that no longer mattered.

"You look beautiful Roberta," Vance said as soon as they were sitting together on a set of wooden steps behind a row of cars.

Hobbs shrugged off his compliment and stayed focused on the task. It was easier this time than in the past. Maybe because she was on duty, or maybe because it was a line she had heard so many times before, worn through and no longer effective.

"Did you tell your guys to assault John Brock?" Hobbs asked him.

Vance laughed. "Whoa, so even out here, you're still all business, huh?"

"Yes, Steven, that's the only reason we're out here and the only matter I care to discuss. Can you please answer the question?"

Vance shook his head. "I have a bunch of different businesses, most of which are decentralized…you know? I don't order hits or anything like that. I'm the guy on the top; I don't really get involved in the details."

"So you didn't order the hit?"

"Why would I order a hit on a high school kid?"

"I don't know. Maybe you sold him drugs and he didn't pay you."

Vance threw his hands in the air. "First of all, who says I sell drugs? Secondly, you think some high school kid is going to work up enough debt to make it worth my time to order a hit on him?"

"You haven't actually answered the question."

"You haven't actually asked me a reasonable question. Did I ever sell drugs to John Brock? No I did not." Vance looked at her – his dark eyes as intense as she'd ever seen them.

Hobbs swallowed and asked in a softer voice, "But you know him."

"Is that a question?"

"Yes."

"Sure, I know John. I know a lot of people."

"He's a high school kid and you're a big presence in the city. How do you know him?"

"I can't remember. I come across a lot of people in the course of a day. Can't say how I meet them all."

"But Greta obviously thought you were involved in his assault."

"Well yeah but she was off the wall…ranting and raving like a maniac. I'd say you should ask her…but I guess you can't."

"Steven, where is the Carpenter family?"

"I have absolutely no idea."

"Steven, look at me." Hobbs shifted until she was sitting a few inches away – the better an angle to stare at him, to survey him, to let him know she was capturing every twitch of body language, every hint of inflection.

"Steven…where is the Carpenter family?" she repeated.

Vance stared back. His voice was even when he responded, his body unmoving. "I have absolutely no idea," he repeated, this time in a slower cadence, each word individually enunciated.

Hobbs looked away. She knew she had to evaluate this conversation and figure out if he was lying. It should have been an easy task given her history with him. Rarely if ever had he looked her in the face and lied to her. His lies were omissions of information, secret meetings and crafty avoidances. But yet, her history with Vance also compromised her; it made her question her own judgment and whether she was truly acting objectively.

The thing was, Hobbs knew of no other suspicious enterprise in or near Vetta Park. Steven Vance had a monopoly on professional delinquencies, as far as she and the police force knew. The names and faces of the petty dealers and corner drug pushers came and went. But there was only one large-scale, skilled operation and that belonged to Steven – a man with enough resources and local political ties to evade capture and incarceration.

"Are you done with me now?" Steven asked.

"Yeah, you can go," Hobbs said.

Steven stood up and faced her. "Hey, look, Roberta, there's one more thing I want to say…and…it's the reason I wanted to meet with you outside – away from everyone. Robbie, believe me, I feel bad about the way things went with us. Over the years. I didn't treat you right and I know I've never apologized or acknowledged how poorly I behaved. I've thought about what to say to you for so many years—"

This was the mea culpa Hobbs had been waiting for five years to hear – the regret for how he had acted, the acknowledgement of the pain he'd caused. And for some reason, even as she'd longed to hear it, she couldn't bear to hear it.

There was something about accepting an apology so many years after the fact that made it insufferable. It was like the nominal payment of a library fee many years after the book had been destroyed in a horrible fire – long after the fine was written off.

There was no way to deal with personal anguish in the parking lot of a police station, in the middle of a workday, at the end of an interrogation that had given her no leads but that she'd have to justify for her Captain. There was no way to hear Steven

Vance's words without reopening a wound she had no time to look after or mend.

So Hobbs left him standing on the steps. He was mid-sentence, rambling apologies and regrets, his face solemn, his voice gravely and sincere.

Hobbs looked both ways, crossed the parking lot and opened the back door to the police station. She could hear him yell after her: "Hey Roberta!" But she didn't look back.

***

Hobbs walked past the cluster of desks, past the bustle of uniformed people in the hallway and into Captain Weaver's office. She was surprised to find it full. Weaver was sitting in his chair, Martinez and Adams were seated across from him, and Rochelle was leaning against a file cabinet near the window. They looked like they were in the middle of something – perhaps a discussion or an exercise – which they promptly suspended when she walked in the room.

"Detective, come in and sit down," Weaver said affably. Without prompting, Adams stood up, vacated the chair and stood next to Rochelle.

"What's going on?" Hobbs asked as she sank into her seat. The air in the room felt different; it was a viscous fog, the culmination of rumors or suggestions that had been abruptly halted but still hung in the atmosphere. Martinez and Adams wouldn't look at her.

"What did you learn from your meeting with Steven Vance?" Weaver asked.

Hobbs cleared her throat. "He says he has nothing to do with the family's disappearance, and I believe him. He also told me emphatically that he didn't ever sell drugs to John. What he wouldn't do is tell me that he didn't order the assault on John.

He kept dodging the question. I think Vance could have ordered the hit…but I can't figure out what the circumstances would have led to that if not drug-related. So I learned that Vance and John Brock did know each other…but Vance kept dancing around my questions about *how* they knew each other too."

Although this information didn't yield any solid leads, it was still good intelligence in Hobbs's opinion. She thought Weaver would praise the work she'd done to glean this information from Vance, but he didn't appear to be moved at all. He sat back in his chair and folded his arms across his chest. "Can you three give us a second?" he asked, still looking at Hobbs. The others left the room.

Hobbs inhaled and waited for Weaver to talk. The air in the room still felt stiff. Although Hobbs knew she had broken some of the rules, Weaver had always been a protector – an avuncular boss who was always in her corner. She figured she would explain herself and he would nod in agreement – like he always did.

But sitting across from his stern face, she realized that she had miscalculated. Weaver didn't frequently reprimand his detectives but when he did, he was cold and severe – and the stories of such rebukes circulated among the police force for days.

"*Why* were you meeting privately with Steven Vance?" Weaver asked sharply.

"I had no choice Captain. It was that or let him go."

"Are you in a position to make that decision?" Weaver asked. His words were sharp, his voice a cavernous grumble. Hobbs had never heard him take that tone with her.

"No sir," Hobbs answered.

"If I'm correct, just this morning, you said you were going to sit this one out. Do you remember that?"

Hobbs nodded.

"So what happened? Or…more appropriately…what's going on between you and Steven Vance?"

Hobbs swallowed hard. Maybe Martinez knew the whole story about her and Steven but no one else did. She was humiliated to have it come up in such a way. The story of her and Steven felt both ancient and fully present – an old folk tale that resonated despite her desires to keep it buried.

"There's nothing going on with us," Hobbs said. "We were together once – a long time ago – but that's all over now. I don't really have any more to say about it."

Hobbs let her eyes run over the objects on Weaver's desk— his desktop computer, his framed pictures of his wife and kids, various folders and papers. If she could just keep her focus on these items, she could ignore the present. Like staring at an object during a blood draw, if she could just concentrate on the inanimate, the acute sensation would pass.

"You say you've moved on, but Roberta, it's clouding your judgment."

"It's not clouding my judgment. I got some good info—"

Weaver's face grew red – tomato-like splotches spreading across his cheeks. "Roberta, you sold out on our most promising lead! Steven Vance is all we have! You think there are other drug lords hiding in the corners of Vetta Park? You said it yourself; the guy knows John Brock, and we're pretty damn sure he assaulted the kid two years ago! But all he has to do is look you in the eyes and say he doesn't know where the family is and you'll believe him! At least make him buy you a nice dinner and take you to the symphony before he tries to fuck you the next time!" Weaver smacked his desk when he spoke, an exclamation point to reinforce his bellowing.

Hobbs waited a few seconds for the room to cool down, for the air that had been scattered and displaced by Weaver's desk-slap to settle. After a few moments, his face reverted to normal too, and she was hopeful that with the eruption of the storm would come a useful dialog. Hobbs could have taken issue with his intrusion into her privacy; the mention of dinner and whatnot was truly not warranted. But she allowed the comment to pass because she wanted to appeal to reason and move ahead.

"Captain, I know you think my judgment is clouded but I can't shake the feeling that he's telling the truth about not knowing where the family is. I'm usually right when I go with my gut."

Weaver acknowledged her by squinting and staring up at the ceiling.

Hobbs waited for his words – the comforting, supportive après-disagreement that he always issued. *I did think that Vance was involved, but I trust your instinct on this one.* Or: *Perhaps I was wrong to question your judgment. If you say Vance isn't involved, we'll see what else we can find.*

But Weaver was neither supportive nor reassuring. "I'm afraid I disagree with you, and the rest of the team thinks so too. Steven Vance and his drug operations are the only link we have tying the family to subversive individuals."

"Well, what about the traffic file? Once they locate the traffic file, we'll have something else."

"Enough about the traffic file! There is no traffic file!" Weaver roared.

Hobbs sat back in her seat, stunned. "What? What do you mean?"

Weaver pressed a button on his phone. "Send Rochelle, Adams and Martinez in here please!"

A moment later, the three came back into the room – their expressions the same as before and their places the same as before – Martinez in the seat next to Hobbs and Rochelle and Adams next to each other against a file cabinet.

"Rochelle, please tell us what you came up with after searching the basement," Weaver said.

All eyes in the room focused on the red-headed young woman, who looked surprised by the sudden onset of attention. "Oh…um…I told the Captain that we combed the entire basement. I'm sorry to say, there was no file about a yellow Ferrari in an accident, and no mention of Greta Brock, Greta Wagner or Greta Carpenter as witness to an accident who later changed her statement."

Hobbs turned back to face the Captain. "So, then, the file hasn't been found yet."

"Or it never existed at all," Weaver countered. "Maybe you remember it wrong."

"No, Captain, I know for a fact. The traffic file *exists*. I wrote the report when Greta changed her mind. I remember her face. I'm not wrong about this."

The room was then completely silent – heads lowered, faces impassive. No one wanted to challenge Hobbs' memory of the report, but it was obvious to her that no one believed her. They saw her as stubborn at best and unprofessional at worst – too stubborn to admit when she was wrong, and too caught in the throes of an old relationship to think clearly about this case.

Hobbs was insistent. "We need to look again. I'll look again. After hours, when I get off of work here, I'll look through the basement and look through the files." She could hear her own voice ringing in her ears and she wondered if she sounded more crazy or desperate. For some reason, she felt a need to prove herself on this case – to advance the momentum even when they were at a stasis.

Weaver huffed in her direction but didn't specifically address her pleas to redo Rochelle's work. "Listen, I think we need to focus on Greta Brock's mother," Weaver said. "Johanna Wagner, we have a name and a most recent location –

Springfield, Missouri. She seems to be a bit of a drifter but I'm sure she's findable if we get some boots on the ground out there. Martinez and Hobbs, get out there as soon as you can and let me know what you find out."

Both Martinez and Hobbs nodded and then Weaver dismissed the group. Hobbs walked out of the office feeling like a once-inflated balloon that had lost all of its air. She was smarting from the professional censure and the loss of credibility. She could have combed through the basement files and found what she was looking for – surely Rochelle and her ilk hadn't combed through every single box in a manner of five days – but now she was to spend the next several days in Springfield, Missouri. She had no choice but to suspend the file search.

Adams followed her to the desk and then asked to catch up with her in one of the interior meeting rooms.

Once they were inside the tiny room, he said, "Roberta, I wanted to tell you that I'm sorry about what happened back there. I tried to vouch for you. Since you'll be in Springfield, I can look for the traffic file in my spare time."

Hobbs knew what she should have felt and how she should have responded. Adams still believed in her and she should have been grateful. She should have smiled at him and perhaps thrown her arms around him – the room was windowless anyway – and thanked him for his help.

But what she actually felt was angry. There was something pitying about the way he looked at her – his eagerness to rescue her from her situation. She wouldn't have needed his help searching the basement if Weaver hadn't forced a temporary geographic relocation and she didn't want a knight in shining armor.

"Don't do me any favors," Hobbs said, sounding more caustic than she intended. "I mean, if you're offering to do it because you think it'll advance the case, then by all means search the basement, but if you're offering because you think it *means* anything, then I don't want your help."

Adams shook his head and threw up his hands. When they landed, he shoved them deep inside his pockets. His face – once willing and friendly – hardened into a grimace. "I offered because I tend to think you're a good detective. Jesus Christ! And you should be *grateful* for my offer, since everyone else thinks—" Adams stopped and rubbed his chin, smoothing the scruffs with his fingertips.

"What? What do they think?" Hobbs demanded.

"They think you fucked the case," Adams said. "That your head is shoved way up your ass over Steven Vance, and that Martinez and Weaver should've listened to you when you asked to be recused from the case. I was the one who took your side."

This information was entirely predictable to Hobbs. If she had sat down and thought about what Weaver and Martinez had been saying before she entered his office, this was what she would have guessed...and yet hearing Adams say it out loud felt like a puncture. Her secrets were coming to light in conversations behind her back; she was no longer the guardian of her past. And even though they didn't know the actual story, it didn't matter.

"Well, I don't need you to *take my side*," Hobbs said. "I can fend for myself with Weaver."

"*Christ*, Roberta, I don't even know why I try with you. I try to offer you help, you get mad at me about it. I try to take your side and we end up in a huge fight, and I just don't understand why I bother."

"Well then save yourself the trouble and don't bother!" Hobbs yelled. She was saying it not for Adams but for all of them. For the colleagues having covert discussions about past and questioning her state of mind. For the young woman who was ever-eager but too incompetent to find a simple traffic file.

And for the drug lord pretending to be a benevolent entrepreneur who had screwed with her for years and was now whimsically tossing out apologies.

Hobbs just wanted all of them to disappear, all of the noise of the day to subside and leave her alone to her thoughts. But instead of articulating herself, she took it out on Adams, perhaps for no other reason than his physical presence and inauspicious timing.

"Fine, you got it," Adams said. He threw open the door and then he was gone.

Hobbs waited a few seconds, stood up and locked the door. She found a seat at one of the tables, buried her head in her hands and sobbed quietly.

# CHAPTER EIGHTEEN

*July 26, 1998*

Roberta Hobbs was in love. Twenty-two years old and freshly graduated from college, she was beautiful and optimistic. Her hair was thick, long and straight, always flowing down her back. Her skin was flawless, even after a night of drinks with him, always with him. She never thought she'd be that girl to drop her friends just because of a guy, but now that she was in thick of it – the eye of the tempest – she suddenly understood everything. What all those love songs were about, the romance novels, the Cinderella stories she'd always dismissed as puerile and illusory. Now it all made sense.

She first saw him walking down the sidewalk on campus. He was older, wearing a business suit while speaking to a few other businesspeople, sandy-colored hair hiding a few forehead wrinkles. Even through the suit she could see that he was muscular, and there was something about his stature that caught her attention. He was a fully matriculated man – not a kid who fumbled with the pen after timidly asking for her phone number. Not a boy who practically drooled after she agreed to go back to his dorm room.

It was all over in a second. She glanced at him and she glided by and saw that he was looking right at her. But still, she had to move forward. At that time, her walk was more of a high-heeled strut, and to pause would be to cut short the illusion.

Roberta thought she'd never see him again, but she was surprised to see him sitting in the booth of the local college luncheonette. Still wearing his business suit, he was alone this time, and he looked terribly out of place compared to the rest of the patrons – none of whom were over the age of twenty-five. Roberta walked over to him and smiled. "Are you lost?" she asked.

He looked up and warmly returned her smile – a ruggedly handsome face. "Not at all. I'm exactly where I want to be. Please have a seat."

Roberta sat down in the bench across from him and noticed that he was sharing his seat with a stack of legal pads. "Are you a professor?" she asked him.

He laughed. "No, I'm in real estate. I was thinking about building a hotel around here. But after today's meeting, I don't think I can justify it to my investors. My name's Steven."

He stretched his hand across the table and she shook it. "Roberta," she said.

That was how it all began – the beginning of everything. It was as if the four previous years of college were just a prelude to this moment. And even though he was quite a bit older, he was still youthful. He was someone she could talk to, relate to, ease into bed with at the end of the day – or sometimes in the light of afternoon.

Everything progressed at light speed, one milestone after the next. She was too excited to experience all of it to wait for the natural pacing of things. Graduation happened and then she moved in with him in an apartment south of St. Louis that overlooked the Mississippi River.

They had only known each other a few months, but Roberta was always looking into the future, casting a vision of their commingled lives – a big wedding at one of his hotels was just the beginning.

Roberta's friends tried to warn her. Most were worried that she didn't know him well enough. One was concerned about the age gap and kept referring to Steven as "the octogenarian". Another said that Roberta had lost her sense of self entirely and had become consumed with pleasing her man, like a 1950s housewife.

"It doesn't matter," Roberta would say. "We're in love."

And she truly, deeply was in love – a feeling more overwhelming and powerful than anything she'd felt before. Everything reminded her of him; every time she was in a conversation, she thought of how it related to him. All she wanted was to be wrapped up with him at the end of the day, asleep in his arms, her face pressed against his chest, with the rise and fall of their respiration in concert.

She didn't dare tell her friends but there were in fact a few things that bothered her about him. The first and most troubling was his role in illegal activities. He had a few business associates who came by every now again – men who were different from the others he regularly dealt with. They were pushy to him and leery towards her. When they came by, they stared at her as though she was a prize Steven had won, an art fixture to be venerated. And when they spoke, they used euphemisms for drugs that didn't hide anything. One of the men once opened a box right in front of her and took out a few packets of white powder. Roberta gasped and Steven glowered at her and told her to leave the room. When he came into bed later that night, he either deflected or lied.

"I'm not selling drugs," he insisted, while pulling her body against his.

Roberta resisted. "But I saw it, the white powder. Cocaine. I've seen it before."

"Mmmm, let's not talk about it," he said, right before rolling over and falling asleep. Roberta turned away and tried to sleep but it took her awhile to drift. Her boyfriend was a drug dealer, and this was a fact she'd have to reconcile with images of him five years into the future – an honest, loving businessman, a husband who doted on her and maybe one or two kids.

Then there was the issue of the future – a topic he refused to discuss. "You're twenty-two years old Roberta," he would say. "You've got your whole life in front of you. Why are you trying to pin yourself down?"

She tried to explain that it wasn't about her but about him. He was in his late thirties, almost forty. Didn't he want to settle down? And she didn't have any qualms about limiting her options; she already knew whom she wanted to spend the rest of her life with. Then he would shake his head or become intimate, pull her into a full-body hug or laugh and tell an anecdote about one of the hapless guys who worked for him.

These issues bothered Roberta but they didn't sway her feelings. She and Steven loved each other intensely and they were going to end up together. That was the only fitting ending to their romance.

And then, everything she felt, everything she dreamed about, everything she thought she knew – all came crashing down one rainy night in October.

\*\*\*

Against her better judgment, Roberta allowed herself to be dragged to a nightclub. It was late in the month, and air was cool and rain-dampened. If it had been her decision, she would have stayed at home under a warm blanket, staring at the barges that occasionally crossed the Mississippi, keeping Steven's place in the bed warm until he got there.

But a good friend was having a birthday, and that led to several pleading emails and phone calls. Roberta was told in a halting, pejorative voice, that she never went out anymore. She had become a ghost since moving in with Steven. So she went.

The club was called The Thirst – and the first things Roberta noticed about it were the deafening pulse of electronica and the long line of hopeful clubgoers who waited to get in. There were five young women in their group, and they took a place at the end of the line, covering their ears and huddling together under a single umbrella.

As the line inched forward, Roberta had her epiphany. She recognized the architecture, the outside décor, even the way that *The Thirst* was scrawled on a sign above the entryway in Bickham Script.

"You guys, this is Steven's place," Roberta said, and her knowledge of several of the employees at work that night afforded them no-cover access to the club as well as the VIP area.

They paraded through the VIP area as though they owned it – and Roberta felt that she kind of did, in a displaced way. They claimed a banquette that overlooked the dance floor, ordered bottle service and made several heartfelt toasts to the birthday girl.

Then Roberta scanned the area and saw something amiss at the far end of the section. There was a girl about her age – blonde, leggy, wearing a tight cherry-red dress. And she was kissing a man who could have been mistaken for Steven.

Of course, it was impossible to see anything from that far of a distance, and through the haze of dancers, wait staff and the occasional puffs from a fog machine. But it was his body language that gave him away. He was leaning into the blonde girl – one hand on the banquette and the other caressing her thigh – a Steven Vance move.

Roberta stood up and made her way over. The whole time, she expected to see the couple pull away and give way to Roberta's mistake. She would politely change course and then tell a funny story to her trustworthy, loyal boyfriend when he came home later that night. *I saw a guy kissing a girl,* she would tell Steven. *And I must have been drunk because at first I thought it was you.*

The couple did separate but only when Roberta was standing directly in front of them. By then, there was no mistaking identity, no changing course. The nightmare was unfolding before Roberta, her worst fear fully realized.

Steven glanced up, saw Roberta, and scooted a few inches away from the blonde. "Roberta! What are you doing here?"

"My friend is having a birthday party," Roberta said, although it was hard to even find her voice, the breath that would allow her to finish her sentence. In one moment, every dream that she had been building up for months was eviscerated, everything she thought she knew was wrong.

"Hi, I'm Shelly," the woman said. "I'm Steven's girlfriend."

If Roberta was shocked and horrified by the presence of Shelly, Shelly didn't seem disturbed at all to see Roberta. She leaned over the banquette and poured herself a shot of vodka, quaffed the beverage and glanced around the room. "I'm going to go look around," she said to Steven, one hand gently placed on his knee. Then she stood up, planted a loud wet kiss on Steven's lips and sauntered away.

"Shelly is your girlfriend?" Roberta asked.

"Yes, Roberta. And I care for her a lot."

These words felt like a dagger. It wasn't enough that he was with another woman, that he confirmed an intimate relationship with someone else. It was this suggestion that he *cared* for her – as a foil for his feelings towards Roberta.

Roberta didn't want to ask the next question but she couldn't help herself. "And what about me?"

"I'm sorry Roberta."

There was a vice clenching her heart inside her chest. The alcohol made her feel woozy and unsteady. She stumbled a bit and thought about how clumsy she looked – certainly when compared to the graceful bombshell in the red dress who was flitting from table to table, casting adoring glances back at Steven.

"But we live together," Roberta said.

"Well, you do live in one of my apartments. But I've been thinking for a while now that you need to move out, find your own place, and move on. I'm sorry; it's just not working for me."

Steven then stood up and joined Shelly at one of the other banquettes in the section. Roberta stayed in her spot for a few moments longer, not even sure her legs could support her if she wanted to leave. Her entire life had been rewritten in a manner of seconds, and in a way that she was completely unprepared for. There was no tenderness – no concern from him. There wasn't even a real apology.

Roberta stayed at his apartment for another week until she found another place with affordable rent. During this time, Steven was a ghost. Roberta saw his images on photographs placed around the home; she saw his handwriting on papers scattered across his desk. But the man himself did not appear – nor did he respond to phone calls or emails. It was as though his decision was not so much a breakup as a purge. Since he'd made his choice, she no longer existed.

When Roberta thought about it later, she realized that his abolition of her hurt the most of all. The surprise sudden breakup was difficult. The discovery that he was seeing someone else was a shock. But to ignore all presence of her was the most demeaning. It reinforced that all the love she felt between the two of them was entirely in her head. Everything he had so whimsically said about his devotion to her was a lie. Had he once loved her or had he never loved her? Roberta would replay their months-long relationship in her mind like a highlight reel, trying to pinpoint the issue, the catalyst.

She left messages threatening to turn him over to authorities, and when he didn't respond, she actually did it. To her surprise, it didn't make her feel any better that he got arrested. She was surprised that in the wake of affection was not anger, or resentment or even a throbbing hurt. It was numbness – a welling up of emptiness, indifferent to sentiment.

This hardened ball of apathy grew over the next few years instead of shrinking. It protected her when others tried to date her, and it helped her cope with her chosen profession. Several months after Steven Vance was arrested in the lobby of one of his buildings by a brigade of law enforcement, Roberta Hobbs decided to become a cop.

*** 

Life on the beat was working out for Hobbs. She was good at her job, even when it involved the most mundane and unpopular of tasks. She could write traffic tickets – sometimes as many as ten a day – even in the face of a verbal assault from tactless recipients.

It wasn't just the traffic tickets. Hobbs worked with the diligence of a woman who had sworn her life to the task. Long hours, short lunches and hard work seemed to define her work ethic – and her co-workers took notice.

For Hobbs, sometimes it was easier to work than to think – easier to stay late and go through files than to go home and figure out her next steps for the evening. At the job, the next steps were obvious, well defined. There was more than enough work for the grunts who chose to embrace it, and that's what Roberta did when everyone else went home.

Steven Vance had moved on too. Three years after the nightclub incident, after his plea arrangement and reentry to the community at large, Vance started appearing in the newspapers again – this time due to community service and large public donations.

Hobbs took notice of Vance's image rehabilitation, his reversal of character – even as she tried not to notice. Every time she read an article about him, she wondered whether he had actually changed. The articles certainly made it seem so.

Then, she got her chance to find out for herself. In July of 2001, Hobbs was walking along the street on her way to work. It was a blisteringly hot day – the kind of day where the pavement seemed to be melting, and the sunshine made a sodden oval in the center of her shirt, where it clung to her stomach. Just as she was cursing her choice of outfit, she saw Steven Vance advancing towards her. He was striding along, handsome as ever, and when he saw her, he broke into a rakish grin.

Hobbs stopped walking, smiled back and incited a casual conversation once he got closer. She had played this part so many times in her head, but when it actually happened, she was surprised that she reenacted it all wrong. She wanted to be unaffected by him, a once-jilted girlfriend who'd since moved on. But there was a twinge of love or lust that still beat whenever he spoke. After five or ten minutes, when he invited her up to his apartment to see his renovations, she agreed. She was surprised by how giddy she felt during the elevator ride, the promise of a once-unbearable outcome that now seemed so auspicious, so certain.

They spent the next six months in bed together and then parted ways in a manner just as ugly as the first time around. She wanted a future and he needed space. And the more she sought it, the more he resisted.

When Hobbs left his apartment the morning after their second breakup, she called him a litany of names and said a bunch of things she didn't even believe. As much as she hated him for contesting the future that she so deeply wanted, she still wanted it.

Steven Vance was big and lumbering, macho and unreasonable. But he could also be candid and open, kindhearted and thoughtful. They had meaningful discussions, comical banter, and they were incredibly physically compatible. Hobbs had no idea whether he was still attached to his old activities, still lording over his old drug enterprises. She suspected as much but never asked. It was better not to know.

This began a decade of what Hobbs referred to as *push-pull*. She would see Vance at a bar or a charity fundraiser, they would anneal their romance with a passionate bedroom romp and he would make promises that appealed to every crucial desire she held for the two of them.

Invariably, they would spend the ensuing three to six months by each other's side, and just when Hobbs grew comfortable enough to declare that *this* time was different, *this* time Vance had grown up, he would pull away.

Each rejection stung just as painfully as the first one, and it surprised Hobbs – who was stoic, emotionless, sensible at the office – that she could be so imprudent in her personal life.

From a rational point of view, Hobbs knew that falling back in with Steven Vance was a terrible idea, and yet it took until the age of thirty-five for her to officially call it quits, and only after a public confrontation. They had taken an off-night during the throes of another torrid affair and she decided to show up at one of his fundraisers – an auction to raise money for a little league stadium. There she found him happily preaching into a microphone, encouraging donations from the audience with an adoring young brunette on his arm – *his new girlfriend.*

The ensuing argument in the parking lot had the composition of a play that had been rehearsed so many times before – same actors, same dialog. He had recently realized that he loved the petite brunette and he was sorry – although he didn't really seem sorry. Before Hobbs stormed away, she declared that she was officially, irrefutably, undeniably *done with him.*

This time she meant it. Hobbs avoided Vance after that confrontation. He was an addiction that required complete abstinence to make way for convalescence. But she also didn't allow for anyone else to fill that gap. No one provided that same sense of thrill, that same fluttery feeling.

And then there was the question of love. *Love* was a word that was thrown around so often in the early days of every Steven Vance tryst. Love was what she was certain she felt for him, why she had stayed in a cycle of bad decisions, the stranglehold that choked her heart. And love was what had destroyed her – kept her from seeing things as they really were, had her believing in silly stories that would never actually happen.

If Hobbs needed to go to great lengths to avoid her former lover, she could do so. But she didn't want to hear anyone sell her on the virtues of love. As far as she was concerned, love was a burning demon, a corrupt concept, and she could live her life without it.

# CHAPTER NINETEEN

*January 11, 2010*

Monday morning in Vetta Park was bitterly cold, a cloudy blanket settling in the air. Greta looked outside the window and marveled at the continuity from lawn to sky – everything a pale, crystal white. She met John at the front foyer area and then drove with him to St. Louis Investigations. She would have preferred to meet with Colt Bundy unaccompanied, but John's winter break was long – a stretch of three weeks across December and January to allow for school building renovations.

Colt met them at the elevators. He shook Greta's hand and then grinned widely when he saw John. "Well, hello John," Colt said. "Nice to make your acquaintance."

John smiled shyly and the trio walked down the hallway into Colt's corner office. Greta and John settled into one of the leather sofas while Colt bent over behind his desk. When he emerged, he was holding a thin novel with a colorful cover. *The Kidnapping at Busch Stadium.*

"Here you go," Colt said, offering the book to John. "It's a book by a local author. When I was your age, I loved mysteries. May be why I got into the business."

John took the book and leafed through it. Greta could see that there were no pictures to provide contextual support. The print was smaller than usual for him. It was also an exceptionally long novel for him – maybe one hundred pages longer than the longest book he'd ever read by himself.

"You can read that while I talk to your mom," Colt added.

"Thanks," John muttered. "The ki...the kin...the kindergarten at Busch Stadium."

Years of special education hadn't affected John's strategy: Say the words he'd memorized with no hesitation, and guess wildly at the words he didn't know based on the first letter.

"It's not *kindergarten*, sweetheart," Greta said softly. "The word is *kidnapping*."

She didn't want to seem punitive or critical – but she felt he needed correction. The word *kidnapping* was phonetically realizable if he just took the time to tap out the syllables.

"Oh, this book is probably not meant for his age," Colt said. "It's meant for fourth grade and up. What is he, eight, nine years old? I can see if I have something."

"He's eleven," Greta said, and then an uncomfortable silence ensued, in which Colt nodded and looked down at his notepad, John closed the book and silently ran his fingers across the cover page, and Greta sat up straighter in her seat and said nothing.

It wasn't Colt's fault; John had a certain look that made his age difficult to pinpoint. For an eleven year old, he had a smaller stature and a skinny build – legs sinewy, arms gawky. He hadn't yet approached puberty so his voice was still a shade higher than many of his classmates and he didn't display so much as a shadow of facial hair.

But lately John had also started adopting some of the character traits endemic to adolescence. Activities that had once given him joy now made him sullen. Once chatty, he was now more often laconic and annoyed by the task of answering her questions. In prior years, when he came home from school, he would sit at the kitchen table and snack on carrots while replaying stories and jokes from the day. These days, he walked in the door and retreated upstairs to the sanctity and comfort of his own bedroom. When Greta knocked, she was told to leave him alone. Solitude was the only request he made of her.

So Greta forgave Colt for misjudging John's age. John's frame and inability to read the title of a book could confuse a well-meaning person. Unfortunately, it set the tone for an awkward meeting. John brought his legs up and hugged them – sulking while he stared at the floor. Colt blushed and apologized.

"I'm really sorry John," he said. "I don't have kids of my own so I get kids' ages wrong all the time."

It wasn't really about the age, Greta knew. It was the inference based on his inability to properly read. These types of situations had been surfacing more and more as John got older.

"John will be fine," Greta said, patting his knee. He lunged away from her to avoid her touch – a sharp jerk towards the edge of the couch. She hesitated for a moment and then chose to ignore it.

"John, can you step outside for a moment so I can talk with Mr. Bundy?" Greta asked.

John continued to sulk and ignore her. Greta had seen this type of behavior from him before, and it amazed her how different he was than his father. When Griffin was angry, he yelled and hurled objects, demanding, flinging and whirring – a theatrical tornado. When John was angry, he took refuge inside of his head. He coped by turning into a statue – mute and expressionless. Greta knew there was no chance John would listen to her so she requested that Colt speak with her in the hallway.

"I'm really sorry about that," Colt repeated, once they were standing next to each other outside the office.

"Oh it's *fine*. He'll be all right. It's just typical adolescence, you know?"

Colt smiled weakly. "So what can I do for you?" he asked.

"I came here because I wanted to thank you, first of all. The information you provided to me last time was really useful, and I was able to use it to get full custody of John."

Colt smiled again – more genuine this time, and wide enough that Greta could see a few dark fillings in the corners of his mouth.

"I'm glad to hear," he said.

"So I have just one more request of you. My ex-husband has a silent business partner for his real estate work and I need to know who that person is."

"I see. When are you expected back in court?"

"No, no, it's not about that." Greta paused for a moment. "The financial and the custody stuff – that's all settled. I just need to know because....because..." Greta waited for a few seconds while thinking of how to explain. There was no easy way to describe what she was thinking. While the court-related issues were all finalized, Greta still worried about her past folding into the present – someone she thought she'd said good-bye to exercising decision-making ability over her family. Like freeing oneself of a cult only to find the leader's invisible hand shaping her future. She finally said, "I have a name in mind and I just want you to confirm whether I'm right."

"Who's that?"

"Steven Vance."

"The real estate mogul philanthropist guy?"

Greta nodded. "That's him."

"Sure. I'll see what I can find out."

"Thanks." Greta went back inside Colt's office and found John sprawled across one of the couches, his head angled and eyes glazed as if half dreaming. *The Kidnapping at Busch Stadium* lay abandoned on the floor.

"C'mon John," Greta said. "It's time to go."

\*\*\*

John's IEP case manager at the elementary school had been Brook Tremble, but that changed when he became a sixth grader. Tremble's middle school counterpart was a small, dowdy, older woman named Sue Chambers.

A few days after her meeting with Colt Bundy, Greta sat at a desk in Sue's office and waited for the meeting to begin. Sue hummed to herself while she arranged papers across the desk. It was a familiar melody – patriotic and puerile, maybe *Yankee Doodle Dandy* or *I've Been Working on the Railroad*.

Sue stopped arranging the papers and sat down at the other side of the desk with a sigh. Greta could tell that the sigh was an indictment – a preface of the unpleasant conversation that would follow.

"Thanks for meeting with me today," Greta started. "I know John has only been at the middle school for a few months but I'm worried–"

"You should be worried!" Sue interrupted. Her voice heaved when she spoke – as though they were projected from a pulpit towards a congregation. "I hate to jump right into it like this, but Mrs. Brock, look at your son's most recent assessment!" She pointed her index and middle fingers towards the various papers while she continued. "John can only correctly decode nine percent of two-syllable words! The intonation and expression is off. His written sentences are completely indecipherable; there are spelling errors, poor letter formation, no punctuation or capitalization, no spacing and many, many letter reversals. And finally, given a list of 20 words, John spelled only two of them correctly! Mrs. Brock, I have seen this type of result from a sixth-grader in the past, but never have I seen it from a child who's been in the Special Education system for three years already!"

Sue Chambers sat back down in her seat. She took another deep breath and waited for Greta to respond. Greta had heard this about Sue from other parents – that she lacked a bedside manner, that she was blunt and pushy. But she'd also heard that Sue was passionate and demanding – that she could be an advocate for her students if she felt they weren't getting what they needed.

To Greta, too much information had been thrown at her all at once for her to formulate a quick response. She almost felt like she was back in grade school again – perhaps in John's seat, sitting numbly while the instructor bellowed names, numbers and statistics that had been tossed too quickly to be comprehended.

"I don't...I don't..." Greta stammered and then stopped herself. There was too much that she wanted to say...and each separate thought made coherence a tough objective. She knew that John was well behind where he should be...but wasn't that why he was continuing to get Special Education services? Wasn't it the school's job to get him where he needed to be? Why was Sue Chambers spouting these scores at her as though she'd done something wrong?"

"Mrs. Brock..." Sue continued in a softer voice – her indignation now caked with a layer of sympathy. "John is very far behind where he needs to be and the gap between him and his peers is *widening instead of narrowing*, and that's something we really need to be concerned with. If we don't help him now, he could lose all interest in school and become – quite frankly – unreachable."

Greta nodded. "What do you suggest?"

"He needs *more*, quite frankly – more than what the school is able to give him. I feel he could benefit from one-on-one instruction. We don't have the resources to offer that at Edwardsville Middle...but maybe you could look into getting him outside tutoring to supplement the work that the school is doing?"

Greta thought about that conversation in Griffin's foyer. Griffin's voice – steady and vexed – insistent that the public schools were fine, that John just needed to work harder and that he didn't need a tutor.

Greta frowned. "I've looked into it, and it's too expensive."

"Well, if tutoring isn't going to work, I want you to consider something else. The Jefferson School is located in downtown St. Louis. Have you heard of it?"

Greta shook her head.

"It's specifically designed for kids who are bright and smart – just like John – but who have profound learning disabilities. It's a private school but they do offer financial aid."

"You think John needs to attend a special school?" Greta asked.

"We've been doing everything we can, Mrs. Brock, but we're bound by budgets and class sizes. I'm telling you this as a mom, because I know how much you care about your son. John is very smart but I've noticed his attitude has changed lately – even from the start of school. I worry that his esteem could suffer because he's not making the progress we'd like to see, and kids this age are very attuned to what their classmates are saying about them. I haven't heard anything specific said to or about John – and we wouldn't tolerate any type of bullying at Edwardsville Middle School. But I'm thinking that he could benefit from being surrounded by peers who are going through the exact same thing as him. Do you understand? Eleven-year old boys are very vulnerable."

"Okay," Greta said softly. "Can you give me the details of the Admissions Director at Jefferson and I'll set up a meeting?"

"Certainly," Sue said. "I'll give you the name of the Financial Aid officer too." She then opened a drawer, took out a notepad and started writing down numbers.

Greta stared at the papers laid out on the desk in front of her while she waited. They were all words and low percentages, points on the low end of a curve, sloping lines that represented poor performance and sentence fragments about unmet goals.

When Sue finished, she handed Greta the sheet of paper and they shook hands and parted ways.

In the car, Greta dialed Griffin's number. She hadn't spoken to him since they'd agreed to cut all ties – not in any real way apart from pickup and drop-off times – but Greta knew she'd need his help for the Jefferson School to be a possibility. It was going to be a painful phone call, but Greta was determined to do or say whatever it took.

Sue's words echoed in Greta's mind while she waited for Griffin to pick up the call.

*Eleven-year old boys are very vulnerable.*

And John certainly was. He was a ship that had run aground – anchorless, rudderless and unique in its predicament. The other eleven year-olds certainly had their own issues, and Greta tried to remind herself of that whenever she saw another mother of an adolescent boy at the supermarket or post office. But the other boys had a foundation that could set their life's course. They could read and write, and if their choices ever steered them off track, they could find their way back using the basics they had learned in elementary school.

John's knowledge of the basics was nowhere. Perhaps he could continue to learn nothing at school and self-teach reading at a later time, like she had. But with each passing year, she grew more worried about the obstacles he faced. It was just as possible that his brain had a window for acquiring new information, and the more he waited, the harder it would be.

Teaching herself to read at age seventeen had been one of the most difficult pursuits she'd ever faced. It required an intense amount of daily discipline that she wasn't sure John had. This is why she needed to act, and she needed to do it right away.

# CHAPTER TWENTY

*February 1, 2010*

Greta had never seen a school quite like The Jefferson School. It was constructed of glass, brick and stone – a long rectangle with a rotunda jutting up from behind. Next to the front entrance, Greta saw a garden – abandoned for the meantime but still demarcated with small pillars and obelisks.

She walked into the front entrance and saw children's artwork in every direction: clay sculptures, drawings, paintings and chalk figures – all hanging from the ceiling or displayed on easels. The words of Thomas Jefferson were etched into stone next to a silhouette carving of his likeness: *For here we are not afraid to follow truth wherever it may lead, nor to tolerate any error so long as reason is left free to combat it.*

"Ms. Brock?" A voice said.

Greta spun around and saw a man and a woman. The man was lanky and grey-haired. The woman was the same height as

Greta, pale and petite. She wore a red business suit and carried a file of papers. "Are you Greta Brock?" she repeated.

Greta smiled. "Yes, that's me."

"Nice to meet you. I'm Joanne Flaherty – Admissions Director for The Jefferson School. This is J.J. Schwartz."

Schwartz smiled and held out his hand. "I'm Director of Financial Aid. Let's have a seat in the corner conference room."

Greta shook their hands and followed them past the front office and through a wide hallway. Everything gleamed and glistened. The rugs were perfectly clean; the ceilings were high and airy, artwork added dashes and pinches of color to every surface. When they reached a conference room, Greta noticed the corner was completely glass, offering a vista of different lime and pea-green gardens.

"Your building is just beautiful," Greta said as they all took a seat around a conference room table. She didn't want to make too much of the school's aesthetics, didn't want to portray herself as a philistine bumpkin from the southern hills of Missouri. And maybe it was just the difference between public and private schools. But every school Greta had seen up to this point was created in the style of pragmatics. The lines were neat and straight, the structures purely square or rectangular. At the Edwardsville schools, hallways were uninspiring, windows needed washing and decorations were sporadic. The Jefferson School seemed like a different breed of building.

"Thank you," Joanne said sweetly. "I wanted to let you know the good news first – that we looked through John's file and he meets the criteria for the school. He clearly has a very high I.Q. and quite a significant gap in reading and writing achievement. We also have space in the sixth grade class…so if you wanted to apply now, we could take him right away, or we could wait until seventh grade if you didn't want to pull him out mid-year."

Greta nodded and swallowed a burst of emotion. Her reaction was sudden and visceral – tears that flooded the ducts of her eyes, sobs that had to be swallowed. Here was a chance for John – the escape hatch she had been wishing for. Here was his chance to flee the path of illiteracy and low self-esteem – a loop that fed on itself and worsened every time he completed a circuit.

"Thank you," Greta said. "Really. You don't know how much it means to me. And to John."

J.J. glanced over at Joanne and then his gaze alighted on Greta. "We know how much it means to all of our students, and we're glad every time we can accept a new student. But…"

He hesitated and glanced at Joanne again and Greta knew that there was going to be some bad news mixed in with the good. Perhaps J.J. and Joanne had practiced this routine before. Lead with the good news and set the mood for the bad. The lowered voice, the furtive glimpses at each other…even the sun seemed to cower behind a mass of clouds as if to participate in the act.

"But…" J.J. continued. "The education here is first-rate and we're able to provide individualized instruction, but there's a cost to that instruction. With tuition and fees, the all-in cost of attending the school is thirty-five thousand dollars a year."

If they expected to her to flinch with shock, she surprised them by continuing to sit there, expressionless. The number so comically, impossibly high that it may as well have been one hundred thousand, or even a made-up number: *sixty-five quadrillion dollars*! She was a stay-at-home mom who barely managed to stretch Griffin's monthly payment across thirty days. Yet the school offered need-based financial aid and she was sitting next to the financial aid officer. Certainly the number he spouted wasn't the actual number.

"How much will I have to pay if I qualify for financial aid?" she asked.

"That's the thing," J.J. said, shifting in his seat. "We've looked at the income tax statements you provided and you don't qualify."

"What?" Greta rang. "How don't I qualify?" If they expected her to get a job to defray the cost of tuition, she would immediately commence a resume campaign. But Greta had no college degree, let alone a high school diploma. She had no prospects for covering the cost of a thirty-five thousand dollar a year school – not even close, and not even when combined with Tuck's salary as a paralegal.

J.J. shifted again and cleared his throat. "Well the financial documents you provided were not only yours but those of your husband…"

"Ex-husband," Greta corrected.

"Ex-husband," J.J. repeated. "We have a very limited ability to offer financial aid and unfortunately, the assistance goes only to the most needy students. John's father earns more than the vast majority of our families. We aren't in a position to offer financial assistance to John at this time."

"But Griffin won't pay for it – any of it," Greta insisted. "He thinks John needs to work harder, that he's lazy. Griffin won't even cover *part* of it. He's opposed on principle."

As soon as she first heard the words *The Jefferson School* – as soon as she was told it was a private school -- Greta had been on the phone, trying to get hold of her ex-husband. Griffin at first avoided her calls but eventually relented – if for no other reason than to stop the flood of messages. And once Greta was able to speak to him, she tried every approach she could think of. She promised him she'd work for him as a housekeeper or assistant, she tried to portray it as an investment in his son, she appealed to his sense of loyalty and paternity. Nothing worked. Griffin, quite simply, was not going to fund any part of The Jefferson

School. The mutually agreed-upon nominal child support payment was the end of it.

"Is Griffin involved in John's life?" J.J. asked.

"Well, he sees him for one weekend every few months," Greta said.

"And does he pay child support?"

Greta nodded.

"I don't know what your relationship is like…what type of agreement you have. But you could look into filing a motion for additional support from your ex-husband if you feel his child support payments are too low."

Greta bit her lip and stared down at her hands. J.J. was proposing that she and Griffin find their way back to court – that they rehash every laborious detail that lawyers had painstakingly covered the first time around. He was suggesting that they toss the custody agreement out the window – the one outcome of the original agreement that had brought her peace.

And who knew what type of judge they would get if they went back at it? The type who sympathized with John's needs or the type who viewed a fancy private school as an exorbitant and unnecessary expense? She couldn't take the risk of facing the latter. She knew that her child support payments were a joke; they were a small fraction – a rounding error – of Griffin's total income and wealth. But the court only needed to find that John was getting an amount sufficient for his lifestyle…and in a twisted, iniquitous logic, it was possible to conclude that The Jefferson School needn't constitute that lifestyle.

Trying to get more child support from the judge was an option available to Greta, but she just couldn't take the chance and risk losing John. Her only hope was to change the decisions of those whose minds were already thoroughly made up: J.J. Schwartz – who seemed certain that she could extract a higher payment from her ex-husband if she tried, and Griffin himself, who felt that his son should just work a little harder.

\*\*\*

Colt Bundy was sitting on the front steps of 12 Avery when Greta pulled into the driveway. She tried to hide her shock as she made her way out of the car. She couldn't even remember having given Colt Bundy her home address – although surely there'd been a credit card billing form or maybe a signed check that listed the information.

Colt looked not exactly pleased with himself – but relaxed, casual as he watched her get out of the car. His white cotton shirt clung a little bit tighter to his biceps than she'd noticed before; his lips had a light sheen of moisture as he smiled.

"Good to see you again," he said brightly.

"Hi" Greta said, and shook his hand. She was still smarting from her meeting at the Jefferson School and suddenly she became aware of how alone she was at that moment. John was still at school. Tuck didn't get off of work for another few hours. And her neighbor, Mary Miller – a woman whose sole purpose seemed to be to lurk and loiter – was nowhere in sight.

"I was in the neighborhood," Colt said. "So I figured I would stop by and chat with you, rather than give you an impersonal phone call."

"That's very kind of you," Greta said. She watched him shift his weight from foot to foot while his eyes assessed her – practically acting out his desire to be invited inside the house – but that wasn't going to happen. Instead, Greta leaned against her car and folded her hands across her chest. She knew she was being uncharacteristically aloof but she was in no mood to be her usual gregarious self. First she'd had to contend with her meeting at The Jefferson School – an ever-tantalizing option that had turned into a mirage – and now she had to deal with a surprise visitor whose intentions were vague.

She let a few quiet moments pass and then Colt finally cleared his throat and spoke. "Well, I wanted to let you know the result of our latest search – your ex-husband's silent partner."

"Oh right! Is it Steven Vance?"

Colt shook his head. "No, I wasn't able to uncover any kind of relationship between Steven Vance and Griffin."

"I see." Greta said, both surprised and disappointed at the same time. She hadn't spoken to Vance in years, but still, he was a known entity. Greta knew that she could find and speak to him if she ever needed to. Had he been Griffin's silent partner, Greta would have had the ear of someone in his inner circle. Instead, someone she didn't know and had never heard of was most likely Griffin's partner – someone who would justifiably never open the door to her.

Colt then took a step closer and smiled. He had probably interpreted her silence as an opening – a hole in the conversation inviting him to overcome his hesitance. "Greta…" he began, in a voice that was both deep and hopeful, a careful enunciation that lengthened the cadence of her name.

Then the rest just spilled out – a streaming flurry of words, perhaps once carefully choreographed. "Greta, I've been meaning to say something for awhile now. I think you're beautiful. I've always thought you were. And now that your divorce and custody arrangement are finalized, I was wondering if you'd like to have dinner with me sometime."

Greta smiled back. In a way, his nervousness was endearing. Colt had the muscular outer shell of a comic book hero. He always seemed charming – the disposition of a salesman. It was sweet to witness a vulnerable side as well – even if she had no interest in pursuing him.

"Thanks Colt," Greta said. "I'm flattered, but I'm already seeing someone."

"Oh, okay, I get it. No problems then." Colt backed away a few steps and tapped a few sheets of folded paper against his palm. "Well, here you go then. It's my findings, as well as a final bill. Stay in touch."

He walked across the street, stepped into his car, gunned the engine and shot up Avery Place – well over the speed limit for their quiet residential street.

Greta watched him leave, amused by his hasty exodus. She then glanced at the first sheet of paper – a hefty sized bill, but not unanticipated. She shuffled it to the back and looked at the other sheet. In bold black lettering, the paper listed a name and description of Griffin's silent business partner. The name itself sent a wave of shock through Greta's body. The other details were superfluous – a street address, a license plate number, a height and weight – all known to her already, based on the name.

It was such an obvious name too, that once Greta saw it, she wondered why she was so shocked and why she hadn't pieced it together sooner: Marcia Brock, her ex-mother-in-law. The woman who had initially funded all of Griffin's ventures. The woman who so vehemently voiced her disapproval when Griffin announced his intentions to marry Greta. The silent witness who sat towards the back of their divorce proceedings and stared at Greta with crystal-blue, unflinching eyes.

This was who had been silently narrating the milestones in Griffin's life – the one who controlled his fortune, with final say in all of his business decisions. It was Marcia Brock who controlled all the strings and Marcia who Greta now so urgently and desperately needed to talk to.

# CHAPTER TWENTY-ONE

*April 3, 2010*

It was a few months after the first phone call, but Marcia was able to find a three-hour respite in her social calendar to allow for a visit. Greta and John drove up on a warm, sunny Saturday – the day before Easter Sunday. When they finally arrived after the seven-hour drive, Greta had to pause and catch her breath before exiting the car.

Marcia's home was a Tudor-style ivory stucco masterpiece. There were pillars and columns, gargoyles and carefully carved topiaries. The two-story home backed up against Lake Michigan, and spread out majestically over what must have been a full acre. A gazebo overlooked sandy bluffs to the left of the house, and a stone-flanked path that led to the beach was on the right. Greta stood staring upward, silent, until Marcia appeared and ushered her visitors inside.

"You've been here before Greta; you needn't gawk like that," Marcia said, although her tone indicated exhilaration. She loved to be admired, adored and celebrated. She handed John's and Greta's jackets to a black-attired butler and led them further inside the house.

The inside of Marcia Brock's mansion was no less remarkable than the outside. There were fifteen-foot ceilings, marble floors, antique furnishings, and high slung crystal chandeliers. Marcia led them through the front foyer, the living room and the drawing room – where an enormous Steinway grand piano absorbed sunlight from the corner windows – and opened a door to her large back terrace.

The three sat down at an umbrella-shaded granite table and gave drink requests to a different butler. To Greta, it felt like she had stepped out of her life and into someone else's, as though she was part of a television show that swapped realities. She had visited Marcia's home before – sporadically, when she and Griffin were still together. But each time felt like the first. It amazed her that someone related to her – even if just by marriage – could have so much.

When the drinks were brought, Marcia took a few sips and folded her hands across her lap. She always looked so put-together, as though she had emerged from the photo clippings of the society pages. On this day, her hair was wrapped in a silk shawl and her white wool dress fitted favorably to her svelte body.

"Thanks for having us over," Greta said after swallowing a few sips of ice tea.

Marcia appeared not to hear her. She motioned for one of the butlers and then jabbed her hand in the direction of the stone path. "I don't know how many times I tell Garcia to use the orchids from the garden and he goes and gets white hydrangeas!"

The butler straightened up and looked vaguely in the direction of a floral arrangement dripping over a marble parapet.

"My apologies, ma'am. I'll talk to him," the butler said. And then he was gone, leaving the three of them alone on the terrace.

Marcia turned her attention to her grandson. "John, you haven't said a word to me yet today. Not one word. Did the cat bite your tongue?"

John shrugged and shifted in his seat.

"Is he mute?" Marcia asked.

"No, he's not *mute*," Greta said. "John, say something. You haven't seen Grandmother in awhile. Tell her about…"

Greta stopped and tried to think of one topic that John could safely mention to his grandmother. Sports were out of the question, as was the hip-hop dance class that she'd enrolled him in. He went for one class and mostly sat on the sideline the whole time, feigning an upset stomach and the promise of eternal embarrassment. She'd tried to get him to take music classes – drums, piano, voice – but he swore he couldn't hold a tune and that reading music was as hard for him as reading English. And school was definitely not a topic for discussion. John was as lost as ever in the sixth grade, with few friends and no ability to keep up with the classwork.

The truth was, there was nothing that Greta could think of that would light a spark within John. He had no apparent hobbies or interests that captured his attention. Greta hoped that perhaps – at age eleven -- they were at rock bottom of prepubescent moroseness and disinterest. Perhaps Marcia would see just how dour her grandson was and insist on helping.

"Can I go inside and watch TV?" John asked.

"I have something for you, John," Marcia said. She stood up and the first butler appeared. She whispered something in his ear and he left the room, returning a few minutes later with a drawing.

The drawing looked as though it had been sketched onto paper-sized card stock. To Greta, it was an opalescent landscape

– tall green hemlocks that surrounded a farmhouse, bright red brick and yellow stalks.

"Did you draw this? With colored pencils?" Greta asked, and Marcia nodded.

"It looks wonderful," Greta said. "I love the different colors."

She appraised it just as she would have a work of art from John – only in this instance she was hoping that her acclaim would rub off on him and he would compliment the drawing as well. John had a way of demonstrating not only lack of decorum but also a frank evaluation of someone's work.

John looked down and Greta could see his eyeballs moving across the paper, while the rest of his face remained frozen. After a moment or two, he said, "Hey, there's hidden numbers! I see a five and a seven, and then two more nines. Hey, it's my birthday numbers – May seventh! I solved the puzzle!"

Greta stood up and walked around the table until she was behind John, her forearms resting on his shoulders. She studied the drawing more carefully, but to her it just looked like a brightly lit glimpse of rustic America.

"No, John," Greta chided politely. "I think Grandmother just drew a nice picture for you."

"The boy is right," Marcia said. "You figured that out rather quickly. And *yes*, the hidden numbers are your birthday numbers and *yes*, I did get you a present. It's a book, and one I think you will love. Alberto can you bring it here."

The butler dutifully left the room while Marcia stayed in her chair, continuing to emit her satisfaction towards her grandson. It was as though she'd finally received evidence of a familial bond, the link that connected her bloodline to her grandson. "Your father used to love these kind of puzzles," Marcia said. "When he was a child, I couldn't buy him enough…and he could always find all the hidden pieces. Why, you must have gotten that from him."

John nodded but didn't say anything. Greta leaned forward and examined the picture again. Only with advance notice of what she was going to find did the hidden figures slowly emerge for her. There was the *2*, creeping out from behind one of the hemlocks, and the *9*, clandestinely fording across a shallow pond.

Alberto returned with a leather-bound book in his hands, and gave it to Marcia, who immediately pressed it into John's hands. "Here you go!" Marcia said magnanimously. "It's *Treasure Island* – my favorite book – and I bought a copy for you. I first read it when I was your age and I *loved* it!"

John opened the book and flipped through the first few pages, then lowered the tome onto the table and repeated. "Can I go inside and watch TV now?"

From her deep satisfaction with her grandson only a few moments ago, Marcia now looked horrified. "Sure," she said. "Alberto will take you to one of the spare bedrooms."

John followed Alberto out of the room, and when the two women were alone, Marcia directed her expression at Greta.

"I honestly don't know what to say!" Marcia said. Her breath was a hot gust on Greta's skin – a waft of opprobrium for the child's behavior.

"He's in a bad place," Greta said. "He needs help, Marcia, and I think you may be the only one who can help him."

"What does he need?" Marcia demanded. "And don't say money. Whatever you do, don't say money. That's the one rule I gave Griffin when he left my house, ran off and got married. You make it on your own out there, just like I did, just like my husband did. When we needed money, we worked harder; we didn't bother our family asking for handouts."

The breath of judgment felt even hotter on Greta's skin, the condemnation even stickier. Greta had to move back a few inches to even think of what to say next. Her appeal to family bonds was a papery intimation; she was as close to Marcia's fortune as any stranger, same as any panhandler. And Marcia's claims of parental sternness were not even accurate. She wasn't the mama bird who kicked her offspring out of the nest and forced them to learn to fly. She was Griffin's silent partner after all, a source of capital and decision-making.

Greta wanted to expose Marcia's misrepresentations but she chose instead to plead to her sense of maternal devotion. Even if Greta was an interloper onto the Brock family name, at least John was kin.

"Marcia, he needs your help. He wasn't interested in the book because he can't read...at that level, I mean. He's had learning difficulties his whole life...in basic reading and fluency. I think he's probably dyslexic. But *Treasure Island* is quite simply above his level. Now there's a school..."

Greta's voice trailed off because the more she spoke, the more Marcia looked confused. And then Marcia wasn't confused anymore but entirely distracted. Her eyes followed the wings of a nearby bird, whose feathers swooped past the women and landed on the twig of a tree.

"Alberto!" Marcia snapped.

The butler hurried over from his perch just inside the house.

"Alberto! Is that a woodpecker in my oak tree?"

Alberto took a few steps towards the tree and made a clapping noise, which scared off the bird. He returned to the table and took a slight bow, his torso pitched forward so he was just a few inches from Marcia's ear. "Is that all, Ma'am?"

"Is that all? Alberto, we've got to do something about these creatures! That woodpecker wakes me up at all hours! Can you get rid of it? Tear down the tree, if that's what it takes!"

"I'll see to it, Ma'am," Alberto said, and trotted back towards the house.

Marcia then turned her attention back to Greta. "I'm sorry," she said with a heavy sigh. "You were saying…that's right, you were saying about John, that he can't read."

"Well, not that he can't—"

Marcia pivoted in her seat and faced the house. "Alberto!" she yelled.

The butler appeared.

"Alberto, why do I have to keep yelling? I'm about to lose my voice. Can you please stay in the general vicinity? Should I start to ring a bell?"

"No Ma'am," Albert responded. "I wanted to give you a bit of privacy. But it's no problem; I will remain on the terrace."

"Alberto, can you please tear John away from the television and have him rejoin us?"

"Certainly, Ma'am."

Alberto left the terrace and returned a minute later with John, who looked slightly dazed. He stumbled forward with a stooped gait, bangs hanging down over his eyes. If there was a silver lining, Greta was proud that John had allowed himself to be torn away from the television. He wasn't smiling but he wasn't screaming about being summoned either.

"Thank you Alberto," Marcia said, and watched her butler scurry towards a different perch across the stone-lined terrace.

Marcia then turned her attention towards John, draping one arm loosely across his back. To Greta's surprise, he didn't shake off his grandmother's clasp.

"Now John…" Marcia began. "Are you excited to read *Treasure Island?*"

John shrugged and paused for a few seconds before responding. "Not really."

"And why is that?"

John shrugged again. "I don't know. It looks long."

"Have you been told that you can't read books of such a length?"

John looked up at her. "I don't know."

"Now let me tell you something Johnny. There's no reason to be afraid of a book just because it's long. It's like being able to look inside someone else's life for a bit longer…being able to really see inside someone's heart and inside his mind. That helps shape our human character. And that's why it's so important to read books. Do you understand John?"

John nodded.

Marcia continued. "I mean, look at me, Johnny. I live alone – ever since your grandfather passed – but am I lonely?"

"I don't know," John said.

"No, I'm never lonely. I'm surrounded by books! I have Jane Eyre and Nick Carraway to keep me company. Anytime I want, I can search for treasure with Jim Hawkins! Do you understand what I'm saying?"

John nodded and swatted his bangs out of his eyes. "Can I go back to watching television now?" he asked.

"*May* I go back—" Marcia corrected. "And the answer is yes, you certainly may."

John left the terrace again – quickly this time and without need of an escort, his shoes flapping against the pavement as he jogged away.

Marcia faced Greta and smiled. "My grandson is very smart, and no one can tell me otherwise. He saw those numbers hidden in the picture I drew right away, without any prompting. If he doesn't like to read, it's because he doesn't think he can…because someone got in his mind and convinced him of what he can't do. Now I like to focus on what children *can* do, let them think they're capable of anything. Then they'll start to come around."

It was this type of logic that raised Greta's dander. She was a calm, rational person. But something about speaking with people who spouted platitudes not grounded in fact as sound advice – something about people who spoke knowingly who didn't know – made Greta want to scream.

Greta had to keep in mind though – she was dealing with a family member. And not just any family member but one who controlled the purse strings, who could change the course of John's fate with a single decision to finance his education.

"Marcia…" Greta said, and then took a deep breath. "John's dyslexia isn't an errant path he's chosen to walk, a button that can be switched off once he changes his attitude. What John needs is more than what I can provide, more than what the public schools can provide. His case manager told me that and she said so very adamantly. John needs a special school to help him with his dyslexia, and this school costs thirty-five thousand dollars a year. They're not going to give me any financial aid because of Griffin's earnings…and Griffin isn't going to help out either. I'm coming to you, begging you really, since you're my last hope. Make it a loan instead of a gift, if you have to, and let me repay you when I can."

Greta's voice was pleading, urging. She felt like the emcee of one of those televised call-in programs – when the host begs and cajoles in the name of charity – desperation dripping from their pores.

And, like so many television viewers, Marcia was unmoved. She flared her nostrils and shook her head. "John's going to be just fine," Marcia said. "Once he realizes how important his grades are, he'll figure out what he needs to do and then do it."

"I could have him read for you," Greta insisted. "Or, I could show you the reports from school, the ones that show how poorly he's doing. Whatever you need to see that might change your mind…"

"Greta!" Marcia said, her voice was a piercing turret that stunned the air. "Young lady, my mind is made up and that's the end of that!"

Greta nodded and sat back in her chair. There was no use in protesting at this point. The conversation drifted away from John and then went further afield – to the topic of food and gardening – anything safe and impersonal. After thirty minutes of chatter, Alberto summoned Marcia and then the elder woman returned and delicately told Greta that it was time to go.

Greta met John at the front steps and they hugged Marcia as distantly as possible – hand clasps on forearms, air kisses and smiles. Greta and John were halfway to their car when Marcia's voice rang out, "Wait! You forgot!"

They stood for a minute on the apex of Marcia's circular driveway – in between a fountain and the front columns. Then Alberto appeared and thrust something into John's hands. Greta looked down and saw that it was *Treasure Island*.

# CHAPTER TWENTY-TWO

*September 26, 2017*

Martinez and Hobbs located Johanna Wagner after five days of searching, checking in with local police precincts, talking with neighbors and following up on leads. A 2007 report of petty theft in Springfield led them to a hairdresser in Mount Vernon. Ten years earlier, the hairdresser had invited Johanna Wagner over for barbecue dinner…and once the ribs, baked beans and cornbread had been devoured, the two ladies sat on twin rocking chairs on back porch and fell asleep to the sound of crickets. When the hairdresser woke up hours later, Johanna was gone, along with an envelope of two hundred-dollar bills that she kept in a kitchen cabinet in case of emergencies.

The hairdresser filed her claim, which had brought two rookie Mount Vernon police officers to Johanna's trailer. She let them inside, politely plied them with ice water and explained that the two hundred dollars had been promised to her for unremunerated housecleaning services. The officers noted in the report that Johanna's trailer was covered in boxes – a labyrinth of them so thick, it was hard to walk or even see around.

"I'm moving," Johanna explained. "I'm sick of this neighborhood." She gave them her forwarding address and never heard from the Mount Vernon P.D. again. Even the hairdresser forgot or abandoned her claims to the missing two hundred dollars.

When Martinez and Hobbs visited the forwarding address Johanna had given, they discovered that it was a tawdry, low-rent motel on the outer edges of Gainesville, Missouri. The structure had traces of powdery white paint, but most of that had chipped away to reveal decaying wood and an insect sanctuary.

The Detectives walked inside the main office and introduced themselves to a woman behind a counter. The woman was late middle-aged and leathery, with tattoos stretching across her neck and down her arms. "Can I help you?" she asked.

Martinez and Hobbs explained that they were looking for Johanna. They provided a physical description based on the ten-year old Mount Vernon Police Report. Johanna was fifty-eight years old, around five feet four, one hundred ten pounds, long brown hair, an athletic build. This was the best they had to go on since she didn't exist on social media or the rest of the Internet, nor did she have a driver's license or any other type of government-issued record. It was as though she lived in the cracks of a registered society, an invisible citizen.

The woman behind the counter was not terribly helpful. She explained that most of the residents of the motel took up permanent residence, and they enjoyed the privacy and parsimony afforded by the low monthly cash-only rent payments. She remembered Johanna but had nothing to say about the woman, other than that she was quiet, kept to herself, and hadn't provided a forwarding address.

Hobbs and Martinez insisted on visiting the unit where Johanna had lived, so the front-desk clerk – after giving both a glare – took them on a tour. The unit was really a one-bedroom cabin near a lake, with the same chipping powder-white paint as the rest. The Detectives knocked on the door a few times but no one answered.

After a few hard knocks, a man appeared from one of the neighboring cabins. His dense, black-gray hair was frayed and he stroked his large, protruding belly while he approached.

"What's goin' on up there?" he asked.

The clerk said "Nothing!" at the same time that Hobbs said, "We're looking for a woman named Johanna Wagner. She used to live at this address but she moved away around two years ago. Do you remember her?"

"Remember her?" the man stroked his belly. "Sure, I still talk to her. Is she in some kind of trouble?"

Hobbs's heart jumped. "No, sir. Her daughter is missing and we thought we should speak to her about it. Can you give us her phone number and address?"

The man looked skeptical so Martinez added, "You may have seen the story of the missing family on the news. Greta Carpenter and the whole Carpenter family."

The man shook his head. "I ain't got a television. I'll get what you asked for and be right back."

Thirty minutes later, Martinez and Hobbs were driving through East Barry County, Missouri. They drove past farmland and penned in grazing cows, stalks of corn and flat dry earth. Eventually they found a section of ten or twelve motor homes demarcated by a green-painted wooden sign: Evergreen Acres.

It didn't take long to find Johanna. By this time, it was early evening, and the residents were out of their homes, all descended on two campfires set up near the asphalt and pebble parking lot.

The Detectives parked their car and approached the group, who immediately ceased their activities and stared at the trespassers.

Hobbs scanned the cluster – mostly kids, a few who appeared to be in their late teens or early twenties, a few older senior citizens planted in plastic chairs and one woman – skinny, five-feet four, with long gray-brown hair tied back in a ponytail.

"Are you Johanna Wagner?" Hobbs asked, and the woman nodded solemnly.

"I'm Detective Hobbs and this is Detective Martinez. Can we speak to you somewhere privately?"

Everyone stared as Johanna put down a vegetable-laced skewer she'd been holding and approached the detectives. Without saying a word, she brushed past them and embarked on a northward trek alongside the lake. They passed the column of homes, then a playground and a smaller parking lot, until they finally reached an isolated picnic table.

"This okay?" Johanna asked. "I'd take you inside my trailer but it's too messy to find a seat."

The Detectives nodded and affirmed that the picnic table was a fine location. There was something about Johanna's demeanor that struck Hobbs. It was her patience, her stillness. In most cases, when she and Martinez showed up at their door asking to interview someone, their subjects were shaky and scared. They tremored noticeably. In unsteady voices, they demanded to know *why* the meeting was happening. They were incapable of waiting for the news – the anvil everyone knew was going to drop.

But Johanna sat patiently and waited for the Detectives to begin.

"Ms. Wagner..." Martinez began. "We're here to talk to you about your daughter, Greta."

After a few seconds of silence, Johanna replied softly: "I'm not sure what you mean. It's been a lifetime since I last saw Greta."

Martinez pulled an eight by ten photograph of the Carpenter family from his satchel. It was a reproduction of the photograph from the master bedroom – saintly smiles on everyone's faces, coordinated denim and white outfits, a choreographed pose of interlaced arms.

Johanna looked at the photograph. She was stoic at first but then something inside of her stirred. She jerked in her seat and put her hand over her mouth. Johanna could see tears forming at the corners of her eyes. "She's so beautiful!" Johanna exclaimed. "I haven't seen her in years. Oh my god, she's so beautiful."

So this was the moment for the trembling and agitating, Hobbs realized – this moment of raw vulnerability. If Johanna was determined to be tough for the interview, she had been defused by the sight of her daughter. It was one of things Hobbs liked about police work – the ability to witness this stirring of emotion.

"How many years since you've seen her?" Martinez asked.

"Years," Johanna answered, still staring at the photograph. "Years and years, maybe fifteen, maybe twenty? At some point, you just lose count."

Martinez stopped writing and both he and Hobbs afforded the woman a moment of silence. It was obvious Johanna wasn't going to be able to provide any leads, and in front of them lay the task of telling her that her daughter and family were missing.

"Look at this little girl," Johanna said, running her finger over the pig-tailed image of Olivia. "That is *exactly* how Greta looked when she was a baby. I can't believe it."

"Yes, they're a beautiful family," Hobbs said. "And we came here to talk to you because they're missing. No one has seen or heard from them since September 6."

"Oh god," Johanna said. She turned back to the photograph and ran her index finger over each family member's faces, one at a time – as though she could rouse an answer from osmosis.

"It's strange," Johanna eventually said. "My daughter has been missing for decades. I don't even recognize the woman in this picture. This is a full-grown woman with children of her own. The girl I lost was a girl. She was like a little pixie – petite and fragile. She wore her hair up every day. She loved pop music. Every day I wait, Detectives. You never stop *waiting*. Every day, I wait for news. And now – two decades later – you're here to tell me that my missing daughter is missing. I don't even know what to think about it."

The tears that had formed in Johanna's eyes fully matriculated and tumbled down the woman's face. She sniffled very quietly and buried her head into her elbow. Hobbs could see tiny heaves moving the back of Johanna's head, and she leaned over to place a hand on the older woman's shoulder.

"I'm so sorry," Hobbs said. "We don't want to stir up any more pain." Peripherally, Hobbs could see some small children lined up at the far edge of the lake. They were presuming to skip stones but in actuality, they stood and stared at Johanna and the detectives, fingers coiled tightly around rocks and pebbles. There were no other adults in sight.

"Can you tell us why Greta left home?" Hobbs asked.

Johanna lifted her head. She swallowed and paused, and during this moment, the color of her face shifted from red to normal. She cleared her throat and her voice came out clear.

"I named Greta after my grandmother. She was a tough old lady, stubborn and strong-willed, living in Germany until they came to America. And now, here we are. My little Greta was exactly like her namesake. Always stubborn and terribly strong willed. She never listened to me. She never paid attention at school. She always got into trouble. I just fought with her all the time. When she was sixteen, the principal called and told me she stopped going to classes. Then I found her with a bunch of her friends, under the concrete bridge near her high school, smoking cigarettes. And I yelled at her, boy did I yell at her. If she was younger I'd have smacked her too but by that age, she was as tall as I was – maybe taller. I told her she could go to school or leave the house. She chose to leave. When she was sixteen years old. The last thing she said to me was that if she left she would never come back. And she never did."

"Did you report her missing to the police?" Martinez asked.

Johanna shook her head. "No. I assumed this was some kind of a stunt – that she'd find her way back to me. And it took two years for me to finally figure out that she wasn't coming back. By then she was eighteen, legally an adult. What could I do?"

Martinez nodded and Hobbs looked down at the picnic table. The surface was patchy and bug-eaten, with knife carvings of initials and love declarations every inch or so.

"Where did she end up by the way?" Johanna asked. "How far away did she get?"

"Vetta Park, Missouri," Martinez answered. "Ever heard of it?"

Johanna shook her head.

He pulled out his phone and showed her their town on a map. "It's just twenty miles south of St. Louis or so. Parts of it are really nice, right along the Mississippi River."

"So she never left the state," Johanna said. "She could have driven back to me anytime she wanted."

"Maybe she didn't have your address," Martinez suggested. "You've moved around a few times."

"She could have found me if she really wanted to find me. You all found me. Any decent investigator could find me. If she really wanted to find me, she'd have found me."

Hobbs wasn't sure how to respond to this claim, so she dug a business card out of her wallet and handed it to Johanna. "Thank you so much for talking with us," Hobbs said. "If you think of anything else, let us know. And if we find anything, give us your phone number and we'll keep you posted."

Johanna shook her head again – this shake was more vigorous, a statement of refusal. "No, I don't have a phone. Won't deal with the phone companies anymore. But I can get mail here if you want to stop by or write me a letter."

Hobbs smiled politely and nodded. She and Martinez stood up and shook Johanna's hand and were just heading back south along the lake when Johanna called out to them.

"Hey! Detectives! You said that some of the homes in…in…that town, Vetta Park, were really nice. Was Greta in one of those homes along the river?"

Hobbs took a few steps back towards the picnic table. She glanced across the lake at the kids – most of whom had lost their interest in the interview and were throwing stones into the water. It was an idyllic snapshot of childhood, Hobbs thought. Kids barefooted and grit-faced, playfully enjoying the mud and the lake, autonomous and self-governed on a cool September evening. For some reason, it made Hobbs envision little Olivia playing by herself in the backyard, under the watchful observation of Mary Miller.

"Not in one of the homes along the Mississippi," Hobbs said. "But Greta has lived for years in a very nice home on a good street."

"A good street…like friendly neighbors, that kind of thing?"

Hobbs nodded. Mary Miller was the only neighbor she'd personally met, but Adams and Martinez had canvassed the street in the week after the family's disappearance. They had described all the neighbors as friendly, responsive, and appropriately concerned about the matter at hand.

"And still no one knows where my girl went?" Johanna asked, but it sounded more like she was saying it in disbelief to herself – rather than asking the Detective a question.

Hobbs answered anyway. "That's correct," she said. "As far as we know, nobody knows."

# CHAPTER TWENTY-THREE

*September 28, 2017*

Hobbs could tell she was interrupting something. It was early morning – the streets tranquil and the sky still dark – and she had shown up at the precinct an hour earlier than usual.

The lights were still off in the main area of the office – the cattle pen they sometimes called it. Only Weaver's office was illuminated, the white-yellow light creeping underneath the doorway. Hobbs could hear men's voices too. They were muffled drones from that distance, but the voices clearly belonged to Weaver and Adams.

Hobbs walked over until reaching the doorframe of the office. Weaver had been speaking but stopped as soon as he saw her. "Detective Hobbs, I'm surprised to see you here. It's early, isn't it?"

Hobbs nodded. "I had a lot of work to catch up on since I've been in Springfield." She then stepped fully inside Weaver's office and lingered behind the empty chair next to Adams. Her mind sprinted in different directions while she waited to hear what they would say. Surely they were having a private meeting – although the door was open. Had the decision to send her to Springfield been deliberate? Why was Weaver meeting privately with Adams when no one else was in the office?

And then there was the issue of Adams himself. Hobbs hadn't spoken to him since their fight the week before. She had thought about him the whole time she was in Southwest Missouri but couldn't bring herself to reach out. Seeing him in the chair in this clandestine meeting with the boss was unsettling. Somehow Adams looked leaner than he had just a week before, cheeks more defined, and somehow this made him seem older, more serious. She was both surprised to find herself still attracted to him and unnerved to think about what he might have told the Captain about her or about the two of them.

After a moment of quiet, Hobbs thought Weaver was going to ask her to leave, but instead he directed her to close the door and have a seat. She did as instructed and gave Adams a vague half-smile when she sat down next to him.

Weaver held up a folder. "Do you recognize this?" he asked.

Hobbs shook her head.

Weaver opened the folder, took out a piece of paper and started reading. "February 5, 2005, 3:15 am. Corner of Memorial and Olympic Boulevards. Collision involving a yellow Ferrari and a white Chevy Silverado. Reporting officer is Lawrence Hardy. Officer Hardy took the statement of a witness, Mrs. Greta Brock. Witness claims she saw the Ferrari run a red light and hit the pickup truck at a right angle, nearly pinning it underneath. Two injuries were reported, no deaths, and one driver declined medical attention."

Weaver stopped reading, looked up and waved the file again. "Now do you recognize it?"

Hobbs smiled. "Yes, of course. But where did you—?" She glanced at Adams, whose expression revealed nothing.

Weaver continued. "Then, there's more from the next day, Sunday February 6, 2005. This time the reporting officer is one Roberta Hobbs. In the comment area of the report, you wrote, 'Greta Brock, witness to the accident, arrived at the police station at 9:30am. Ms. Brock changed her story to report that the driver of the Chevy Silverado, who she does not personally know, was the at-fault driver. Witness claims the Silverado driver ran the red light and not the Ferrari driver as she'd previously stated. Witness says she also does not know the identities of the driver and passenger in the Ferrari.'"

Weaver stopped reading and looked up.

"Is that all it says?" Hobbs asked.

Weaver looked back down at the page. "No, there's one more thing. You wrote, 'Witness seemed scared.'"

After letting this comment sink in, Hobbs said, "So we should investigate the identities of the Ferrari and pickup drivers."

"Yes we certainly will," Weaver said. "Now at least we have names."

"How did you find the file?" Hobbs asked.

Weaver used the file to point across his desk to the seat next to hers. "Adams found it...in the basement last night. He asked to meet early this morning to discuss it."

Hobbs looked over at Adams and nodded as if to thank him. His way of accepting gratitude was to smile sheepishly and look down. He seemed aware of the weight of her expression and was unable to match it by looking directly at her. Instead he studied the floor and ran his fingertips across the edge of his chair.

"Where in the basement?" Hobbs asked. "I thought Rochelle gave it a thorough sweep."

"It had slipped underneath one of the filing cabinets," Adams said. "It must have fallen out during the move and no one saw it."

"I see," Hobbs said, still staring at him.

"Well, we've got names and phone numbers," Weaver said. "Let's start with the Ferrari drivers, Arthur Forsett and Will Carter. Adams, I want you to reach out and let me know what you find. Hobbs, stay in here and let's talk about your meeting with Greta's mother."

Adams stood up, took the file and left the room. For the next thirty minutes, Hobbs debriefed the Captain on the details of the meeting with Johanna Wagner. Weaver seemed to listen attentively while she spoke but there wasn't much useful information to glean and she was distracted anyway.

For the whole time that she was speaking and answering questions, Hobbs' thoughts were circling on something else. *Thousands of files in the basement and Greta Brock's traffic file is coincidentally the one that falls underneath the filing cabinet? No way.*

\*\*\*

Adams was leaning back in his desk chair, chatting on his cell phone. His legs were perched up on his desk, crossed at the ankle. Roberta had never seen him this relaxed at the office before, and it seemed to her that he was sending a signal. He was *fine*, unwound, loosened up. He wasn't bothered by her presence in the office – and when she sat on the edge of his desk and crossed her arms, he responded by laughing at whatever the person on the other end of the phone call said. It didn't sound exactly right though. It was more like a warble, a bird's off-tune trill.

"You're right, you're right," he said. "Oh okay. I'll see you tonight. Okay, bye."

Adams brought his phone away and tossed it onto his desk. "Roberta, hi! Good to see you back!"

It seemed like an act and he was playing the part horribly. There was too much exaggeration – too much of a caricature of the newly single guy at the office.

Roberta uncrossed her arms. "Dean, I'd like to talk to you."

He smiled. "Okay, talk."

"Not here. One of the meeting rooms please."

"What, am I in trouble?"

"Let's just go. Please. Five minutes." She stood up and walked into one of the tiny meeting rooms. It was the same room where they'd broken up and now it seemed different to her – the off-white color a bit more shaded, the size more claustrophobic. This room was tainted; it had history. And she had to suppress her emotions and forge ahead just to be inside of it again.

Hobbs didn't look behind her but knew Adams was following her. When he walked inside, he closed the door but lingered near it.

"What is it?" he asked.

"Tell me where you found the file," Hobbs said.

"I told you. I found it underneath one of the file cabinets in the basement."

"That's bullshit," she said. "Someone was holding on to that file, and you know who it is."

"So…what if I do know who had the file," he said. "What makes you think I'd share that bit of information with you?"

Hobbs sighed. "Because we are colleagues and we treat each other with mutual respect. Dean, you know how much I care about this case. I've never worked so hard on something that led nowhere. Every other case has been *solvable*. This one – it's like all the leads are pointing in a circle. And each day that passes…"

Hobbs stopped talking because there was no need to complete the sentence. Adams knew the statistics. Every day that passed without any credible leads increased the risk of it becoming a cold case – unsolvable, an infinite question mark. And the possibility of police involvement made the case even more problematic.

"I found the file in Martinez's desk drawer," Adams said. "I looked through your desks while you were both out of town."

"What?" Hobbs felt her pulse accelerate. She swallowed hard, sunk into one of the chairs and rested her palm against her forehead. "That's not possible," she muttered. She could forgive the violation of her desk. She didn't keep anything personal in there anyway – always cognizant that Vetta Park employees could be fired at-will, their desk contents searched and reclaimed.

But it was this indictment against Ray Martinez – her partner for five years. What did she know about Ray? He was a family man, with four small children, mostly boys. He went to church every Sunday and talked a lot about football. He was a compassionate, caring man. He always asked Hobbs how she was doing. He seemed legitimately concerned for her wellbeing. He covered for her. He had her back. He was her partner. It wasn't possible.

But it was possible. In this line of work, you learned quickly that you never know the truth about anybody. There were no surprises about human nature. You never, ever knew.

Adams walked over and sat down next to her. "I'm sorry," he said. "I didn't want to tell you before I talked to Martinez. I know you guys are close."

Hobbs took her palm away from her forehead and gazed at Adams. He didn't seem like he was pretending anymore. He seemed genuinely concerned for her and this show of affection only sent her further into a tailspin of mistrust of her own instincts. Hadn't Ray Martinez always seemed authentic? When they were searching the family's house, speaking with potential witnesses, reviewing the facts of the case? Hadn't he looked at her genuinely, with doe-eyed fondness, sometimes squeezing her shoulder and offering comfort? *Don't worry, we'll get to the bottom of it*, he always said.

Meanwhile he had been at that meeting – the one in which Weaver had questioned her memory and possibly her sanity. Martinez had been there, just as virtuous as always, the traffic file safely buried in his desk drawer.

Hobbs was *pissed* – but just as much at herself as she was at Ray Martinez. It was history repeating itself – her tendency to trust the wrong people. There was no better justification than this for her desire to be left alone. She felt vindicated in breaking up with Adams, even though it hurt. It had been the right thing to do.

"I just can't believe it," Hobbs said quietly. "Where in his desk did you find it?"

"In the very bottom drawer, tucked under a bunch of other files. Either it's been in there awhile and he forgot about it or he did a very good job of hiding it." He chuckled. "I almost missed it."

Hobbs shook her head. "I can't believe it," she repeated. "What are you going to say to Weaver?"

"I'm not going to say anything to Weaver. Are you kidding? He would have Martinez fired or reassigned. I'm going to talk to Martinez first, see what he has to say for himself."

Adams' confrontation with Martinez was the last thing Hobbs wanted to be a part of. There was the admission that Adams had been snooping around in his desk. Then there was the confrontation itself – an attack on Martinez's integrity, the pressure for sensible answer.

Hobbs wanted no part of any of it. But she also thought about the Carpenter/Brock family portrait – four smiles on ostensibly innocent faces. She thought about Johanna Wagner's anguish. The thought that Martinez had anything to do with the family's disappearance made Hobbs feel sick inside. But if there was a reasonable answer for his sheltering of the traffic file, she wanted to be the one to hear it.

*** 

Det. Martinez didn't come into the police precinct that morning. He called Hobbs on her cell phone, explained in his hurried way that one of his kids was sick, and that he'd show up later in the afternoon. The conversation came and went so quickly that Hobbs didn't have a chance to say what she had prepared to say: *We need to talk as soon as you get here.*

Without Martinez, Hobbs spent the morning and early hours of afternoon checking out Arthur Forsett and Will Carter. Both men seemed clean. Will Carter had a DUI from years back, but neither had any other criminal history or outstanding arrest warrants. Arthur Forsett didn't even have so much as a moving violation.

Once she'd done the research, she determined that an in-person interrogation wasn't warranted. Instead, Adams placed a phone call, first to Will and then Arthur. Thirty minutes later, Adams and Hobbs were both in Weaver's office, discussing the case.

"What'd you find out?" Weaver asked.

Adams looked at his notes. "Alright, we know that Greta changed her story about the car accident that Will and Arthur were involved in. First she said they were responsible and then she said they weren't. At the same time, Will and Arthur were in Vetta Park because they were meeting with Greta's husband at the time, Griffin. You know Northman Shopping Center?"

Adams looked up, paused, and Weaver abruptly snapped to attention. "What? Oh, yes. Northman. I go there every time I feel like I need to lose a few thousand dollars on an article of clothing."

Adams smirked. "Well it used to be a big empty lot owned by the Brock family. Will and Arthur were in town for their company Carter Commercial Development – to buy and develop that land from Griffin."

"How much do you think Carter Development paid Griffin for the land?" Hobbs asked.

"What, I'm supposed to guess now?" Weaver asked. "I don't know, how much does land go for? It's a pretty upscale part of town so I guess…one-hundred grand?"

"*Five* hundred grand," Hobbs answered. "They paid ten-thousand dollars an acre for fifty acres."

"Wow," Weaver said. "That's quite a payout."

"At that time, it was the most paid per acre in Vetta Park," Hobbs said. "We're thinking that Griffin didn't want the deal to fall through. He must have told Greta to change her story to keep the money guys out of trouble."

"Okay," Weaver said. "What else?"

Adams read from his notes again. "Will and Arthur say that in 2009, Greta came to visit them, very unexpectedly. She didn't know anything about the deals, just that they were involved with her husband, and she wanted some details. At that time, their company Carter Development was involved in *another* deal with the Brock family that was about to close."

"Which deal was that? Did it close?" Weaver asked.

"Yes, it closed a few months later. Riverfront Harbor Pavilions…sound familiar?"

Weaver thought for a few moments but then shook his head. "Doesn't ring a bell."

"It's right on the River, up in St. Louis. It was acres and acres of empty land until the Brock family sold to Carter Development. The payoff for that deal was six million dollars."

"Six million dollars, Jesus! I'm in the wrong line of work!" Weaver said. "So it sounds like the Brock family has been doing pretty well."

Hobbs nodded. "It would seem so." She had been to the Riverfront Harbor Pavilions a few times. Three large two-story brick-and-glass structures, they housed shops and restaurants right on the banks of the Mississippi River. Sightseeing boats docked and departed from the bottom level, mostly teeming with tourists. The St. Louis Arch loomed over the structures, offering a comprehensive view of its steel panels. Hobbs could understand the basis for a hefty payout for that land.

"You think Greta saw any of that money?" Weaver asked.

"That's the funny thing. I don't think so," Hobbs said. "She stayed in the same house in the same solidly middle class neighborhood. It doesn't seem like her expenses ramped up at any point. And that deal was right around the same time as the divorce, but technically after the divorce was finalized. It's possible she didn't see any of that money. I wonder if she even knew about it."

"What about after the Riverfront deal?" Weaver asked. "Any other deals?"

Adams shook his head. "Nothing. That's the last these guys ever dealt with Griffin or Greta."

Weaver was pensive for a moment. "You trust these guys?" he asked. "You get the sense they're hiding anything?"

"I mean, I only spoke to them over the phone," Adams said. "I didn't get to see their faces. But they seem legitimate to me."

"Any relationship with Steven Vance?" Weaver continued. "Vance is in real estate too; maybe they overlapped on a project. Have you found anything that links them to him?"

"Nothing," Hobbs responded. "Vance does exclusively night clubs and hotels, all in this area. Carter does mixed-use commercial space – mostly high-end malls and condos. And the Carter Company is primarily in Chicago and the northern Chicago suburbs. They claimed the two deals with Griffin Brock were the only deals they've done south of Bloomington, Illinois."

"So what we've got here is a dead lead," Weaver said, and smacked the top of his desk with enough force to knock a few papers onto the floor.

Hobbs understood his frustration. She had spent so much mental energy on this traffic file – convinced that once it could be located, it would be a Holy Grail of information. Through all the doubts and uncertainties Hobbs had about their two leading men under suspicion – Griffin Brock and Steven Vance – she held this traffic file in the back of her mind, convinced it would implicate one or both of the men. The file would provide a footpath through the dead underbrush of worthless leads towards the actual perpetrators and possibly the family itself. She had been certain.

But the traffic file didn't yield any of its imagined promise. The file was itself another dead lead – implicating no one except possibly a Vetta Park police detective whom she'd known and trusted for years.

\*\*\*

Detective Martinez finally showed up at four-thirty. He looked disheveled – clothes wrinkled, eyes swollen, hair dark in a scruffy heap. While serving himself a cup of coffee in the snack room, he caught sight of Rochelle and explained that he'd been up all night, peeling vomit off the walls of his son's room.

Adams walked over to Hobbs. "Are you ready?" he asked quietly.

"I want to do this myself," Hobbs said. She could see that Adams was prepared to disagree but then he caught himself. He had taken a breath but then he closed his mouth. Instead of speaking, he pressed his lips together, nodded and walked back to his desk. She was on her own.

Hobbs walked into the snack room and fixed her own cup of coffee. While she waited for the machine to spit out the hot liquid, Rochelle sauntered off and Martinez eagerly regaled her with stories of sick children. He seemed more chirpy than usual, and Hobbs couldn't tell if this was by design or a side effect of sleep deprivation.

"Let's go into a room and have a chat," Hobbs said, once the coffee was in her mug and his story had ended.

If Martinez suspected that something was off, he didn't show it. He followed Hobbs into the main conference room and sat down next to her. It was a larger, more spacious room than the one she had used to speak with Adams. The room had windows and curtains and was decorated with sketches from Vetta Park schoolchildren.

It was only once they were sitting beside each other – Martinez sipping his brew, Hobbs trying to formulate the right string of words – that he grew impatient. "What's this about?" he asked.

Hobbs waited another few seconds before responding. When she spoke, her words were carefully constructed, her pacing slower than usual.

"Do you remember the mysterious missing traffic file – the one in which Greta changed her mind? The file I swore existed even though no one could find it?" Hobbs stared at Martinez as she spoke – waiting for his conduct to change, for him to become startled or argumentative. Instead, he was unmoved.

"Yeah, of course I remember," he said. "Did you find it?"

Hobbs stared at her partner, speechless. She looked in his eyes, studied his face. There was no palpable difference in his demeanor – no eye twitch or beads of sweat. She wasn't sure what to make of his lack of a response. *Could he have been framed?*

"What's this about, Roberta?" Martinez asked.

"Ray, we found the traffic file…at the bottom of your desk!" she said.

He puffed audibly and put his hand over his mouth. "Oh shit!" he said. At last, the light bulb had gone off, the understanding of the situation's significance.

Hobbs was also slightly relieved that he wasn't going to point the finger back at Adams or claim to have been set up. It was clear by his reaction that the culpability of the missing file lay with him.

"What the hell happened?" Hobbs asked him.

Martinez still had his hand over his mouth. He ran the other hand over his hair, and once a few seconds had passed, he crossed both hands in front of him and stared down at them. "What were you doing in my desk?" Martinez asked.

"Answer my question first," Hobbs instructed. "And then I'll answer yours."

The problem was, she realized, they were both detectives and decent interrogators. They knew how to set a mood, how to scare a witness, how to capitalize on weaknesses. Martinez had always been her partner in interrogations and now they were pitted against each other, like two experts in a chess game – grand master against grand master. She wasn't sure whether she'd made the right choice keeping Adams out of it. He was young and had a much more aggressive style – a manner she didn't feel like putting up with. But at least Adams' presence would have put more numbers in her corner and made the questioning feel less symmetric.

Martinez eventually answered. "Roberta, what happened is that I had the file in there and I completely forgot about it," he said. "It must have been in there for years. If I had any recollection about it, I would have brought it out sooner, I swear to you."

"You admit putting the file in your desk?" Hobbs asked.

"Yeah. Years ago."

"The fact that it was years ago doesn't make it any better, Ray!" Hobbs said. "We have systems in place. What was the file doing in your desk in the first place?"

"What were *you* doing in my desk in the first place?" Martinez countered. "You said you'd answer my question if I answered yours. Were you digging around in my desk?"

"Yes I was," she lied.

"Why?"

"Because…" Hobbs' mind raced. She wanted to lob a softball excuse – *I was looking for a lost pencil* – but she knew Martinez too well. He would see right through anything that wasn't the truth. Even though it was Adams's truth and not hers – it was the only reason she could give.

"I figured someone was probably hiding the file," Hobbs said. "I remember very clearly taking down the information, even though it was over ten years ago. If the file wasn't in the basement, I figured it was in someone's desk…and I started with yours."

"Why'd you start with mine?"

"Physical proximity," she answered. "It was the closest desk to mine. Believe me, I was completely shocked when I found it."

"Did you tell the Captain?" Martinez asked.

"My question next, Detective," she said. "What was the file doing in your desk in the first place?"

Martinez gritted his teeth and looked around. The main door had a rectangle of clear glass, and people were bustling just outside. The ring of telephones and rustle of people created a consistent murmur of noise. But no one appeared to be focused on them.

Martinez sat back and ran his fingers along his chin. "There used to be a private detective in St. Louis named Colt Bundy. He sometimes requested information. I think I must have pulled the file about eight or nine years ago and I forgot to put it back. I forgot all about it until just now."

"Used to? Are you still…?"

Martinez anticipated the end of the question and shook his head. "I haven't talked to Bundy in a few years. I don't know if he's still in business or moved on to someone else in the PD or what. We ended our arrangement."

"Your arrangement? You must have been getting paid a pretty decent amount to put our cases at risk like this."

"It was a stupid thing I did years ago and I regret it," Martinez said. "But that doesn't mean…"

Hobbs held up her hand and shook her head. She didn't want to hear any excuses or justifications. She was fighting off a sickly feeling – bile creeping across her throat, or maybe it was anger. She knew that officers sometimes ran ex-lovers or former bosses through their databases. But this was something different – an arrangement, meaning secret meetings and money exchanges. It changed her view of her partner. Now he was dishonest, compromised – even if he had nothing to do with this case.

"I haven't told the captain yet," Hobbs said weakly, answering a question he may not have remembered he asked.

"Oh good. Thank you, thank you," Martinez gushed.

"But that doesn't mean I won't," Hobbs clarified. "Let's wait and see if this Colt Bundy person checks out."

"Okay, sure."

And then they were quiet, while Hobbs again searched her mind for the right words to a question. It was embarrassing to even have to ask it, but she knew she would regret it if she let the moment pass.

"Ray…" Hobbs began. "Did you have anything to do with the Carpenter family's disappearance?"

"No, god, no," Martinez answered. "Lord as my witness, on the lives of my kids, I had nothing to do with their disappearance. Are you kidding me Roberta? This is all because of an oversight, something I forgot about. My heart goes out to that family. If I knew where they were, I would say something."

Hobbs nodded. She had nothing more to say to Martinez. "Okay. Let's go back then." They both stood up and made their way back to the cattle pen. Hobbs thought about Martinez's words – both his confession and his avowal of his own innocence regarding the missing family. The funny thing was, even though she no longer trusted him…she still believed him.

***

It was late when Hobbs finally left the station that evening and she felt like she could use a drink. Since the break-up with Adams, she had fallen into her pre-boyfriend habits, which included a late night drink at the dive bar a few blocks away.

The Red Lion was claustrophobic and dark, and stank of stale air and cigarettes, even though indoor smoking had been banned there for years. Hobbs loved the anonymity of the place – that she could show up by herself, sit at the bar for thirty minutes drinking Scotch and no one would say a word to her. It was the kind of bar for introverts like her – where people could be alone in the company of dozens of others. Shortly after their first hook-up, Adams had suggested accompanying her to the Red Lion.

At the time, she shrugged aside the suggestion. The Red Lion was for singletons, not couples, and she felt an ownership towards it like it was her own private discovery. The rest of the police station hadn't yet encountered the bar – or maybe they'd already discovered it and moved on – and that suited her perfectly.

But on that particular night, as soon as Hobbs sat down on her wobbly black bar stool, she saw Adams out of the corner of her eye. It wasn't hard to identify Adams by the top of his head. He had spiky brown hair and a thick, muscular neck that reminded her of an Olympic shot putter. She only doubted herself when she saw a manicured hand reach across the back of his neck and squeeze his shoulder. Surely, she had the wrong guy.

But as soon as she saw him, he turned around and locked eyes with her. It was in fact Adams, and the manicured hand belonged to a woman by his side – a woman he was leaning up against.

The woman looked no older than twenty-five. She had a cropped t-shirt on that exposed her belly button, and tight white jeans. Her hair was long, straw-colored.

Hobbs felt like she was looking into a prism at someone else's life – the image of her ex-boyfriend and another girl refracting the light at odd angles, the way they moved next to and against each other a blurry, distorted display.

The bartender walked over but Hobbs shot out of her seat before he could say anything. She pushed her way through the crowd and into the outdoors. The whole time she could hear Adams' voice behind her. "Hey Roberta!" he called out. "Roberta!"

The problem with Vetta Park at nine p.m. was the absence of ready cabs, cruising down Centennial Avenue with their lights ignited, waiting to pick up bar stragglers. Instead, the roads were mostly empty – save for a few speeding motorists – and it gave Adams time to catch up with her.

"Roberta, wait, just wait," he said once he'd reached her. "I actually came here thinking that I might run into *you*. I wanted to talk outside of work and I didn't want to…I mean I didn't know how…"

Hobbs was surprised to see that Adams actually looked nervous. His face was red-blotted – a stain that stretched north from his neck and into his cheeks. He seemed to be searching for the words that would keep her from walking away, and he delivered them in a hurried cadence.

"…I didn't arrange to meet Madison here. She went to my college. We took some pictures on her phone and that's it."

Then it was silent between them for a moment. Hobbs had been dreaming of this time together with Adams since the break-up. A time to talk about what had happened away from work or either of their homes. This cracked sidewalk just outside of a noisy bar on a sleepy September evening seemed like the perfect non-subjective venue.

There was so much that Hobbs wanted to say to Adams. In fact, she thought that if she started to open up, a chain of emotions might be vomited up – declarations and sentiments, heartrending narratives of her time without him.

It was better to be bottled up – better for their work relationship, better considering the huge age difference between them, better in the long run anyway. And so, Hobbs took a few steps back, flashed a carefully crafted smile, and broke her own heart.

"It's fine, Dean. You and I were just having fun anyway. It was never serious. Go back in there and have a great time with Madison. I'll see you in the office tomorrow."

Without waiting for his reaction, Hobbs turned around and walked back to the station alone.

***

September 29, a Friday, Hobbs ducked out at lunch and drove to the St. Louis Investigations office downtown St. Louis. She didn't tell Weaver where she was going or who she would be speaking with. At this point, any mention of Colt Bundy would lead to Detective Martinez, and then to his inevitable firing. If Bundy checked out, Hobbs figured, there would be no need to mention him to Weaver at all.

Hobbs arrived at the tall glass building, rode the elevator to the tenth floor and surprised Colt Bundy in his office.

"Hi, I'm Detective Hobbs," she said, with a quick flash of her badge. "Are you Colt Bundy?"

Colt stood up and met her in the doorway of his office. Hobbs was surprised by how diminutive he was – squat legs on a muscular frame, almost artificially tan skin and dark hair. He had a wide, genuine smile though, and after nodding yes and shaking her hand, he led her to a seat on his couch.

"Is there some kind of trouble?" he asked.

"No, no trouble," Hobbs said. "I just want to talk to you about Greta Carpenter. Do you know who she is?"

Colt nodded. "Ah yes, I remember her. She was Greta Brock when I knew her. I read that she and the whole family have gone missing, right?"

"Yes, that's correct."

"Are you close to finding her?" Colt asked.

"Let's leave the questioning to me, okay?" Hobbs said. She wanted her voice to remain neutral, indifferent, the archetype of the in-charge detective. But there was a voice in the back of her head at all times reminding her that twenty-three days since the last sighting of the family and the Vetta Park Detectives were no closer to locating them than on day one.

Colt seemed to have sensed her anxiety because he opened up and told the story without any prompting and from memory. Greta had come to see him, back in 2009, looking for leverage in a losing divorce case. He had given her names of Ferrari drivers in a car accident from 2005. Colt stood up and swayed across his office. He opened up a mini-refrigerator, took out a bottle of water and pointed it at Hobbs.

"Can I get you one?" he asked.

"No, that's...thanks, I'm okay," Hobbs said.

Colt closed the fridge, placed the water on his desk and opened up a file cabinet behind the desk, his back turned towards the Detective.

Hobbs stiffened and cupped the edge of her revolver.

The detective then pivoted to face her, and Hobbs could see that he was holding a file. She immediately slackened.

"I have their names, if you want. The two guys in the Ferrari," Colt offered as he made his way back to the couch.

Hobbs agreed and took down the names, even though as he spouted out the names and the correct spellings, she knew the information was useless – leads that had already been scrubbed.

Colt adjusted his position on the couch, crossing his legs at the ankles. "You know, Greta only came to see me one other time," he said. "Not too long after her first visit. She wanted the identity of Griffin's business partner."

"Yeah? Who is that?"

"His mother – Marcia Brock."

"I see. And that was the last time you saw Greta?"

Colt threw up his hands, palms upward. "That's it. Last time."

Hobbs paused to draw out the moment. She wanted to ask questions about his infiltrating within the Vetta Park PD, and more than that, she wanted to send him a warning to stay away from them. But she was too tangled in her concern of finding the Carpenter family to want to delve into the issue of police impropriety.

"Anything else you can tell me about your meetings with Greta?" Hobbs asked. She was gathering up her items, shifting her weight on the couch, getting ready to leave. The question was a standard wrap-up question for the end of interviews, meant as a catch-all that typically caught nothing.

But there was something about the way Colt Bundy moved, the way he cocked his head back with a subtle but obvious twitch that led Hobbs to believe there was something more.

"Mr. Bundy…" she led.

He faced her and she could see that his eyes were wide, his expression baffled – as though he was on the brink of finishing a puzzle but couldn't quite get the pieces to fit together.

"Well, I just thought of something," he said in a voice that seemed both bewildered and startled, a pitch higher than his usual tone.

"What did you just think of?" Hobbs asked, and she reminded herself to remain patient as brought his eyes back and forth across the room. He seemed to be registering, sequencing and revisiting his thoughts instead of looking around or even at her.

Finally, he leveled his eyes directly at Hobbs and stated, "Greta said she thought that Griffin's silent business partner was Steven Vance. Before she found out that it was Marcia Brock, she thought it was Vance."

If this was supposed to be an a-ha moment, it was lost on Hobbs. This bit of information was neither surprising nor newsworthy. Greta had an established relationship with Vance and it wasn't a stretch to think he might be working with Griffin.

"I don't understand why that's significant," Hobbs said.

"Because they're both *gone!*" Colt said. "First Greta's family and now Vance…they've up and left Vetta Park and just disappeared."

"What are you talking about?" Hobbs asked. Now it was she who felt taken aback. "Steven Vance hasn't left town! We just brought him in for questioning last week."

"Well he left, probably right afterwards," Colt said. "Trust me, I have a client who…let's just say he's one of Vance's creditors, to the tune of a few pennies. When my client couldn't reach Vance, he hired me. And I have been unable to locate him, which is extremely rare for me."

Hobbs was perched at the edge of the couch. It was a position she'd assumed when she had been prepared to hop up and leave, and with Colt Bundy's revelation, she stayed in that pose and tried to figure out what was going on.

There was an obvious, textbook reason why a person of interest would mysteriously leave soon after being questioned. But the Vetta Park police weren't close to connecting Steven Vance to the family's disappearance. In fact, his vanishing – if it was true – was the closest reason they had for distrusting him.

And it wasn't just that he'd left, but if Bundy's account was correct, he'd left in the same abrupt vein as the family. It was as though some unexplained force was shaping the lives of certain Vetta Park residents – as though at any time, she could get a phone call that would make her pack a few bags and leave town forever. But it was an improbable scenario that had now happened twice – two entities distantly related but who must have been more closely aligned than their detective work had uncovered. Clearly, they needed to work harder at tying one to the other.

"Are you sure Steven Vance left for good?" Hobbs asked. "He's not just on a getaway for a week or so?" She knew that as soon as she returned to the station, the primary concern of the police department would be to track Vance down. But she wanted to hear from the private detective who had a few days lead on her.

Colt shook his head. His face was hardened, decisive. "I've done everything in my power to find Steven Vance and I'm very good at my job, Detective. The man is *gone*."

# CHAPTER TWENTY-FOUR

*March 11, 2011*

Tuck couldn't have chosen a more perfect restaurant for their night out. It was a small Italian place, open-air, overlooking the Mississippi River, and sporadically layered with heat lamps to make the cooler air seem just right.

They were seated at the best possible table with the nicest views. Greta at first attributed this to luck or coincidence...but as soon as Tuck got down on one knee and requested her hand in marriage, she knew he had planned the whole thing.

Greta said yes without hesitation and soon the whole place erupted with cheers. Waiters stopped by their table to wish them the best, and one table sent a few congratulatory drinks over to the lucky couple.

The diamond ring itself was stunning, in Greta's opinion. It was a solitary round diamond, affixed to a gold band – a symbol not just of the eternity of love but the hardness of perseverance.

Greta and Tuck spoke throughout the evening of their plans for the future – a timetable for Tuck to move in with her and John, a simple courthouse wedding and maybe even one or two more children.

It was all so fun and exciting – the planning that made her feel the momentum of her life moving ahead. They spoke ebulliently over stuffed prawn and lobster tail, crowned half-rack of lamb and filet mignon.

While they were waiting for the dessert course, she let her gaze rest on the ring – a new ornament to enclose her slender finger – an accessory that felt strange to wear. She was quiet for a few moments and Tuck noticed.

"You look sad," Tuck declared. "Why don't you tell me what you're thinking about?"

Still staring down, Greta exhaled a sigh and fingered the ring with her right hand. "My mother," she said. "This is the second wedding I'm going to have where she won't be there. She's never even met Johnny."

"So call her," Tuck said. "If you're looking for a reason to get in touch with her again, this is as good a reason as any. Tell her you're getting married and you want her to come to the courthouse. She can be our witness."

Greta shook her head. "I can't. I don't know how to reach her. She's moved around a lot, changed her phone number."

"Well, you know a private investigator, right? Get in touch with him and hire him to find your mom. I bet he could do it."

Greta shook her head again and kept her gaze downward. It was hard to explain to Tuck – a man so logical, whose thoughts seemed always rational, algorithmic. This wasn't a problem that could easily be solved. "Too much time has passed," Greta explained. "I don't think either of us would recognize the other."

"So it's a pride thing," Tuck said, and Greta could tell by the way she snapped her head up and frowned at him that he instantly regretted saying it.

"Let's not focus on the past then," Tuck added. "This is our happy night, our celebration of our lives being together forever. Let's not let anything sour it."

Greta blinked back the tears that had formed in her eyes, nodded and raised a champagne flute. She and Tuck returned to the task of planning. The wedding was going to be small and unceremonious, practically bureaucratic. But it was still exciting to think about details such as date and attire.

Greta's mood was lifted by the end of the meal, and she was so buoyed by her news that when she got home, she forgot to knock on John's door before bursting in.

"Johnny, guess what?" Greta exclaimed – although in the same instant, she forgot why she had come into his room in the first place. John's room stunk – a hybrid of incense and weed. There was a fog in between the door and the window – a cloud of stench and haze that hung in the air. Behind the fog, two bodies leaned out the window, their faces obscured. As soon as she came into the room, the bodies recoiled, jumped back into a military stance and tried to clear the air by waving their palms.

One of the bodies belonged to John, and his shock soon gave way to anger. "Mom, you're supposed to knock!" he yelled.

The other body belonged to a neighbor named Robert – a gawky teenager with spiked hair dyed purple. He was older than John by a few years, and although he'd played at their house occasionally as a child, Greta hadn't seen him for a long time.

Here is what Greta did know about Robert: that he had been expelled from the local public schools starting in elementary school, that he had a record for vandalism and drug possession and that he attended a school for children with behavioral concerns.

Once the haze dissipated and Robert could see Greta more clearly, he said, "Uh, hi Mrs. Brock. See ya later." He then reached forward and snatched a plastic bag from the top of John's bed, but before he could cross the threshold of the doorway, Greta held out her hand.

"Leave it with me," she ordered.

"Aw, come on, Mrs. Brock."

"Leave it. With me." Greta repeated.

Robert thrust the bag into her hand and disappeared behind her. Greta looked down and studied the bag.

"Mom, you need to knock before you come in," John repeated. "This is my room!"

Greta sat down on John's bed. She ran her fingers across the comforter's stitching and thought of what to say. She looked at her son's face, hoping to garner some type of insight – a regret-laced frown from being caught with marijuana or an optimistic gaze from the talk that they were about to have. But instead, his face was hardened, cheeks sunk, eyes fixed on the ground.

He sighed heavily as if to emphasize the taxing nature of whatever drawn-out dialogue was bound to happen. First there was the offense of her uninvited entry, and then she made herself at ease on his bed and was going to force a conversation.

"John, I can't have you smoking pot in my house," Greta said, in a voice that was meant to be soft but convincing.

John was quick to respond. "That wasn't mine. That was Robert's pot."

"Are you telling me right now that you didn't smoke any of this?" Greta asked. But the question was worse than rhetorical; it was an invitation for him to lie to her. The question was answered by the redness of his eyes, the smell that secreted from his lips every time he opened his mouth.

And when he did – predictably – lie right to her face, he didn't even flinch. "Mom, I'm telling you. I didn't smoke any of it. It was all Robert."

To Greta, just as bad as the act of smoking pot at the age of twelve was the ease with which he looked right at her and lied. It was a worse case than her baby growing up and assuming the rebellious rites of adolescence. He had learned to be deceptive, dishonorable…and it didn't even seem to bother him.

"Well I don't want you hanging out with Robert anymore," Greta said. "He's a lot older than you and he's a bad influence."

"Really?" John asked. "Well then I guess I won't be hanging out with *anyone* because Robert is my only friend!" John took a book off of his shelf and threw it on the floor in protest, then jumped onto the bed and hid under the covers.

Greta shifted her position on top of the bed to allow him to completely unfurl and thought about his declaration. He rarely gave her any insight into his social world and she wondered whether he'd spoken the truth or was exaggerating.

"What about Jacob? Matthew? Or Tyler?" she suggested to the shrouded lump on the bed, spouting a few names that had come home on class lists.

John remained frozen in his current position – neither moving nor speaking. When Greta thought she detected a tuft of hair creeping up from his swaddle, she reached out and gave it an affectionate scratch. He shrunk down further in response.

Greta tried again. "Johnny, are those boys not nice to you?"

His response – muffled and garbled – stung her. "Stop calling me Johnny. Call me John. *Everyone* is not nice to me. They say I'm an idiot and they're right. Only Robert is nice to me."

Greta placed her body next to John's and tried to quiet the hollow feeling in her heart, now furiously pumping. She was both ferociously angry and heartbroken – split between the desire to march up to the school and scream at everyone and cry on the bed with John.

"It's not true John; you're *so* smart. Remember the tests you took. The tests that showed you have a really high IQ. It's just that your brain processes things a little differently, that's all."

"Yeah, okay, mom, whatever. The tests say I'm smart."

Greta realized the futility of pointing over and over again to the tests. Maybe it worked when he was a kid but it wasn't going to work anymore. He *was* smart, but he was also sensitive and impressionable. Empirical evidence demonstrated every single day that he couldn't read – not really, not like the other kids – and he could barely write. Telling him that he was smart against a rising chorus of classmates telling him that he was stupid was just pointless.

"You know, John, I taught myself to read when I was a teenager – several years older than you are now. I think I may know some good techniques. Do you want to work with me – maybe for a little bit every day after school? I think that would really help."

John shot up in bed and yelled, "Mom! I know how to read!" His voice was loud, livid. Her suggestion, while well intentioned, had embarrassed him. And his avowal that he knew how to read was another falsehood. But unlike the last one, this one made Greta worry that he was lying to himself, too afraid to accept the reality that both of them knew.

"Can you please leave now, Mom? I'm tired and I want to go to bed."

Greta nodded and stood up from the bed. "Good-night John. I love you." She leaned forward to kiss him on the cheek and was surprised that he let her, although didn't move to reciprocate.

As she left the room, Greta was overcome with the feeling of powerlessness. Her only child was plunging down a slope and she had no idea whether this was the beginning, middle or end of his descent. She had tried to intervene and she swore to continue to try...but it was hard to feel capable of making a difference. John was strong-willed and introverted. As long as he refused to accept his constraints, he was bound to self-soothe with the likes of Robert and his inauspicious remedies. Greta worried about what the future had in store.

It was this future that lay before her that had shifted so dramatically throughout the course of the night. At the beginning of the night, the future was a long promising arrow, pointing towards comfort, marriage and love. But it had flipped and reversed as soon as she entered John's room. Now the future was a question mark at the end of a tunnel, and the hope that John would find his way out before it was too late.

# CHAPTER TWENTY-FIVE

*September 23, 2013*

Olivia Noelle was two weeks old when Greta brought her home from the hospital. Despite her prematurity, she was a beautiful baby…not round and plump, but soft and pink, with wrinkly skin and a tassel of downy hair.

Mary Miller was the first neighbor to stop by. "I knitted a baby blanket," she said, placing it on Greta's shoulder and then bending over to get a closer look at Olivia, who was fast asleep in the crook of Greta's arm. "Oh what an absolute beauty!" she squealed.

Greta smiled, thanked the older woman, and led her into the living room. The sofa was covered with baby blankets, burp cloths, pacifiers and other baby accouterments, but somehow they found space across from each other.

Mary held out her arms. "Can I hold her? Please?"

Greta obliged and handed over Olivia. The baby stirred and fussed, but eventually settled down in Mary's arms.

"How is Tuck doing?" Mary asked. "Is he here?"

"No, he's at work."

"And how about you, dear? How are you doing?"

Greta sighed and thought about what to say. Mary Miller was a neighbor she spoke with once a year at most. The older woman was lovely...but not a confidante – and not someone Greta wanted to receive her avalanche of personal issues.

First there was Greta's physical state – her body, which felt like it was on fire. She felt emotionally drained – exhausted to the point of feeling shattered. And finally, the fact that she hadn't slept in days and felt practically catatonic at all times.

"I'm good," Greta replied. "Just really tired."

"And your other child...James...?"

"John."

"John yes, is he driving already? I sometimes hear him and his friends late at night outside my window," Mary said pointedly.

"He's only fourteen so he can't drive yet," Greta said. "But I guess he does have a few older friends. I hope they don't bother you."

"Oh, no, no," Mary said, but her voice was a whisper directed at the sleeping baby in the bend of her arm.

Greta was surprised to find herself relieved. If John's friends were an annoyance to the neighborhood...well, that was another notch on the list of grievances she would take up with him at some point.

Hard rock music suddenly blared from the floor beneath them – a cacophony of electric guitar and drumming.

"Is that John? Or a houseguest?" Mary inquired.

"That is John," Greta answered, and she hopped up from the couch with an alacrity that sent a quiver of pain through her body. Somehow her anger was able to assuage her pain receptors, and she raced to the basement to find the door to John's room locked.

Greta pounded on the door. "Let me in!" she yelled.

The noise subsided and Greta heard footsteps, then the door opened. John stood on the other side, his hair straw-thin and long enough to reach his upper chest. He had dark stubble across his upper lip and jawline – a shaggy adolescent determined to appear older than he was.

"Why are you pounding on my door?" John asked.

"Why aren't you at school?" Greta asked. "It's ten-thirty on a Monday."

"I thought you would be at the hospital," John said.

"That doesn't answer my question," Greta said. "Do you skip school every time you think I'm not home?"

John shrugged. "It was raining and I missed the bus. Didn't want to bike over and I didn't think you were around. I'm not missing anything. It's just a long day of study halls anyway."

"John, your entire day does not consist of study halls," Greta said. "I think that would be a violation of state requirements. Now come on and I'll take you to school."

Greta stayed resolute but she had to chase some oppositional thoughts from her head. She had no reassurance that the school was meeting any of John's needs and she wasn't certain that a day of study halls would have been any less didactic than the curriculum he was receiving. Every year, Greta was amazed that the school passed John into the next grade and since he didn't show any outward indicator of progress, she had resigned herself to trust in a system that didn't seem to be working.

"Ugh, school, I hate school!" John said, but he laced up a pair of sneakers and pulled his backpack from under the desk.

Greta smiled at him. "Just don't be like me. I stopped going to high school and every day I wish I'd stayed in and paid attention."

"Right," John agreed. "You only ended up with a nice house and two *amazing* children!"

Greta laughed and lingered by the doorway until he joined her. It was so rare between the two of them these days – a moment of levity. Every interaction between them seemed fraught – the decision to move his bedroom down to the basement to make room for the baby, the constant nagging about homework or study time, the friends he chose to hang out with and of course, the worry about his incessant time on the computer.

These seemed like normal worries of any parent of a teenager, but to Greta, they felt exaggerated – as if somehow, John's predilections for isolation, experimentation and rebellion were more harmful than they were for other teenagers.

First were the two boys John hung out with: Robert was constantly at her house and then there was a new friend, Tai Gausman. These boys seemed to exist in a permanent fog – their eyes inflamed and their appetites voracious. Greta watched their interactions with her son whenever she could, suppressing her antipathy to their existence, her knowledge about their obvious extracurricular activities.

She told herself it was okay as long as they didn't exert their influence over John – and as far as she could tell, they didn't. John was coherent, ever-present, and he never avoided her even while his friends raided her refrigerator and succumbed to laughing fits. *It's just them*, she would tell herself. *It's not him*. His room smelled fine and his behavior was normal, so she let it go.

But the problem with teenagers was the startling buffet of issues that threatened them. Even as Greta chose not to address John's friends' drug use, there were other concerns she didn't know how to ignore. John locked himself in his room most days – not to huddle over magazines or alter his state of mind (so far as she could tell) but to be on his computer. He was protective about his activities as well. The boy who still constantly misplaced his backpack and forgot to comb his hair was fastidious about passwords and screen locks, so it was impossible for Greta to tell exactly what he was doing.

Greta let this go on for a while, hoping it was just a phase, until she couldn't take it anymore. Perhaps it was the new feeling of distension in her abdomen unleashing hormones and an overbearing feeling of maternal rigidity, but she reached her breaking point just after John turned fourteen.

It was early March 2013, the weather just showing signs of warming up, when Tuck and Greta sat down with John and talked to him about the dangers of unsupervised internet use – a little family intervention. John seemed genuinely interested in what they were saying at the time, nodding frequently and saying all the right things. He showed them all the websites he visited – mostly news and sports sites, and occasional music videos.

Greta watched his guided tour through his computer activities with an ounce of skepticism. She felt there was more beneath this little display that John would never show them and they had no means of discovering on their own.

This is why, as Greta scanned John's bedroom while she waited for him to finish packing his bag that morning, her eyes alighted on a black blinking computer monitor.

She wasn't even sure what stirred her to cross the room and study the screen. Nothing about the monitor itself was particularly telling – it was white font on black background, a blinking cursor, and the rest was indecipherable, a lattice of letters and symbols.

What surprised her was John's reaction. He leapt through the room as though his mother had unearthed a body bag, cutting through the air until he landed just in front of her, his right palm on the computer table.

"Mom!" he yelled. "Don't go through my stuff!" The computer screen went blank and then John pointed to the door. "Stay out of my room!"

It took a moment for Greta to piece together exactly what had just happened. Instead of leaving, she stood in place, her eyes darting from the computer to John. "What are you doing on the computer John?"

"Nothing!" he yelled.

"Then why are you acting like this?"

"Because you're invading my privacy! You're always up in my business! Now come on, I'm already really late for school!"

John had a way of insisting that betrayed his message. His eyes had darted just to the right of hers, his upper lip curled to cover the beads of sweat. It was this way with him – and it had always been this way – that she could tell when he was lying to her, omitting something from her. And she desperately wanted to sit down with him again in a momentous face-to-face, to tell him how much potential he had, how harmful whatever he was doing on the computer could be. But at that moment, he was already by the front door, opening it quickly and shutting it again and whining about how she was making him even later to school.

She could also hear the piercing shrill of her baby's cry, a scream so dramatic that it echoed clearly through the floorboards.

"Greta!" Mary called out. "I think your baby's hungry!"

Greta took a deep breath and turned out the lights to John's room as she headed upstairs. The momentous face-to-face conversation would have to wait.

# CHAPTER TWENTY-SIX

*November 1, 2015*

Greta was folding laundry in Olivia's room when the baby toddled over to her, a thin book trapped under her arm.

"Read this one, Mommy," Olivia said, reaching up and pressing the book against Greta's torso. She was over two years old now and pudgy, her hair white-blonde and her eyes blue. Olivia's aesthetics reminded Greta of herself as a child but her demeanor could not have been more different.

Greta remembered being wild and obstinate when she was younger – a rambunctious pit bull who couldn't conform to expectations. By contrast, Olivia was easygoing and malleable. She played quietly, she entertained herself and she loved books. Every morning, while Greta was folding laundry in Olivia's room, the child toddled over and requested her mother read at least one of the many books in her room.

Greta put the pile of clothes in a drawer and reached for the book Olivia had chosen. *Jacob Gray Wants a Dog.*

"Oh I remember this book," Greta said, and then swallowed as the memories inundated her – first, reading this book to John when he was very little, and then, watching him struggle as he tried to read it to himself.

Greta pulled Olivia onto her lap in the rocking chair and opened the book. "Jacob Gray wants a dog," she read.

Olivia melted into her mother's embrace and put her thumb in her mouth.

Greta turned the page. "I will love my dog. My dog will love me too." She turned the page. "I do want him. I will take care of him. I will give him food to eat."

The door to Olivia's room swung open and John walked in. "Oh, hey Mom," he said.

Greta turned sideways and looked at him. She was doing that more and more these days – studying him as though he was a boarder in the basement. It wasn't that his personality or proclivities had changed over the years – he still spent as much time in front of the computer as he had at fourteen and hung out with the same friends; it was his appearance. He constantly tried on new looks – always dyeing, growing or shaving his hair. On that particular morning, she thought that he looked like an ephebe in rocker's clothing – a boy growing into a man but still clinging to gawky rebellion.

The changes weren't limited to John's appearance. There were a few adjustments to his schedule too, now that he was in the eleventh grade. Edwardsville High had a work-study program for students like him – those kids who did better when their hands were put to use instead of their minds. John went to school some mornings and to work at an auto body shop other mornings. Greta wanted to intervene and steer him back to full-time schooling but he actually seemed to like working on cars.

When she saw John in the driveway examining an engine – hood up, his face burrowed behind it – she could occasionally hear him humming. Likewise, she had never seen his mood so lifted as when he solved an engine problem. He actually sat down with them at family meals on occasion and told them stories about auto work with a sanguine tone he'd never used when talking about school. And so, Greta bit her tongue and stayed silent despite her ability to see the long game.

On that morning in early November, John stopped into Olivia's room to say good-bye before he walked up the street to work. "I have two pickup trucks the guys want me to take a look at," he announced.

Greta shifted and pulled Olivia off of her, then stood up and handed the book to John. "Can you please read this while I run to the restroom?" she asked. It was more of a command then a request he could deny, and as Greta shot off towards the bathroom she could hear Olivia screeching behind her, "Book! Book! Book!" and John responding, "Okay, okay."

When she returned, she lingered in the doorway to Olivia's room while listening to John read.

"My dog will play with Spot," John read effortlessly. Then he continued: "Spot lives ac…ac…access the street."

The word was *across* and Greta could feel her heart sink. Sixteen years old and he was still obstructed by two and three syllable words. It was all so anachronistic – six years had passed since she'd first bought him the book and it was as though no time had passed at all. The difference was that he was optimistic back in those days, a freckled, bright-eyed child who got frustrated when confronted with words he didn't know. When he was ten he was still striving, still hopeful.

Now he was sixteen and resigned. The struggle was familiar to him, and he'd long since stopped trying to overcome the blockade.

"I will wash my dog in the sink," John continued. "I will use sssooo…shhh…soap? Ssss…shhh…I will use…oh hey, Mom."

Greta had taken cover behind the frame, biting her lips while she tried to mentally toss the word to him. *Shampoo.*

John shook the baby off of his lap and tossed the book to Greta. "Gotta go," he said as he passed her in the doorway.

No sooner had Greta gotten back into position with Olivia – the toddler bent, shrimp-like against Greta's torso – than the twin slams of car doors from outside made her jump.

The noise itself caromed across Olivia's bedroom. It sounded ferocious, dangerous, as though there were a right and a wrong way to slam the door. And yet, Greta was still surprised when she heard the screams. First the shouts of men and then a shriek that was unmistakably John's.

Greta hoisted Olivia into her crib and screamed, "TUCK!" as she raced out of the room, loping through her house like a sprinter. When she reached the front yard, she saw two men attacking John, who was curled on the sidewalk in the fetal position. The men weren't tall but they were burly, each wearing a denim jacket, blue jeans and boots. One man – bald, coated with arm and neck tattoos – was kicking John in the ribs.

The other man – skinny, with curly hair – was leaning over John and smacking his face.

"STOP IT!" Greta screamed as she ran across the yard. Both men looked up at the sight of her and stopped their assault. The bald man took a few steps backwards. Greta hadn't thought about what to do when she reached the scene – whether she was putting herself in danger or risked making the situation worse.

It was only when she was leaning over her son's furled body, cradling his head in her hands and rocking him slightly, that she became aware of a third man – a driver in a red convertible. The incident seemed frozen in time -- the perpetrators as still as statues while the driver stared at them.

And then she heard Tuck's voice behind her, thunderous and bellowing – and life moved in fast-forward again.

Tuck descended upon them, both hands rolled into a fist. He was tall and athletic, half a foot taller than the curly-haired guy. Before Tuck could land a punch, the men were gone – two figures who leaped into the awaiting car and sped away.

Greta turned all her attention to John. He was unconscious but still breathing, with a red, bloody jaw that was beginning to swell up. Greta held her body aloft, trying to cradle him without smothering him. She could hear Tuck's strained voice as he spoke to an emergency dispatcher.

"We need an ambulance at 12 Avery Place! Please come right now!"

She looked down at John's body and stroked the top of his bangs across his forehead. "You're going to be okay, Johnny," she said over and over again because she couldn't think of what else to say. In the distance, she heard the wail of sirens.

Tuck was still shouting into his phone. "No! We don't know why, and we don't know who it was!" His voice sounded strained – a sibilant yell.

Greta stayed on the ground with John until the ambulance arrived and then she rode with him to the hospital while Tuck drove separately with Olivia.

Once at the hospital, she wasn't allowed to see John right away, so she sat with Tuck and Olivia in a waiting area. The room had metal benches and vinyl chairs, a vending machine and a mounted rack of magazines with some children's books.

Tuck passed the time reading to Olivia but all Greta could do was pace silently. The wait to see her son felt endless, a drawn-out agony in which she could feel the passage of every minute. Eventually a doctor showed up and told them of fractures, bruises and contusions. If there was a silver lining, the doctor assured them that John would eventually make a full recovery from his injuries.

When he was finished speaking, the doctor told them they could visit John in his room, although Olivia was too young and had to stay behind.

It was silently agreed that Greta would go back and Tuck would stay in the waiting room with Olivia – but Greta paused before she allowed herself to go back. It was as though she wanted to take measure of the situation, to prepare for what she was about to see.

And then she nodded at the doctor and followed him around a corner, into an area where small rooms encircled a nursing station. In one of those rooms, John lay unconscious on a hospital bed, his arm tethered to an IV drip, his right index finger wrapped in a plastic sheath. There were tubes and cords coming out of him, trussing John to machines that blinked and beeped.

Greta managed not to gasp when she saw his swollen, discolored face -- but she couldn't prevent her tears from falling. He looked like a character in a play – an impersonator of her son wearing a patina of rose hip colored make-up.

"He's going to be okay," the doctor assured her. "We've given him some medicine for the pain. He'll be out of it for a little while."

Greta nodded and wiped the edges of her eyes. "I'm just going to stay for a little while," she said in a weak voice, as she took a seat in a nearby chair.

The doctor looked down at his pager and left the room without saying anything.

For the rest of the day, Greta stayed in that spot and watched John sleep. He opened his eyes every so often but these were short, fleeting moments unaccompanied by cognition.

At some point in the afternoon, Greta texted Tuck to take Olivia home and assured him she would call a cab when she was ready to leave. But she never felt comfortable leaving John's side.

Instead, she kept a vigil that night, her mind occupied with all the assorted thoughts to tell him once he woke up.

Greta needed to let him know how much she loved him; that much was clear to her. But just as important, she needed to express to him the weight of his choices, the burden of responsibility over his life that was once entirely hers now shared with him. She needed him to take stock of his life's course and change it – to confront his beating as an opportunity to turn his life around. And she needed to do all of this before it was too late.

*** 

John woke up around noon the next day. He surveyed the room – listless and glassy eyed. When he focused on his mother his lips parted into a half-smile.

"What happened?" he asked, his voice grainy and weak.

"You were assaulted," Greta responded. "How much do you owe them?" She had practiced asking that question all morning – a tone of voice that was entreating instead of judging, a query that should have been easy enough to answer.

But he surprised her by sticking to his story. "Mom – I don't…"

Before he could say anymore she was in front of him, her face ruddy and her eyes narrowed. She felt the same burst of adrenaline that she'd experienced when she heard his yells from the front sidewalk – a crazy jolt of energy that made her want to rip the lines to his machines and shake him until he came to his senses.

"Don't. You. Dare. Lie. To. Me," she said, glowering at him, her face suspended a few inches above his face as though disembodied.

John's expression changed and she wasn't sure whether it was fear from seeing a side of her she'd never displayed before or the physical manifestation of a decision to start being up-front with her.

"I don't owe anything," John repeated. "I hacked this guy's computer."

"You...what?"

"His email, actually. I hacked into it."

"Who? What?" Greta asked. This wasn't the confession she had been expecting. She was prepared to hear about drug deals and unpaid bills, loans from the wrong sort of guys to finance a well-hidden drug habit. "What does that mean, John? Pretend I was born in the Stone Ages and please explain it to me."

John sighed. "My friends...they, uh, sometimes...ummm...are they going to get into trouble if I speak honestly?"

"No. Please be honest."

John continued. "My friends sometimes, you know, smoke pot or something else. Nothing hard or anything. But the guy who sells to them often complains about the bigwig at the very top. Says the guy in charge doesn't treat anyone well and that he brags about how he has an in with the cops. So you can't say anything to the cops about my assault. Mom, I mean it."

Greta exhaled, closed her eyes and opened them very slowly. "I won't say anything about this to the cops, John."

"Anyway, this guy at the top is such a hypocrite, Mom. I recognized his name because I've seen him profiled in the local paper for, like, donating to charities. He's got this public image where he's basically the Pope, and meanwhile he's selling drugs to guys like Tai and Robert. I promised Tai I wouldn't tell anyone the name but I didn't promise to do *nothing*. I thought it would serve this guy right to knock him down a few notches."

"But Johnny…" Greta started. She stared down at her hands while she thought about what to say. The words flowing through her mind were too abrasive, too candid. Only a child would hear the name of a dangerous public figure and think to put him in his place. This was an undeveloped mind – a kid who lacked the proper judgment to stay far away.

John continued. "It was so easy, Mom. I hacked into his email and then I sent a bunch of stupid messages to him from himself. They weren't trolling or anything, just dumb. It was just to have some fun with him. I guess he got the message."

Greta exhaled and looked over at the machines in his room. There were the monitors, pulsing and beeping, and the slow drip into his arm from the bag. She then looked up at the fluorescent lighting and spoke to him in an admonishing tone that she wondered if she should have used months, maybe years ago.

"Well this kind of behavior isn't okay, John. Are you at all surprised that he got the message? Or that he sent you a message back?"

John countered her rebuke with silence.

Greta looked at his bruised face and asked, in a softer voice, "How did he find out it was you, anyway?"

"I told him it was me. I put my signature on everything I do. I'm not some coward, hiding in my room."

"Oh Johnny," Greta said, and closed her eyes while she rubbed the edges of her fingers against her temples. This was his puerility again – an arrogance endemic to being fifteen.

"Are you mad at me?" John asked.

Greta took John's left hand in hers. Anger was one of the many emotions she was acutely feeling.

"I think…" Greta began, and then she moved closer until she was leaning over him. At this closeness she could smell him now – a metallic whiff of blood and gauze, and the faint hit of soap.

"I'm thinking so many things right now," Greta said. "First of all, I think you need to find some new friends. I think you're hanging out with people who don't value you. They don't see all that you're capable of, all that you can do. And I guess I didn't see it either. I spent so much time focusing on your limitations and not enough time seeing how gifted you are. I don't want you ever hacking into anyone's email ever again – no matter who they are – but I do see that your brain works in amazing ways, John. You see hidden things that the rest of the world just overlooks. Don't waste your life, Johnny. You can give the world so much."

John pressed his lips together and looked at her. Tears clung to the edges of his eyes. She thought he might refute her – shake his head like he typically did, or cover his ears. But this time, he just looked at her with a face that seemed so blank, so innocent.

Greta squeezed his hand again and continued. "I think we should pull you out of Edwardsville High. That school has done absolutely nothing for you except introduce you to the likes of Tai Gausman."

"But what will I—?"

"When you're not at the auto body shop, you can sit down with me and we will work on reading and writing. Johnny, I've been in exactly your shoes. I know how hard it is and I can teach you. I've been telling you this for years and you've never listened to me."

John made a fist with his hand, and Greta wasn't certain whether this was involuntary or not. She cradled his fist with her palms and brought it up to her cheek. "Listen to me now," Greta whispered.

John straightened in his bed and unclasped himself from her grip. He unclenched his fist and stared down at it as though it was an alien appendage with its own thoughts and motives.

"I can work with you," John eventually said. "So, it'll be, what? A few hours here and there to get better at reading and writing?"

Greta nodded. "Yes. Every single hour that you would otherwise be at school."

"Hmmm," John said. He seemed to be weighing the prospect but Greta knew that he would do it. He had asked a question about the time commitment, which was a momentous step forward from every other time that she'd broached the topic.

"Do you think you can clean up your act, John?" Greta asked. She looked directly at him, wanting to convey the seriousness of the question, the necessary prerequisite for her vision to take shape.

"What do you mean?" he asked. "I already told you I'm not on drugs."

"I believe you that you're not on drugs," Greta said. "I'm talking about less time on the computer and less time with Tai and Robert."

She expected a fair amount of pushback from this part of the proposal. Tai and Robert were not directly behind John's assault...but Greta saw them as encumbrances to John's forward trajectory. It wasn't just that they regularly engaged in drug use – John had admitted as such, even if their influence hadn't reached so far as to ensnarl him in it. It was that every time she saw them they were brooding or complaining, attired in all black and protesting the world and their place in it.

Greta knew these behaviors were typically teenage; she even saw some vestiges of herself as a sixteen-year old – a defiant and strong-willed creature, one willing to sacrifice her most precious connection with her mother, to upend the very notion of home, rather than admit she was wrong.

If only someone had gotten to her when she was sixteen – sat her down and made her visualize the future she was shaping for herself. If only she had given herself the chance to turn it all around.

"Yeah, I can agree to that," John said.

"Really?" Greta stared at him and tried to figure out whether it was really that simple or whether he was just trying to appease her.

John took his time answering her. He pressed his lips into a thin line again and held back tears. When his words finally did come out, he sounded coarse – pinched air and uneven sound. "I want my life to change," he said, and then he repeated himself. "I want my life to change."

"Well let's change it then," Greta said, and it took all of her self-control to remain perched casually on his hospital bed instead of smothering him with affection.

"Oh, one more thing," Greta said. "I think I know the answer to this question, but just to be sure…who is this guy at the top you were talking about, the one whose email you hacked? What's his name?"

"I'm afraid if I tell you, you'll get Robert and Tai in trouble. I don't want them to get in trouble."

"John, I promise you, I will not get them in trouble."

"Okay." John took a deep breath. "His name is Steven Vance."

\*\*\*

Vance did not want to be found – that much was obvious. Greta tried calling the number listed for his real estate business, but the receptionist simply took down her information and pledged a callback that never manifested.

Greta didn't want to sit around and wait, and she wasn't the type to concede defeat. She had a message that she wanted to convey to Steven Vance and the more he evaded her, the stronger her drive to deliver it to him.

One evening, she showed up at The Thirst – aware that she looked out of place among the sea of partygoers. Greta was stern-faced and engrossed with her mission. Clad in a t-shirt, jeans and sneakers, she was able to charm her way past the velvet rope after listening to a brief lecture about dress etiquette from the bouncer.

Once inside, Greta stepped into the flush of music and strobe lighting. She passed young women selling tubes of alcohol and swarms of gyrating bodies. One man stretched an arm out as she passed to try to slow down her pilgrimage.

"Hey hey!" the man said. He had dark-framed glasses and a crew cut, and he looked only a few years older than John. "Why are you in such a rush? Sporting the casual look, I like that."

Greta just smiled at him and moved on. She found the staircase and just as she had started her ascent, she caught sight of Steven Vance coming down.

He was larger than she remembered – heavier, more muscular. His hair had greyed slightly and his skin looked weathered but he was still attractive – he still looked recognizably like the man who had set her up in an apartment years ago.

When Vance passed her, he allowed his eyes to rest on her for just a moment before moving on – a split second of eye contact with no hint of recognition. Then he whiffed past her.

"Steven!" Greta called out and he halted on his step and spun around. He looked at her, studying her more closely from the vantage point of a few steps below, but didn't say anything.

"Do you remember me?" Greta asked.

Vance walked slowly back up the steps. When he reached her step, he gave a half smile. "Greta?" he finally said, but he seemed unsure of himself, and just as she was about to nod and explain her presence, his phone buzzed.

Vance picked up the call. "Yeah. Yeah, I'm coming right now. Right now." He put the phone back in his pocket and asked, "Are you going to be here for awhile?"

"Yes, I actually came here to talk to you."

"I need to take care of something. Can you go and wait in my office and I'll be there in a few minutes."

Vance waved an arm and a beefy security guard appeared on the steps. The guard escorted Greta up the remaining stairs, back through a hallway and into a large, square-shaped office with glass-paneled walls that overlooked the downstairs dance floor.

He left the room and then Greta took a seat on the couch. The beat of the music droned into the room and occupied her until Vance made his way back.

This time, when he came into the room, he greeted her with a warm hug and sat across the coffee table from her in a large armchair.

"Greta, you still look amazing," he said affectionately. "What have you been up to all these years?"

"Well, I'm married now and I have two kids," Greta said, and she pulled her phone out of her bag and placed an image in front of Vance. It was a candid photo of Olivia – blonde, pig tailed, wearing a tutu, playing in the backyard.

Vance shook his head. "Beautiful. Just like her mom," he said.

Greta took the phone back and sighed heavily. "And here is a photo of my son John." She changed the image and placed the phone back on the coffee table beneath him. It was a photo of John from the hospital bed – eye and jaw swollen, head wrapped, tubes spreading out from his bony frame.

Vance picked up the phone and stared at the image for a little while. Greta could tell that he was calculating. He looked like a chess player caught at a decision point, his tongue curled upwards behind closed lips.

A minute later, Vance asked. "This is your son?" When Greta nodded, he cocked his head and murmured, "I had no idea." Then he handed the phone back to her and ran his hands searchingly across his lower chin, as if stroking a phantom beard.

"Your guys really beat him up pretty good," Greta said. She glared at him, perhaps hoping to provoke a staring contest…but Vance's eyes were everywhere: on the ceiling, on her phone, which was now a blank screen, on her sneakers, then back up to the ceiling. He had the *decision point* expression on his face again – the tentativeness about what to say, whether to insult her intelligence by denying his involvement or whether to confess to crimes he likely didn't even discuss with close confidantes, let alone a near stranger.

Greta felt like she was bearing witness to Vance's internal struggle. These two contradictory sides of Steven Vance now juxtaposed against each other – the public image of benevolence he fought so hard to portray and the dubious dealer who operated in the dark.

Greta tried to back him into a corner. "These were your men who took him out," she said. "Don't try to deny it. I know how you work."

Vance didn't flinch. He smirked widely and without apology – lips stretched to the edges of his lower jaw. After a few moments he said, "I don't know why you're coming in here like this or what you expect me to do. All I ever did for you was provide money and housing. I took you off the streets, Greta! If it weren't for me, you'd still be homeless and illiterate, pouring people's coffee for two bucks an hour. Truly no good deed goes unpunished." Vance grunted and pulled his phone out of his pocket. He started swiping and tapping as if he had already moved on from this visit.

Greta had anticipated his martyr defense and she responded in a calm tone. "Steven, I am grateful for all that you did for me years ago. But that was in the late nineties and this is now. I didn't come here today to pick a fight. I just want your guys to leave my son alone. That's all. "

She waited to see if he would accept his role in John's beating by agreeing to talk to his men – or if he would counteract her claims with evidence of John's own crimes. But Steven Vance remained unmoved. "Sorry but I had nothing to do with your son or with the guys who put him in the hospital. I gave up that business years ago."

"It must drive you crazy," Greta said softly. "You've taken such measures to project this image. You want everyone to think you're such a good guy…but I know the truth about you."

Vance stood up and walked towards the door. If she was expecting a confrontation or staunch denial, he didn't play the part. He was unflappable as ever – his denial a refrain that oozed smoothly from his lips.

"I wish your son a speedy recovery," Vance said, holding open the door. "I'll have my receptionist send flowers to his hospital room."

This angered Greta more than anything – more than his repeated repudiation of responsibility. She leaped from the couch and stood a few inches from him, so close she could smell tobacco and whiskey on his breath. "You'll do no such thing! You leave him alone!" she yelled. And then, because her anger had swelled into a vicious storm – a torrent of vehemence she could no longer contain, she said through gritted teeth, "I have bought a gun and been to the firing range, Steven. Don't think I'll hesitate to use it if you guys go near him again. You leave my boy alone!"

Greta walked out of his office and left The Thirst. Back inside her car, she caught her breath and every emotion she had been feeling seeped out of her. She sobbed in the front seat while clutching the steering wheel, staring up at the club.

Thirty minutes later, she felt stable enough to drive home. The confrontation and emotional release had a cathartic effect. As she climbed into bed next to Tuck that night, she felt lighter, her next move elucidated as clearly as if she'd been considering it all along.

On Monday morning, November 9, 2015, Greta drove to the St. Louis office of the FBI and gave an official statement about Steven Vance.

# CHAPTER TWENTY-SEVEN

*October 2, 2017*

Hobbs knew a federal agent when she saw one. Hunky, military-grade seriousness, thick-shouldered and slackened jaw. She knew as soon as she walked into Weaver's office on Monday morning and saw the young man occupying one of the seats across from Weaver's desk.

"Hobbs, you're just in time," Weaver said. "Agents Eversgard and Waldron came this morning to talk to us about Steven Vance."

The hunky man stood up, walked over and shook her hand. "I'm Eversgard, with the FBI, nice to meet you."

He pumped her hand once and then – just as she was about to give her name – he made a sliding motion to her right, where Dean Adams was standing. "Hi," he said in a deep voice. "Eversgard, FBI, nice to meet you."

There was another man sitting in the other chair. He was older, gray-haired, with wiry glasses, almost comically nerdy. He stood up and nodded at Hobbs and Adams but didn't bother to make his way over. They waited a few moments and then Martinez walked into the room.

"We're all here," Weaver said. "Shut the door."

Martinez closed the door to the office and the three of them advanced closer to Weaver's desk. They found bookcases and window ledges to lean against, forming an outer periphery to the inner circle that the seated gentlemen had formed.

Eversgard cleared his throat and folded his arms across his chest. "We understand you're looking for Steven Vance. You can call off your search; he's under our protection. He's been moved to a safe location."

Hobbs swallowed hard and sat forward. "Can you tell us why?"

Eversgard looked up at Hobbs, over at the other Vetta Park police and then back at Weaver. "Steven Vance is an informant for us. He's been giving us information about the Islava drug operation, based in Mexico City. He's been working for us for almost two years. Last week, he gave us a particularly useful bit of information that helped our agents locate a cross-border tunnel. Our guys seized a few tons of marijuana and cocaine, and several AR-14 assault rifles. He also gave geographic details that allowed Mexican authorities to find and arrest Raoul Islava. That's when we felt it was necessary to move him into hiding."

"Steven Vance has been working with you for two years and you never felt the need to bring it to the attention of the Vetta Park Police Department?" Weaver asked.

The older agent leaned forward and made a steeple out of his fingers, which he laid against Weaver's desk. "With all due respect sir, the Vetta Park police department has been looking the other way for years. Steven Vance has a known drug operation and somehow this city has allowed him to rise to the upper echelons of its elite. Just last year, he donated thousands of dollars of drug money to build a little league field and you all threw a party for him. His money is drug money. And he launders it right through this city."

The room was silent for a minute. Hobbs waited to see how Weaver would respond. She'd never before seen him face reproach and now the criticism was harsh and real – delivered in front of subordinates no less.

But Weaver was not, by nature, an explosive man and he accepted the censure with a long single nod and a contemplative stance. He inhaled and opened his mouth as if to say something but nothing came out.

Hobbs shook her head. She was aware of this notion about the Vetta Park police – that they were glorified traffic cops, bumbling about as though jesters in a slapstick comedy. And here were these agents with their arrogance and authority – who clearly shared this view without having to say it.

"When did you first start talking to Vance?" Hobbs asked.

"Like I said…" Eversgard responded. "Almost two years ago."

"Why?" Hobbs asked. "What happened almost two years ago?"

"Someone came to see us," Waldron answered. "Someone with a bit of knowledge about his inner workings. It wasn't a perfect road map but it gave us enough to haul in Vance and get him to inform on his suppliers."

"Was that person Greta Carpenter?" Hobbs pressed.

"For their own personal safety, we don't reveal the names of informants, not even to police departments," Waldron stated.

Captain Weaver stood up and took a few steps towards his squad. "Hobbs, what are you getting at?" he asked.

"It was Greta!" Hobbs exclaimed. "Don't you see? It would have to be Greta. She lived in his apartment in her late teens; she would have seen some stuff. And almost two years ago is the date that Steven Vance's people attacked John. And she must have gone to the FBI as retribution for it."

"We don't reveal the names of informants," Agent Waldron repeated.

But there was a shift in his voice as he said it, an almost palpable air of acquiescence. Hobbs had figured it out and Waldron was neither going to agree nor try to fight it. She knew if the name were wrong, he would have said so with a manner of superiority. But the name was right, and the agents allowed it to be absorbed by the room.

"You do know that she's missing, right?" Hobbs asked. "She and her whole family...they're gone."

"We are aware that they've gone missing," Eversgard said. "We know you brought Steven Vance in for questioning on September 20. We told him that he didn't have to subject himself to your interrogation but he insisted on coming in and speaking to you anyway."

"Why do you think he would come in if he didn't have to?" Adams asked.

"Well..." Eversgard shifted his whole body to the left until he was facing the three Vetta Park PD subjects. His eyes roamed over Hobbs – not in a suggestive way but in an appraising gesture, as though he were sizing her up. When he answered, he seemed to speak directly to Hobbs.

"I don't know what history you two had, but he said he wanted to try to get out some personal stuff. I don't know exactly...clear the air, say good-bye. That's why."

Hobbs met Eversgard's stare but didn't say anything right away. She thought about her off the record talk with Steven Vance in the back parking lot of the police station. At the time, if she'd only known he was about to go under witness protection, would she have acted differently? Hobbs thought about how she walked away during Vance's apology – as though his words meant nothing to her. Just a few years earlier, that apology would have carried all the weight of the world and she never would have forgiven herself for walking away from it – leaving his explanations dangling in mid-air. But at the time, the world looked different, and it was even different still. Now she knew she'd likely never see him again. The partial apology before she cut him off was all the closure she was ever going to get from their little love story. It would have to suffice.

Hobbs brought her mind back to the missing family. "At the time, we believed that Steven Vance had a connection to Greta Carpenter; he was our best lead for finding out what had happened to her and her family."

"But you were barking up the wrong tree," Waldron said decisively. "Steven Vance had nothing to do with that family's disappearance."

"How can you be so sure about that?" Weaver asked.

"Several reasons," Waldron explained. "First of all, there's no real motivation. He doesn't know who turned him in but let's just say he thinks it might be Greta. Two years later, just about the time that he's providing his most valuable insight to us, he also decides to make Greta and her whole family disappear, sabotaging any hope for freedom? Witness protection doesn't exactly make you a free man but it's better than being behind bars. Secondly, he's been under our watchful eye for the past two years. We've monitored his calls, read his emails and listened in on his meetings. Not once has the Carpenter or Brock family come up. Vance has made no mention, given no inkling that they're even a blip on his radar screen. Right now, quite frankly, he's got bigger fish to fry than a Vetta Park paralegal, his wife and their two kids. And the third reason is just logistics. If he took them out or ordered a hit, he would have either had to do it without us knowing or we'd have to be involved, complicit. And before your imagination takes you to places you shouldn't be going, I can assure you that that wasn't the case."

Waldron's phone buzzed and he stood up, leaned forward to shake Weaver's hand and gave a polite wave to Hobbs, Adams and Martinez on the other side of the room. "We have to get back now," he said, and just hesitated at the door long enough to allow Eversgard to give a hasty farewell and join him. Two minutes later, Hobbs looked out the window and could see them as figures in the parking lot – the husky and the lean sauntering through the rows, as if foils in a police drama. They got inside a black, unmarked SUV and sped off.

Once they were gone, Adams closed the door to Weaver's office and returned to his space against the bookshelf, while Hobbs and Martinez assumed the seats the agents had vacated.

"Well, what do we think?" Weaver asked.

His underlings were quiet at first, and Hobbs felt they had a good reason to be. It was as though the agents had sucked the competence out of the room – as though they had diminished a once diligent, capable police force. They had appeared from mid-air to show neophytes what major leaguers looked like. Worse than just arrogant and didactic – they'd also stripped them of their biggest lead. Steven Vance was the family's only connection to any type of crime syndicate and Hobbs had never been more certain of his involvement than when she'd learned – only three days prior – that he'd disappeared. Now his disappearance had a police-underwritten explanation and they were back to square one.

When no one answered Weaver's question, he tried a different tactic. "Let's reassess the case," he said. "If we assume that Steven Vance had nothing to do with this, who does that leave us with?"

The room was quiet. Weaver allowed the stillness to settle into the room and then he said, "Talk to me about Griffin Brock."

"He has a solid alibi and no motive as far as we know," Hobbs responded. "There's nothing that indicates any anger towards the family, no behavior in the past month or so that was out of the ordinary. And he has nothing to gain by their death or disappearance."

"I see," Weaver said. He exhaled a puff of breath and drummed his fingers on the top of his desk. "What about those investment bankers? The real estate guys in Chicago?"

"Nothing," Adams answered. "Also no motive. They haven't dealt with Greta or even Griffin for years. They bought land years ago and then moved on."

"So what are we missing?" Weaver asked – in a voice low enough that Hobbs wasn't sure if he was speaking to them or himself. She hated to admit that they were no closer to an answer than a month ago when she'd first inspected the Avery Place house with Martinez.

There was only what amounted to an abandoned life, a black hole that had swallowed an entire family. They were now in a science fiction movie that left four intelligent, experienced members of the police department mute and uncertain.

The rest of the day was an assignment of futility. She listened to the tip line they had established for the family and quickly ruled out dead ends. Adams and Martinez reviewed the files they had amassed over the month to see if anything new jumped out at them.

At ten after six, Martinez ducked out and by ten after seven, Adams closed the file, rubbed his eyes and announced to Hobbs that he was done for the evening too. "There's a Chinese food restaurant over on Centennial. I'm going to go and grab a bite."

He stood up and lingered for a moment by her desk. Hobbs wasn't sure whether he was inviting her to join him but she felt silly inviting herself. After a second or two, Adams said, "Do you want to join me?"

Hobbs said, "No, that's ok," and watched him leave. She had answered more out of instinct than desire. What she yearned for and what she allowed herself to do were at complete odds with each other – as they often were.

She stayed for another hour at the police precinct but got nowhere with the tip line or the files. The Carpenter family disappearance was the most frustrating case Hobbs had ever taken on. There was no coupling of time spent with resolution of the case. Most of her cases had a linear bend; a point where she could justify the hours with the conclusion her work had revealed. Not this one.

Hobbs left the precinct and got in her car, heading for home. But as she got closer to her house, she was overcome by the notion that this wasn't where she wanted to be. She wanted to be back in Adams' fold – talking with him about the case, cracking jokes with him, lying next to him.

It was so difficult for her to turn the car around, to head in the direction where she'd just come, to rehearse the words she was going to say – but she did it anyway.

She felt like she was taking a leap over a one hundred foot crevice – and this uncertainty left her with a dizzying, nauseous sensation. She could make it to the other side or she could fall into the cleft – emotionally drained and embarrassed – and there was no way to tell which way the conversation would go until she jumped.

\*\*\*

The host stand at the front of China Garden was abandoned, so Hobbs led herself to Adams's table. The entire restaurant was a box-shape so it was easy to identify the only diner sitting by himself – his napkin folded formally in his lap, his chair arranged to face a poster of the Great Wall.

Even in the dim lighting, Adams saw her approaching from the other side of the restaurant. He stood up as she neared and gestured towards the seat across from him, his mouth too preoccupied with a fried chicken dish to say anything.

When Hobbs sat down and Adams finally swallowed, he cleansed his palate with a sip of water and said, "I didn't expect to see you here."

A waiter appeared and Hobbs ordered a glass of iced tea and a pork dish. Once they were alone again, Hobbs said, "I came because I wanted to talk to you about my past. With Steven Vance. I wanted to give you the full story." Adams was quiet for a moment so Hobbs added, "if it's something you want to hear."

"Sure, I'd love to hear it," Adams said. He put his fork down and leaned closer to her across the table.

"Well…" Hobbs said. "I'm not sure what you already know but Steven Vance was my first real boyfriend. You probably already knew that."

Hobbs waited for an affirmation or denial from Adams but he did neither. He balled up his napkin, placed it on the table in front of him and waited. His eyes were fixed on her in a way that normally made her feel uncomfortable. She fought her instinct to shrink away from his stare, and instead, she returned the gesture.

"It sounds very strange saying it out loud…well, not strange really but common, incredibly common. He was my first boyfriend and I was madly in love with him and I was already mentally picking out the tablecloths for our wedding registry when I caught him cheating on me. And then he dumped me. And ghosted me."

"Ghosted you?" Adams

"He ignored me; it was like he couldn't stand to be in my presence. And when I think about it now, I think he probably felt guilty and didn't know what to say. Because somebody who just didn't care…maybe that person would have accepted my calls or talked things through. I don't know; maybe I'm being too gracious about his motives."

Tears spilled down Hobbs's cheeks and landed on the tablecloth. They made fat juicy circles, a sprinkle of moisture that revealed the dark brown wood beneath.

Adams had never seen Hobbs cry before and he reached forward and held out his hand. At first Hobbs crossed her arms but then she slackened and allowed him to take her right hand in his.

"Over the years, he kept coming back to me and I kept taking him back. I know it sounds stupid but he allowed me to believe he'd changed and every time, I believed it because I wanted to believe it. During those years, I didn't open myself up to anyone but him. I really thought that he was the one for me. But, of course, he's a very damaged person and he didn't treat me the way I deserve to be treated. I can't tell you what it's like to be in love with someone who thinks you're not worth shit. It hurt *a lot.*

"And then, a few years ago, I guess I just woke up and finally realized that was it. I needed to give up the idea of him. And this…epiphany…well, it changed a lot about the type of person I wanted to be. I couldn't trust my judgment. I stopped thinking life was one big romance novel waiting to happen to me. A piece of me hardened that I didn't think would ever soften again. I think that toughness is what you see…what a lot of the guys on the force see. I think that's why I have a tendency to push you away when in reality…" Hobbs sighed and didn't finish her statement.

The waiter came back and brought Hobbs her food. She unwrapped a pair of chopsticks and pushed the pork around her bowl but didn't eat anything.

A few seconds passed, in which neither of them said anything. Then Adams leaned forward, scratched his chin and asked, "What's the reality?"

"What?" Hobbs had been staring down at her food but she looked up at him – into his eyes, a rich umber shade, seemingly darker than usual.

"You were saying something…before the food came," Adams said. "You said that you have a tendency to push me away but in reality…"

"Oh…I don't know," Hobbs said quickly. "Sorry, I got distracted."

It was far from a measure of deflection or an attempt to put up a wall. Hobbs felt like words had been streaming out of her mouth unfiltered, like hallucinogenic rants. She felt the warring pieces of her – the part that wanted to be uninhibited, open and vulnerable pitted against the part that had learned the consequences time and again. She needed to be careful, defensive. She had sat in that seat before, even though the recipient of her affections was a very different person.

Adams accepted her response and the silence returned. He looked around the restaurant while finishing what was on his plate. Finally, he placed his fork and knife together, sat back and asked, "When we brought Vance in for questioning, was that the first time you'd seen him?"

Hobbs nodded. "Well, the first time in a few years. After the last breakup, for the longest time, I would imagine what it would be like to bump into him – maybe on the street or at a charity event. I would have imaginary conversations with him in my head – thinking about what I would say and how he'd react. Sometimes, I'd be tossing a drink in his face or slapping him across the face. I've been so angry about it for years…I didn't even entertain the notion that I could see him again and be civil."

"But you were quite civil, actually," Adams said.

"I was – because it was different from what I imagined, once I finally took him off of that pedestal. He was no longer this larger than life local celebrity shining down on the proletariat. He looked…older and defeated…in a way."

"Not the invincible guy you had made him out to be?" Adams offered.

"Not at all. I saw a desperate, lying con man whose empire was collapsing. I guess moving on allowed me to see through different eyes. Seeing him made me realize that there was nothing he could give to me that would make my life any better. He didn't actually hold any cards. It was on *me*. I need to move past it…or stay angry and guarded forever."

Adams nodded and moved into the seat next to Hobbs. He reached across the place setting and held her hand in his. The tears shed earlier had abated. On Hobbs's face was a look of resilience, an anger that had shifted to softness.

"I'm telling you this, Dean, because…" Her voice drifted off as she took note of the distractions surrounding them – waiters bustling among the tables, a clattering in the kitchen, diners seating themselves, eating food, paying checks.

"Because…" Hobbs continued, staring at his face the whole time. If he was getting impatient, he didn't show it. He looked interested, his eyes tender, his rakish gaze frozen on her.

She took a few deep breaths and tried to settle herself. Her thoughts were racing, clouding her good judgment, yelling at her. *Jump! Jump! Jump!* As if her ability to protect herself had become a labile barricade – protected for so long and now carelessly tossed aside.

"Because I've fallen for you," Hobbs finally said. "I don't know if you think I'm too old for you or it's strange that we work together. There are probably a million reasons for us not to be together. But don't let my indifference be one of those reasons. If I've acted like it's casual to me, or that I don't care, or that I don't really want this, it's not true. The truth is that I'm in love with you and I want to be with you."

Hobbs sat forward in her seat, still staring at him, still clasping his hand. Her thoughts were still muddy, her heartbeat racing; her stomach felt like a pool of slurry. It was as though she had jumped from a cliff after all.

But the funny part was – as Hobbs waited for him to respond, she also felt a sense of peace. It almost didn't matter whether he would reciprocate or not – whether they would spend the night together or whether he would form an expedient excuse and swiftly duck out of there. Hobbs knew what lay beneath her and it wasn't jagged-edged limestone or craggy rock. After taking the leap, all she could feel was the exhilaration of forward momentum, the echo of her voice – as clear and sharp as ever – and the safety net of self-reliance waiting for her at the bottom.

# CHAPTER TWENTY-EIGHT

*October 11, 2016*

There was a knock at the front door of Avery Place and then the shrill melody of the doorbell. Greta placed Olivia on the floor of her bedroom and trotted towards the front of the house. "Coming!" she cried out.

When she opened the door, she was surprised to see Griffin. He looked handsome as usual but also a bit haggard – unkempt hair and a slouching stance.

"What are you doing here?" Greta asked, and realized just as the words cascaded out of her mouth how unfriendly she sounded. It wasn't that Griffin wasn't welcome in his former house; it was just odd to have him ringing the doorbell on a Tuesday morning.

Back before John was driving, when the custody agreement dictated a sporadic paternal visit, Greta would drop off John at Griffin's residence on the east side of town, and Griffin would return John to her home on Sunday evening. Not once did either parent venture outside of the car. They co-parented like distant acquaintances, each maintaining their own insulated orbit around the other.

"Nice to see you too," Griffin said.

"I'm sorry," Greta responded, opening up the door wider to allow him entry into the split-level foyer.

"How are you?" Greta asked, once she closed the door behind him. Then, before giving him time to respond, she added, "Congratulations on your wedding, by the way. John had a great time; he told me all about it and showed me some pictures from his phone. You two look very happy together."

Greta's sentiment was sincere and she hoped it came across that way. Griffin's new wife was in her mid-twenties and blonde – someone who could have been confused for Greta from a distance. Even though Griffin looked tired this morning, he had looked ecstatic in John's pictures – a wide grin in every shot, blue eyes sparkling as they rested on his bride.

"Thank you," Griffin responded stiffly. "And congratulations to you on your baby."

"My baby is over three years old now," Greta said with a smile. "But thank you."

That was all the conversation she could think of to cover the vast span of time since they'd last spoken – a mutual congratulations on the milestones they'd been informed about through John. Just as Greta was starting to think about how to gently nudge him to give a reason for his visit, Griffin blurted out, "My mother had a stroke a little over a month ago. I wanted to make sure you knew."

"Oh no. I'm so sorry," Greta said. "Is she going to be okay?"

Griffin shook his head. "I'm afraid not. She'll need constant care so she can't live alone anymore. Her Lake Michigan house is going to be empty for awhile – I just got finished firing all of the help – and I'm moving her into an assisted living facility closer to here."

"That's terrible. I'm so sorry Griffin," Greta repeated. She thought about Marcia Brock and how incongruous it was to imagine the iron-fisted woman in an assisted living facility. Marcia had always been so *sharp* – laser-tongued, quick witted. It was difficult to imagine the older woman soliciting help from anyone other than her trusted cache of butlers.

"Thank you," Griffin said. "I wanted to let you know because she's lost her eyesight but she's…she can…" Then he paused and stared down at the tile. Greta thought he was about to become emotional – the most typical response she could imagine, given the circumstances, but Griffin remained stoic. He pressed his palm against the wall, took a breath and continued. "My mother can still speak and the other day she asked about you and John. She said she wanted to see you."

Greta was caught off guard by her own immediate physical response – a distention of the heart, a rising of her spirits. She never knew she cared that much for Marcia until the words came out of Griffin's mouth. Although she could be difficult, Marcia was good-hearted and benevolent towards the charities she cared about. She hadn't come through for John when Greta had requested help, but Greta knew the older woman profoundly loved her grandson.

"I'd like to see her too," Greta said. "And John isn't home right now but I know he'll want to see her when he gets back."

Griffin then nodded, reached into his pocket and took out a piece of paper. It had a name written across the top: *Northman Assisted Living Facility*. There was a room number, a caregiver's name, hours for visiting. Griffin took a few steps back and seemed just about to turn around and walk out the door but instead he stopped.

"Something else…" he said. "I've been wanting to tell you for a little while…I noticed that John has been reading lately."

"Yes," Greta agreed. "It's been a long journey but he can finally read." She expected him to thank her or to acknowledge the difficult road John had faced.

Instead Griffin said, "And to think that all he had to do was work harder. It was that simple."

Greta let out a surprised laugh. "Griffin, it was not as simple as that. John always worked *very* hard…but he attended a school that completely failed him – for years – until he didn't see any hope for himself. I tried for so long to give him the one-on-one instruction he so desperately needed but he always pushed me away. Only after he was attacked and thought about where his future was headed did he allow me to work with him. And that is what we've done *every single day* since. It's been so hard, Griffin. Some days we can barely get through the lesson but we always push through. So, *yes*, he can read now. But don't you dare try to simplify it by saying he just needed to work harder. When I look at him I see a boy who is finally equipped with the skillset to overcome his struggles – after so long. To me, John is a hero."

Griffin paused and looked at her but didn't argue with her. Greta knew he viewed her as some sort of howler monkey – always yelping and wailing, prone to hyperbole. And she knew that trying to make him see things from her perspective was a futile endeavor.

So instead of pushing her viewpoint, she ended the conversation by thanking him for coming by, repeating that she and John would visit Marcia and closing the door behind him.

Greta had to chuckle as she headed back up the stairs. This had been their first face-to-face meeting in years, and they couldn't even last five minutes without squabbling. At least she was divorced and Griffin's antics weren't something she had to worry about anymore.

***

Three weeks later, on a cold, dusky-gray Saturday in November, Greta and John visited Marcia Brock at the Northman Facility. The building was newly constructed – a ten-story rectangle of orange and yellow siding that offered partial views of the Mississippi River.

The outside was bright enough, but as soon as she walked inside, Greta was imbued with the sense of gloom. First there was the smell – a mix of pine cleaner and antiseptic. Then the faces of the residents who were sitting in the front lobby – expressionless, weary or half-asleep already. Most had wheelchairs and oxygen tanks that were tethered to their nostrils. It was a far cry from the pillars and rolling topiaries at Marcia's previous home.

Greta and John signed in and made their way to Marcia's room. Once inside, Greta had to suppress her lament from the sight of her former mother-in-law. Marcia was a hunched wraith – an emaciated figure in a blue hospital gown, with a white bandage wrapped across her eyes. She was sitting in an upholstered chair while a middle-aged woman with wispy brown hair was crouched next to her, stirring a bowl of applesauce.

The caretaker turned her head. "Are you relatives of Marcia?" she asked.

"Yes," Greta said. "I'm Greta, her daughter-in-law, and this is John, my son."

"Greta and John, you're here!" Marcia exclaimed. "Oh, sit next to me! Johnny, sit next to me."

John did as he was instructed, assuming a seat on the couch, and the caretaker took Greta aside. "She's been blinded by the stroke but she's otherwise in alright shape."

Greta nodded. "Okay."

The caretaker went on. "But she's a bit emotional, still adjusting to her new setting I think. She's having a hard time with it."

Greta looked around at the apartment. It was large for apartment standards, with a kitchen, long hallway and sweeping views of the River. But it was miniscule compared to Marcia's former house and held none of the woman's personal accents – not that she would have been able to appreciate them anyway.

The largeness of this apartment only made it seem emptier. And Marcia, who had once been such a commanding presence in her house that she carefully choreographed where her own personal servants would stand – now was a hindered figure in the corner of the room. It seemed like a tremendous transition to have to accept.

"I can understand she would have a hard time," Greta said.

The caretaker nodded, picked up the bowl of applesauce and left it in the sink. "I'm going to let you all have some time alone," she said, then left the apartment.

Greta walked over to the living room and crouched next to the chair. "How are you, Marcia?" she asked.

"Oh, I'm terrible, just terrible," Marcia responded. "I can't read my books. I can't call anyone. I can't figure out how to use this telephone. I can't see the television screen. I can't see anymore. I used to watch the light come into the room in the morning. Did you know that?"

Greta patted the older woman's hand. Her skin seemed translucent – the blue veins protruding and intersecting each other. "I didn't know that," Greta said. " It sounds very peaceful."

"Oh, it was," Marcia said. "I'd get up before the sun and then sit by my window with a book. I could watch the sun rise over the lake – brilliant hues of red and gold. There was something so special about it – starting out in the dark and then being lifted by the sunlight every single day."

"I bet it was…" Greta paused and thought of what to say. Eventually, she said, "I bet it was magic," because she couldn't think of how to describe it.

"I didn't realize it at the time," Marcia said. "Because it's just what I did. But now I can't do any of it. I can't get up and walk to the window. I need Elizabeth, my caretaker. I can't watch the sunlight. I can't read any of my books. This is how it's going to end, I guess. The last part of my life will be in the darkness. I guess this is how it's supposed to be."

"Marcia…" Greta said and reached out so she was holding both of the older woman's hands. She thought of what to say – how to appease her former mother-in-law. She had always considered Marcia Brock to be so finicky and hard to satisfy. And now – when Marcia was mourning the loss of a basic human facility looking for Greta to mollify her – Greta still couldn't find the right words to say.

Instead, John spoke up. "I can read to you," he said. "If it's your books that you're missing."

Greta gasped and looked over at John. It wasn't just his suggestion – a show of compassion completely divorced from the behavior he displayed in his early teen years – it was those five words: *I can read to you.*

Those were words she had never heard him say to another person – not herself, not a teacher, not a counselor. Reading had been so wrapped up in feelings of inadequacy and self-loathing for his entire life.

Now all of that had changed. Greta wanted to cry and laugh at the same time, pick him up off of the couch and twirl him around like a whirling dervish. But she knew he hated when she made a big deal out of things so she refrained from saying what she really wanted to say: *Look at how far you've come. Look at what you can do now, what you've accomplished. I think you're exceptional, John, and I always have.*

"That's so kind of you to offer, John," Greta said.

"That would be lovely," Marcia agreed. "You can select a book from the shelf in my bedroom. I would love to hear you read it."

John stood up and walked into the bedroom and Greta moved further away to give him space to sit down next to his grandmother. When John came back, he was leafing through a hardcover of a few hundred pages. The image of a boy and a pirate at the helm of a ship was on the cover.

"You gave a copy of this book to me a few years ago," John said, kneeling down next to Marcia. "*Treasure Island*, do you remember?"

Marcia smiled. "Yes, of course I remember giving it to you. Did you ever read it?"

John laughed. "No, I think I threw it away. But I'll read it to you now."

He opened the book and balanced it on his lap, while moving his finger across the first page of text.

"*Squi...squire Tre...tre...lawney, Doctor Lively...no...Doctor Live-sey, and the rest of these gen...gen..tle...gentle...men having asked me to write down the whole... whole... par...tic...u...lars about Treasure Island ...*"

Greta listened carefully while John read. He stumbled over several words, got a few vowels wrong, paused between phrases...and his pacing was slow. But he was moving through the book after all, and Greta closed her eyes and listened to him.

John continued for another thirty minutes and then slapped the book shut. "I think I'm getting tired," he said. "I hope that was okay."

"That was wonderful, John," Marcia said. "The highlight of my day, really. Can you come back tomorrow?"

John took his phone out of his pocket. "I have to work at the auto shop tomorrow, but I can come by and read more later in the week."

"Yes, please, grandson," Marcia said and then she called out, "Greta! Are you still here?"

Greta walked over. "Yes I'm still here."

"Where are your hands?" Marcia asked.

"Right here," Greta said, and she placed her hands once again over Marcia's.

Marcia turned her palms upward and held onto Greta. "Thank you," the old lady said softly – her voice so faint that Greta wasn't even sure she'd heard correctly. Then Marcia whispered – louder this time, and with a sudden strength, "Thank you thank you thank you."

# CHAPTER TWENTY-NINE

*June 5, 2017*

Marcia Brock's health steadily declined. Each month that passed since the stroke seemed to offer a new array of health concerns. The winter brought pneumonia, bronchitis and a lung infection that kept Marcia isolated and confined to her bedroom. Family was allowed to visit, provided they were healthy and wore a mask at all times.

Greta got into a rhythm of visiting once a week, and John went by himself three or four times a week to read to his grandmother. Greta knew that John's visits meant everything to Marcia. She could tell by the way the old woman responded to John's voice – the way she stirred and smiled, followed along with his reading, and leaned towards him like a plant bending towards sunlight.

Still, every time Greta visited, Marcia made it a point to pull her former daughter-in-law closer to her, to lean forward and whisper in a feeble voice. She told Greta that John's visits were the best part of her day, that he provided motivation for her to wake up each morning.

Greta worried about the type of pressure this placed on her eighteen-year-old son, but for his part, John seemed to enjoy these visits with his grandmother. It took three months to finish *Treasure Island*, and in winter he moved on to *The Great Gatsby* and other classics.

Now it was early May, John had finished the last pages of *Jane Eyre* and the temperature outside had been steadily in the 70s. There was hope that summer weather meant fewer viruses — that Marcia could accept more visitors and spend some time outside.

But the morning that John and Greta visited, it was clear that Marcia would not be rising out of bed anytime soon. The old woman looked just as debilitated as ever, lying on her side in a loose coil, her hair matted and her eyes glazed.

Elizabeth explained that Marcia's health had taken a turn. In addition to the chronic bronchitis, Marcia had a kidney infection and was in pain in her limbs from arthritis.

"How are you Marcia?" Greta asked, and she softly rubbed the old woman's back as she crouched down next to the bed.

"Is that you Greta?" Marcia asked, her voice a rising lilt, a chirrup of optimism.

"Yes," Greta said. "I'm here with John. Do you want him to read to you?"

"I don't think I can listen to any books today," Marcia said.

"That's okay," Greta said gently. "We can just sit here with you."

Greta took a seat on the bed and motioned for John to do the same. They sat in silence for a few minutes, the lack of sound broken only by an occasional bird chirping, the prattle of water from the toilet, which every so often jetted for no reason.

Twenty minutes passed, and then Greta placed a hand on Marcia's shoulder and leaned forward. "We're going to head out now," Greta whispered.

"I'm so…alone," Marcia responded. "Griffin, he never comes to see me. I never talk to my son. He moved me from Winnetka to his backyard and he never stops by. Why do you think that is?"

Greta shrugged. "I don't know." When it came to Griffin's behavior, there was a long list of actions that Greta had given up trying to understand.

"I wish I could call you," Marcia said. "Sometimes I just want to hear my grandson's voice. When I'm trying to go to sleep sometimes, I imagine that he's reading to me."

"I'm sure that helps."

"I'm still tired," Marcia said. "I'm just so tired."

"Get some sleep," Greta responded. She wanted to leave for Marcia's sake as well as John's – to blunt the sights and sounds of a dying grandmother. John was now an adult, but Greta still wanted to protect him. She wanted his memories of Marcia to be culled from the first seventeen years of his life – when Marcia was a robust, intelligent, strong-willed woman – not now, when she was wilting away.

But John was not one to stew in his grandmother's grievances. The next time he visited, he brought with him a burner phone.

Marcia was still immobilized and morose, a hooked figure lying on her bed and looking out into darkness. John ran her fingers across the buttons.

"This is how you dial us, okay?" he said. "The phone is prepaid so you don't have to worry about a calling plan or any of that. Anytime you want to hear my voice or talk to my mom, you give us a call. Okay?"

"Okay," Marcia agreed, and she hugged the phone towards her body. "Thank you Johnny."

When John left that afternoon, he was certain that he'd solved at least one of Marcia's problems. She would no longer be as separated from them as she'd been before. His voice could be as close as she wanted it to be, with a device he had instructed her how to use – a device she kept close to her body.

This is why John was surprised that she never used the phone. Instead, he was the only one to use it – almost three months later.

# CHAPTER THIRTY

*September 4, 2017*

Grandparents were supposed to die. John knew this to be true even though he'd never had any experience with an ailing grandparent before. The problem was that he felt cheated by the whole thing. With two remarried parents, he was supposed to be swimming in grandparents – and yet he was about to go from one to zero.

There was no living grandfather on either side of the family, not that he knew of. His new stepmom's parents ignored him, as he was basically an adult when they came into his life. His stepfather Tuck had no parents. And then there was Johanna Wagner – a woman whose virtues were extolled in all of Greta's stories, the woman for whom he was named. And yet, much like other fabled legends, this woman had never materialized, nor did John know anything about her that had taken place in the last twenty years. Johanna was flawless simply because of her lack of existence – her perfection about as realistic as that of a storybook character. It was only pigheadedness and pride that kept John from meeting his grandmother, Greta always insisted. It was not the older woman's fault.

This left Marcia Brock. Marcia was John's only link to the older generation...and now she was dying. For the first seventeen years of his life, John observed Marcia from a distance. They saw each other infrequently, and when they spoke on the phone, Marcia talked about hobbies that held no interest for him at all – bird watching, gardening and book clubs. It had taken a medical catastrophe and a move for Marcia to fully come into his life, for them to see their common ground and enjoy time together.

Now their time was getting more and more shallow; John could see it every time he visited. Some days Marcia was fully engaged and some days she just lay on her bed and stared out the window while he read to her – the occasional nod or smile her only gesture.

The end was coming soon for Marcia, and they both knew it, and this unavoidable truth made John alternatively morose and enraged. He had always pictured death as a sudden clap – a flicker to black – the way it always seemed to go in the movies.

Instead, for Marcia it was a gradual decay – the glaringly tedious fading away – during which time her skin became alabaster and her pain was only muted by the regular intake of pills.

Every time John visited her throughout the month of August and into September, he wondered, *is this going to be the day*? And the constant questioning and wondering about the inevitable also drove him a little crazy.

Hours at the auto shop were the worst. John had too much time inside his head, too much time to attend to his thoughts. He wasn't even surprised when Mitchell Davis called him into his office and questioned him about his attitude of late.

"What is it?" Mitchell asked. "What's going on? Can you tell me? The guys think you're going to blow your brains out."

"I'm not going to blow my brains out," John said as he stared down at the floor. It was too personal to explain to someone like Mitchell and not a conversation he wanted to have anyway. He ran his finger across the spongy orange cushion of his chair.

"Is it girl trouble?" Mitchell asked.

"Huh?"

"What's troubling you? Is it over a girl?"

"Oh…um, no."

"School work?"

John shook his head.

"Family issues then?"

John didn't say anything.

"John, is the matter that's troubling you about your family?" Mitchell insisted.

"Yeah, I guess you could say that." John could feel the tears well up and he wiped his eyes with the back of his hand. He didn't want to let go in Mitchell's office, not in front of this man that he barely knew on a personal level, not with the line of cars and customers waiting just outside for him.

Mitchell leaned back, grabbed a tissue box and tossed it over his desk to John. John looked at the box but refrained from taking a tissue. He was able to stem the tide, to keep the tears from falling.

"What's going on with your family?" Mitchell asked.

"Just…there's something bad that's going to happen…and I guess I'm just waiting for it to happen," John said.

"Oh. Huh. This…thing you mention…is it illegal?"

"No."

"Is it something you want to talk to me about?"

"No."

"Do you want to take some time off of work to deal with it?"

"No."

"Well, great talking with you John. I wish you weren't such a chatterbox but…you know…we can work on that."

Mitchell smiled but John kept his focus on the floor – nervous that if he looked up, he wouldn't be able to control whatever muscle was preventing a stream of tears.

"Can I go back to work now?" John asked. "I was working on a car that needed new brakes and the customer is hanging out in the waiting room until I finish."

"Sure, John. Go right ahead."

John stood up and tried to walk out of there as normally as possible. He didn't want to brood, to languish, to make a display out of his emotions. Apparently he had been doing enough of that at work.

As John sauntered back to his workstation he thought he could hear Mitchell yell out: "Let me know if you need anything!" but the cacophony of sounds made it impossible to be sure.

# CHAPTER THIRTY-ONE

*September 7, 2017*

There was nothing particularly unusual about the morning the Carpenter family disappeared. Greta woke up early, cooked breakfast for the family and sat at the table in jeans and a sweatshirt while she drank coffee and read emails on her phone. Olivia emerged first – her fine blonde hair matted against her head, her Minnie Mouse pajamas billowing out from her tiny frame.

"Is Daddy awake?" Olivia asked as she claimed a seat at the table.

Greta shook her head but Tuck soon proved her wrong. "I'm awake," a deep voice grunted from behind the doorway and then Tuck stumbled into the kitchen to pour himself a cup of coffee. Greta could feel the kitchen floor shudder beneath his tread as he grabbed a plate of eggs and then sat down with them.

Breakfast lasted about ten minutes – its usual length of time. Tuck wolfed down his food and hastened out the door to work.

Greta and Olivia lingered a short while longer but there were errands to run, appointments to keep. Greta was just about to clear the table and start the day when the phone rang.

***

John Brock's hollow, broken voice was on the other end. "It's me," he said. "Grandmother's gone."

Greta swallowed hard and thought about the right words to say to him. It surprised her that she was trembling a little – as though she hadn't spent the past several months anticipating this call. Maybe because she had expected the news would come from Elizabeth or one of the caretakers at the assisted living home – not John. Maybe because there were recent days where Marcia seemed okay, almost jaunty and energized, and it had fooled Greta into thinking there was more time.

"I'm so sorry John," Greta said.

"She passed away this morning," John continued, providing details Greta had forgotten to ask. "I was here with her. Dad too. She must have known. As she was lying there, she was saying all kinds of things."

"Really? Like what?" Greta asked.

"She told me she was sorry," John said, his voice breaking.

"Sorry for what?"

"For one thing, she said she should have given me the money for The Jefferson School years ago. And she apologized to Dad too – said she was too strict when he was younger and should have been nicer to him. And she said we're her two favorite people and she can't choose between the two of us, and she's sorry she did it this way. We kept asking, 'Sorry you did what this way?' And then she'd say in this weird voice that she was sorry she made it a race, that she never wanted it to be a race. And she said there was a sailboat. She kept talking about a sailboat. Sometimes it was us on the sailboat, sometimes it was Dad and his new family and sometimes it was the characters from *Treasure Island*. Dad said she was having hallucinations."

Greta leaned against the wall and closed her eyes. There was a lump in the back of her throat large enough to taste.

"Mom? Are you still there?"

"I'm still here," Greta said. "What do you think she meant by all of that?"

"I have no idea. Oh and also…she gave us both a picture – a drawing – said she had spent months working on it before she lost her vision, that it had to be perfect, and that it was hard to do. She said she just asked her caretaker to make a photocopy – one for me and one for Dad."

Greta kept her eyes closed and thought about the afternoon on Marcia's portico when the older woman had given John a drawing. It would have been seven years ago – maybe more. Greta remembered how John had regarded that drawing – the promise of a gift, more valuable to him than the gift itself. She remembered how John had solved a puzzle that Greta wasn't even aware existed. And finally, she remembered how the sun shined down that day – blanketing their skin in slatted shades, the older woman hurling demands at her butlers.

"Mom?"

Greta cleared her throat and brought herself back. "What's the drawing of?" she asked.

Greta felt like she could sense John grinning. "Well, Grandmother drew a picture of her house. The lake is behind it, and there's a gazebo and the house has all these columns and there are all these gardens. The one she actually drew was in color. Dad got that version. They gave me the photocopy."

Greta thought about the woman's house. It would have been impossible for her to recreate such an image in a two-dimensional way, even with fully functioning eyesight. There were too many details, too many floors, too much granite, marble and ivory, and too much color.

"That's very nice," Greta said, because she couldn't think of what else to say.

"But here's the thing about having the photocopy…" John continued. "I can see it. It's almost easier for me, I think. I can see what she wanted us to see."

"What she wanted you to see?" Greta asked. "What do you mean?"

"There's numbers in the picture, four of them, and she overlaid them with the portrait of Alden Brock that hangs in the drawing room. And then, at the bottom of the portrait, she wrote the word *safe*."

Greta could feel her heart beating faster. "What do you mean, numbers? What are you saying?"

"Numbers: 39, 20, 53, 76. I can see them, just as clearly as I saw my birthday in the drawing she made for me years ago. And below the numbers is the word *safe*."

"Listen…listen to me…" Greta took several labored breaths between her words. It was all becoming clear to her as her heart beat furiously, and her legs felt rubbery, like they could no longer support her body.

Those numbers etched on a depiction of a painting in her home, talk of a sailboat whose occupants could have been John's family or Griffin's family, a race between John and Griffin, a puzzle that both of them could solve. Greta wasn't sure if she was deciphering or inventing, if she was lucid or delirious.

As her thoughts churned, she felt like she was creating a portrait of a fable, or perhaps a television drama – a life foreign to Greta's. But then again, hadn't Marcia's life always been unfamiliar to Greta? The excessiveness of it all, the extreme luxury…was there anything that Marcia's money couldn't buy? Greta felt her throat constrict.

"Mom?" John asked.

"Yes," Greta said, but her voice sounded foreign. "Did you say your father got the same drawing?"

In her mind, she heard the older woman's voice – shrill and singsong, sweeping across the patio. *Your father used to love these kind of puzzles* she had said to John. *He could always find all the hidden pieces.*

"Yeah," John said. "Actually, he got the original and I got the photocopy."

"How long ago was this?"

"I don't know. Maybe twenty or thirty minutes."

"Okay, let's go. We need to move. Now! John, stay there and we'll pick you up." Greta stayed on the phone a second longer and waited. She waited for John to ask her why they had to hurry or where they were headed, but he did neither. He said a quick good-bye and they hung up the phone.

\*\*\*

The drive up I-55 North felt surreal to Greta. There wasn't much to look at outside her window – farms and cornfields mostly, with occasional rest stops dotted along the way. In the back seat, John dozed while Olivia massaged the white-blonde hair of a doll that she kept in the car.

Typically, their car conversations were lively affairs, with everyone talking over everyone else, competing for airtime. But this morning was different, since the weight of uncertainly hung above them.

They had packed up and left as though their entire lives before were just a prologue. And the aspect that bothered Greta the most was that it could all have been fiction – a dream shaped by her vast imagination, fed to her through her son via his grandmother, who had lost all of her faculties in quick succession and was on the brink of her own demise.

Just as Greta could imagine the de-masking of a wall, the opening of a safe, the discovery of cash and maybe directions to a sailboat, she could also imagine a different outcome: a safe that didn't want to open or that didn't exist in the first place, or an angry ex-husband who had raced past her to the holy grail and emphatically laid claim. She could imagine a return to their home on Avery – forlorn faces and demoralized spirits. And in this, possibly more realistic version of the tale, she would emerge as the cheerleader like she always did. At least Grandmother knew the love they felt for her. At least the old woman had tried to right some wrongs in the end. Wasn't that more important than the fulfillment of a pot of gold at the end of a rainbow?

It was this moment of looking out the car window and imagining the pep talk Greta would possibly have to give to her family when John spoke up from the back seat.

"I...uh...left my cell phone at home," he said. "I forgot to bring it to Grandmother's and I'm guessing you guys didn't pack it for me."

"I threw a bunch of your clothes into a bag for you," Tuck said. "But I didn't come across your cell phone."

"Great," John said.

Tuck then chuckled and started patting his pockets with his left hand while still steering the car with his right. Eventually he switched which hand was doing the patting and which was steering. After a minute or so, he turned his head to the right and glanced at Greta. "I left mine at the house too," he said. "I always seem to forget it when I need it the most, don't I?"

Greta pulled her phone from her jacket pocket and stared down. Her phone was old – seven years at least – and its age gave way to its inability to keep battery power. That particular morning, even after an all-night charging session, the phone's battery had expired sometime earlier on the drive.

"I think we are officially off the grid," Greta said.

"Mom, people survived for years without cell phones," John offered from the back seat.

"Not that you would remember," Greta responded. Then she placed the lifeless phone back in her pocket and resumed the job of looking outside the window. She tried to be optimistic, to envision everything going as planned -- but there was one thought that kept pulling her back, a nag that had originated in the rushing current from the house and was now made bigger by their apparent lack of a communications device.

"Tuck ..." Greta said. "You sent an email to your office, telling them you might be gone for awhile, didn't you?"

"Oh sure," Tuck said. "Yeah, I did. I think so."

"You think so or you actually did?"

"I did, I did. I'm sure of it. I mean, who knows how long we'll actually be gone though."

Greta sighed and tried not to analyze whether there was a tremble in his voice, a cadence that drew the end of his statement to a high note, his giveaway for uncertainty.

She needed to restrain herself from this exercise because the conjuring of worst-case scenarios was an ugly habit of hers – probably from the time that John was a child and she projected abduction scenarios every time he took a ride on his bicycle.

Besides, wasn't this worst-case scenario that she was thinking about wrapped up neatly in their best-case scenario? In the best possible case, all of her irrational musings came true and the Carpenters became wealthy seafaring nomads. In the most likely scenario, they returned to Avery Place within the next day or so, returned to their usual routines and had a story that was at the same time slightly embarrassing and highly entertaining. *The time they followed Greta's whimsical imaginings.*

Greta turned on the radio and focused on the music. She didn't want to think about the future, the logistics, the mistakes she may or may not have already made. She just wanted to look at America's rolling farmland, to revisit all the poignant memories of Marcia Brock from the past year, and to allow the future to unfold as it was going to happen.

*** 

Marcia's home was locked when the Carpenter family arrived, but Greta knew where to find the key. It was hidden in the same spot as eighteen years earlier – underneath the third stone in the path that led to the beach.

Greta opened the front door and the rest of her family sprinted through as though propelled by a giant gust of wind. John was first and then Tuck, with Olivia hoisted on his hip.

"Slow down!" Greta called after them, but she sprang up the steps just a few feet behind.

Upstairs, she made a right and went into the drawing room. John and Tuck had just removed the portrait of Alden Brock from the wall and all three of them sighed in unison when they beheld the shiny gray rectangle of metal on the wall.

"So there is a safe," John whispered and then he got to work rotating the dial. Every time he reached a number, he whispered it out loud before turning the dial the other way. Tuck and Olivia stared at John while Greta tried to calm herself by focusing on the recently removed portrait. She looked at Alden and studied his features – long, pointed nose, saucer-shaped eyebrows. It was an ample distraction for the period of time when the only noise in the room was the whisper of numbers and the whirring of metal.

At last, there was a clank and the safe door opened. Another sigh in the room – this one more like a collective gasp. John reached inside and started taking things out, narrating as he handed each item to Tuck.

"This is a photo of a sailboat," John said. "And this looks like a map of a marina. Here are instructions for a boat...thr---...thr--...throttle. This is a picture of a reserved parking space at the marina. These must be the keys to the boat. Oh, and here's a page where Grandmother wrote: The Boat is Stocked. Go Have an Adventure like Jim Hawkins."

John held up a piece of paper with his grandmother's instructions spooled across the page in red ink.

"Is there anything else?" Greta asked, her voice shaking.

"Oh yeah, further back." John stretched forward until the safe had entirely consumed his arm. When he reemerged, he was clasping a burlap sack the size of a laundry bag. John looked inside and started laughing. "It's money," he said giddily. Then he stared inside the bag for a bit longer before carefully handing the bag to Tuck. His laugh became sharper, more vigorous, almost delirious. "It's Benjamins!" John declared. "A shitload of Benjamins!"

Tuck placed the papers and the keys on the floor and used two hands to open the bag wider. He superficially sorted through the items near the top and allowed a few bundles of wrapped bills to topple out. "Greta, there must be hundreds of thousands of dollars in here!" Tuck said. "Maybe more!"

Greta realized then that her heart was pounding. She tried to calm herself, to steady her respirations, to find stamina in her wobbly legs. She knew that this moment was critically important – the crucible for the family's future course, and she wanted to make sure her decisions were rational.

"Are we sure we can consider all of this ours?" Greta asked. "Grandmother never explicitly said it was for us."

Tuck glanced up from the bag with a stoic expression but John looked distraught by this suggestion. "Mom, of course this is for us!" he said. "Grandmother gave us the picture with the clues and apologized for making it a race. She even mentioned the sailboat. It's a race and we won!"

Greta shook her head. "But instead of rushing out to the marina, should we stick around for a bit? Maybe tidy things up back at home, maybe show our respect at Grandmother's funeral, since she's done so much for us? We can take the sailboat out after."

"No," John insisted. "Grandmother didn't leave us a note telling us to attend her funeral. She left us a note telling us to go have an adventure on the sailboat."

"Greta, I know this is going to sound strange but I agree with John." Tuck said. "Just because we got here first, I wouldn't consider the race to be over. If Griffin discovers any of this, he'll claim the rights to it. He'll tie us up in probate court. It's better to ask forgiveness than permission, right? If we want our sailboat adventure, we have to take it now."

Greta looked at the faces of her family members: Tiny Olivia, who was looking around while sucking on her index finger – oblivious to the conversation around her. John, who was calm and hopeful, staring at his mother with a tacit but desperate expression. And then there was Tuck, who pressed his lips together while he dug deeper into the bag of cash.

"Okay," Greta said at last. "Okay."

# CHAPTER THIRTY-TWO

*September 18, 2017*

Marcia Brock's funeral was simple and elegant. Griffin sat in the front row next to his wife and infant son. When the time came, he trotted up the stairs, stood behind a podium and delivered a moving eulogy about a caring mother who had lived a full and rich life.

There were other tales as well. Marcia's longtime closest friend stood up and told stories from Marcia's college years – well kept secrets of playfulness and mirth, pranks that Marcia had participated in, which kept the funeral-goers amused.

There were five speakers in all, and the common thread across all of the exaltations was that Marcia was benevolent and charitable. She gave profusely and without any expectation of reward or recognition.

When all the eulogies were done, when Marcia's memory had been invoked and her spirit had been blessed, a few of the closer family members gathered around her gravesite and watched as her coffin was lowered into the ground. One of Griffin's cousins asked about John's absence but Griffin just shrugged it off. "Teenagers," was his response. Until that moment, he hadn't given much thought to his older son. There had been too many other matters to think about.

It was a perfect mid-September day – sunny sky, light autumn breeze that caused a rustle in the branches – although Griffin still shivered as he watched the box go into the earth.

After the gravesite ceremony came coffee, pastries, petite fours and light appetizers at a relative's house in Evanston, Illinois. Griffin walked from room to room while his wife tended to the baby upstairs. He felt like the mayor of the funeral, the way that everyone came up to him – not just to offer their condolences but to regale him with stories. After an hour, he could feel the suspension of his face – cheeks frozen into a half smile, voice nearly hoarse from saying "uh-huh, uh-huh" so many times.

Finally, there was refuge in the laundry room. Griffin stood next to the washing machine and stared at a pile of folded clothes. At last there were no suppliant people, no stories from decades earlier, nothing he needed to respond to. There was just the emptiness inside and the muffled chatter that leaked in underneath the door.

Griffin thought he might stay in there for a while – after all, he had his cell phone with him and could always feign a work emergency – but the door trembled and then an obese, bearded bald man stepped inside.

"Thought I might find you here," the man said.

"Please," Griffin said. "I just need a few moments to be alone."

"You don't recognize me but we've met before," the man said, and he extended his right hand. His fingers were chubby, with dark sprouts of hair, and what looked like a class ring was strangling his ring finger. "I'm Wade Wilson, your mother's estate attorney."

"Oh right, right," Griffin shook the man's hand, and tried to avoid the sensation that his hand was being swallowed by the grasp of Wade Wilson.

Wade smiled. "I'm sorry to chase you down like this but I'm about to leave town for a week and I thought you might like a back of the envelope estimate. Again, this is just our best estimate so the final number will be a few off in either direction."

"Oh right, of course. I'd like to hear," Griffin said. He tried not to appear too eager to hear the numbers, like a kid about to receive a prize or a grown man about to hear the much-awaited details of his inheritance.

Wade unwrapped a sheet of paper from his pocket. "Naturally, all of her holdings, bank accounts and real estate were left to the trust, which lists you as sole beneficial owner. We estimate the house on Lake Michigan will sell for $7 million and that, combined with the rest of it, leaves a total of $8.5 million."

Wade placed the paper back in his pocket and waited. Griffin knew that this was the moment he was supposed to smile and give a muted cheer – his ebullience restricted by the gravity of the situation. But even though the number was high on an absolute level, it was still low based on his expectations.

Griffin had been entertaining dreams of unlimited wealth – where men made donations in the range of several million and had buildings and libraries named after them. He had dreams of multiple residences across cities – Aspen, Ibiza, New York and Pacific Palisades. All these visions would now have to be tamped down and reshaped. He could still be a player, but not in the manner he'd been expecting.

"You look disappointed," Wade said.

Griffin frowned. "I guess I didn't realize that nearly all of her net worth was wrapped up in the Lake Michigan house. What about the Hamptons house? My parents owned a house by the water in Southampton where I used to play when I was a child."

"Marcia sold it – years ago – and I think most of the proceeds went to charity."

Griffin sniffed and nodded. Of course, his mother had been charitable – hugely, extravagantly charitable, at the expense of her trust and her heirs. That had been the reigning theme of her funeral after all – tales of giving to children's hospitals, animal shelters and political campaigns. Ironically, just as she was ever eager to give to established charities, she was quite stingy when it came to family members.

Griffin had been given a starter loan for his real estate business but only after he'd promised to make her a silent partner. She funded some of his real estate ventures, but she expected to be compensated as though she were a venture capitalist sitting on the Board, an arms-length financier who demanded smart investments.

And now Griffin knew – if Marcia's final, bizarre ramblings were to be believed – that Greta had come to Marcia asking for money for John to attend The Jefferson School back in 2010, and that she'd been turned down. Most likely Marcia had used the same refrain that she'd repeated to Griffin his entire life – handouts made you lazy, lethargic and robbed you of the zest to work for yourself. Meanwhile, Winnetka Animal Shelter had received an enormous donation that year. It was Marcia's money, and Marcia's prerogative to spend how she pleased, but in Griffin's view, the allocations didn't always make sense.

"What about the safe?" Griffin asked. "The one behind the painting in the study."

"We got to the house right after we took your call. Our agents opened the safe and…I'm sorry to say Griffin…there was nothing inside," Wade said.

Griffin nodded and took a deep breath. He remained in the same position but darted his eyes across to the far edge of the room…until he was staring at a pile of old towels on the floor.

"Is that not what you expected?" Wade asked.

"I don't know what I expected," Griffin said with a shrug, his eyes still lowered. "The safe was something that I always knew about, but never knew the details. My mother would make reference to it but only in jest or passing. If I had to guess, I think that at various times it probably had cash…although who knows."

"Griffin, your mother had three quarters of a million dollars in a checking account, and more in mutual funds. That's all part of the trust that will go to you. I don't know why…"

Wade's voice trailed off and Griffin wasn't sure whether he had censored himself or not come up with the right wording.

"What about the car?" Griffin asked. "My mother drove an Aston Martin. Have you searched the car?"

"No, we haven't searched the car," Wade said. "I don't have the keys on me, but stop by the office tomorrow, we'll get you the keys and you can do a search if you like."

"Okay, thanks Wade. I appreciate it," Griffin said. He was partially sweating now, a film of perspiration that treaded across his forehead and behind the ears. He knew he looked a little crazy and he felt that way too. Maybe the tragedy of his mother's passing would afford a bit of leeway when Wade spoke about him to his colleagues. Maybe his mother's passing had clouded his thinking and confused his memories.

Here he was, grasping at intangibles, as tenuous as air, and hoping to spin straw into gold. What he didn't know how to explain was that it wasn't just the number…the number could have been eight figures, or nine or ten. It was that lifetime dream of the safe – that moment the metal clacked and the door opened. It was the fabled riches beyond the door that he had spent years thinking about, that seemed to get larger, more exotic with each deliberation.

And wasn't it just fitting that the safe had been completely empty? His mother wouldn't have been able to fulfill any of these lavish, puerile fantasies and so she'd left it empty for him and moved all of her wealth into interest-bearing electronic accounts. Wasn't that the intelligent thing to do?

He just needed to accept it, to override the drone in his mind that something was wrong, something wasn't adding up, and accept the number. The temperature in this laundry room seemed to be rising with each minute, or maybe the problem was his proximity to Wade Wilson, who seemed to be absorbing all the oxygen in the room, leaving little space and air for Griffin.

Griffin wiped his forehead with the back of his hand and was surprised to find it dripping. Those towels in the corner now seemed like more than just an eye fixture; they were a downy comfort when he felt close to passing out, a source of dryness when he needed to look presentable. As he toddled towards the back corner of the room, he could sense Wade reaching an arm out to him, an attempt to bring him back.

"Hey man," Wade said. "Are you okay?"

Griffin picked up one of the towels and wiped it across his face. He closed his eyes and felt the flicker of darkness, the cool soft threads against his tingling skin.

Everything felt okay again and everything would be all right. The number was more than sufficient to provide for his family for a lifetime. He might or might not search the Aston Martin once all of Marcia's assets were turned over to him, but whatever he found or didn't find would be just fine.

"I'm okay," Griffin finally answered, and he listened to his own words echo around the small room. "Let's get back out there, okay? I'm fine."

# CHAPTER THIRTY-THREE

*October 13, 2017*

Detective Hobbs blinked underneath the florescent lighting of the police station. She had been sitting at her desk for an hour already, reviewing files and reports that she'd already reviewed, waiting for that moment when something new would jump out at her – something she'd missed during the first iteration.

Outside the wind was howling – so loud she could hear its squeal from her desk. Branches tapped at their windows – newly bare from the loss of foliage. Hobbs tried not to be distracted. She bent her neck and brought her eyes to the top line of the page, which was a report from the interrogation of Griffin Brock. She needed to focus, to clear her head, to read every line as though she'd never read it before.

A bang caught Hobbs's attention, and as she lifted her head, she saw that Colt Bundy had ripped through the front door of the police station. He was wearing jeans and a Cardinals jersey, his hair mottled with grease or sweat. He was waving a piece of paper frantically.

"Detective Hobbs! Detective Hobbs!" Colt yelled. "Where are you? I have something for you!"

Hobbs could see Colt freeze on the tips of his toes and search the station. His eyes were roving anxiously across the room as if taking inventory. Hobbs stood up and they locked eyes on each other at the same time.

Colt trotted to her desk, unfolded the piece of paper he'd been strangling and held it in front of her. "It's a letter from Greta," Colt said, his voice stabilizing from its previous hysterical pitch. "She sent it two weeks ago from Manitoulin Island. Here's the envelope. Look at the postmark." Colt produced an envelope from his pocket and pointed to the black scrawling across the postage stamp.

At this point, a small crowd had formed around Hobbs's desk. Adams and Martinez walked over. Even Weaver emerged from his office and stood next to Colt. "What's going on?" Weaver asked.

"Colt Bundy is a private investigator," Hobbs said. "He says he received a letter from Greta Carpenter and that the family is in…Mani….?" Roberta gave Colt a quizzical look and the private investigator finished her sentence.

"Manitoulin Island; it's in Ontario, Canada, along the lake," Colt said. "They're sailing."

"Why did she write a letter to you?" Weaver asked.

"It's not meant for me; the letter is to her mother, who she asked me to track down."

Colt reversed the sheet of paper and pointed to black scrawling. *Colt, please find my mother, Johanna Wagner, and send this letter to her. When I get back to town, I will pay you whatever cost. All My Best, Greta.*

Hobbs recognized Greta's handwriting – the lettering in black felt tip on the dry erase board in Greta's kitchen, the name with the curvy, looping G she'd used to sign the report in the traffic file.

"They're sailing," Weaver repeated.

Hobbs wasn't sure he had asked a question but Colt answered as though it was. "Yes, they've been on a sailboat this whole time. I don't even think they know they're missing."

"How does the Carpenter family have a sailboat?" Adams asked.

Martinez pulled out his phone and keyed *Manitoulin Island* into the maps feature. "It's on Lake Huron," he said. "If someone is after them, maybe they thought this was the best way to hide out for awhile."

"No one is after them," Colt said decisively. "I read the letter. Marcia Brock gifted them the sailboat and now they're having an adventure."

Hobbs smiled vaguely at Colt and then took a seat in her chair. She felt like her brain was suspended and swimming at the same time – looking back and looking ahead, and reconsidering every conclusion she had reached thus far. All this time – and with every similar case – their job was to figure out who the missing people were running from. Who was chasing them? What were they trying to avoid? It was the default position for anyone in law enforcement to get to the crime.

But in this case, the Carpenter family wasn't running from anything or anyone. They were running *towards*....towards the completion of Marcia Brock's conceptions, towards an opportunity that fastened the family together.

There was still a lot about the story that Hobbs didn't know. Why did the family have to leave in such a hurry? Was it Marcia Brock who called from a burner phone, and who gave it to her?

Later that evening, as she nestled next to Adams under the warmth of her bedspread, they relayed their lingering questions and talked about possible theories. Any number of reasons made sense, and the only thing that kept Hobbs from going mad with ambiguity was the idea that Greta Carpenter and family would return to Vetta Park at some point. Hobbs didn't know it for certain, but she believed it to be true. In the meantime, Weaver would assign another case to Martinez and Hobbs… and the days of interrogating, investigating and deliberating would continue like they always had.

Except that one thing was different. Hobbs turned out the light and crept closer to the warm body next to hers. Her relationship with Adams was no longer a secret, held together by surreptitious meetings and repeated avowals for discretion. Their coupling was an open story, a connection that grew stronger as it was made more real.

Adams reached for her in the dark and drew her closer to him. In the darkness she could only make out the faintest trace of his chest and torso. But she could feel his breath against her forehead, the tightness of his clasp as he whispered to her: "Good night Roberta, I love you."

Hobbs smiled and hugged him tighter. "Good night Dean. I love you too."

# CHAPTER THIRTY-FOUR

*Dear Mom,*

*I'm so sorry that it has taken me all this time to write you this letter. I wish I'd reached out to you years ago. Here is what I've wanted to say to you for so long.*

*I walked away from you when I was 16 because I was angry and proud – angry that things were hard for me that came so easily to others, and too proud to turn around when I realized I was wrong. And how I was wrong! The first night away from you, I found a bed in a homeless shelter for teens in St. Louis, after hours of wandering the streets.*

*I was so scared, Mom. I missed you so much. I slept right by an open window and every time a breeze blew in, I imagined it was you. You were watching me, lying next to me, blowing air on me to comfort my pain – like you used to do when I was a kid. Your brown hair tied back in a ponytail, your long arms secured around me. I cried myself to sleep that night, but it was silent kind, the kind of crying you do when you realize you're on your own, your mother is not really there to comfort you.*

*I wanted so badly to turn around and go home…but I was afraid of what you'd say and what I'd have to confess – that I was wrong, that I'd made a mistake. So I stayed gone.*

*But here's the thing. I always missed you and I always thought about you. Every morning, I woke up and tried to smell the pancakes you used to make in the morning. I always brewed a cup of green tea at 4 o'clock in the afternoon, just how you liked it. I started singing the silly rabbit song you used to sing to yourself all the time. You see, I kept you with me – in my thoughts, in my songs, in how I raised my children. You don't know it but you were right there with me the whole time.*

*I know these little rituals and relics don't substitute for you actually being there. You should have been with me for all of it, Mom, and that's my fault and I'm so sorry. I should have said these words in 1995 but I'm finally writing them now. I don't want to look in the direction of Southwest Missouri and wonder which of the smoke plumes coming from a chimney in the far distance might belong to your house. I want to know.*

*So, on to the present. We do have time, Mom. I really believe that. We have the whole future to make up for lost time.*

*I'm currently sailing the Great Lakes on a little adventure, courtesy of my former mother-in-law. But at some point the weather will change and we'll head back to Missouri. The first thing I'm going to do when I walk in the door will be to be to find you and make amends. We will have all the long talks we never had, share all the photographs, re-live all the milestones. You can meet my husband Tuck, and my kids John and Olivia. We can start again.*

*I will come home this time, Mom, I promise.*

*I love you.*

*Your Daughter,*
*Greta*

Greta rested her pen on the table and went up the tiny staircase. John was sitting on a cushioned seat at the edge of the boat, reading a book out loud, while Olivia stretched out next to him and listened attentively.

Tuck was behind the wheel of the boat – a self-proclaimed skipper. Sailing was a pastime he'd learned one summer as a teenager, but he was surprised to find it wasn't difficult to pick up again – especially now that they were further away from the crowded Chicago shoreline.

In a few days they'd be at Manitoulin Island and then Greta would mail the letter. In the meantime, she could finally relax. Greta reclined on a cushioned divan opposite her children and felt the dips and bobs of the current beneath her. She fell asleep to the gentle resonance of her son's voice, and when she opened her eyes again, all she could see was the sky.

# ABOUT THE AUTHOR

Jillian Thomadsen grew up in Baltimore, and has lived in Virginia, New York City and Los Angeles before finally settling in St. Louis, MO. A former finance professional, Jillian now spends her time chasing after her three active boys and repairing all the damage they've inflicted to her house.

Jillian first got the writing bug at age seven, and has been honing her craft ever since. She has written for *Sophisticated Living, ADDitude, ScaryMommy, Today Parenting* and *BusinessWeek*. *All the Hidden Pieces* is her first novel.

Get on the mailing list! Please contact Jillian at jillianthomadsen@gmail.com or Twitter: @JillianA_T

# ACKNOWLEDGEMENTS

It would be impossible to fully acknowledge everyone who supported me throughout this process but I'm going to give it a shot.

First of all, my beta readers Nicole Oppenheimer and Cara Goldberg. Thank you a million times over. Your advice was invaluable and improved the book tremendously.

Thanks to Melissa Abrams who put together a project plan that I diligently followed once I decided (6 months later but who's counting) to actually stick my neck out and self-publish. I'd have been lost without your guidance.

To all of my friends who helped throughout the way: Jen Jim, Robyn LeBoeuf, Jackie Jarvis and Michele Weiss, who put me in touch with their author friends or other people in the publishing world that they knew. Thanks to Becky Marbarger who assured me an unyielding social media campaign when I revealed my social media inhibitions.

Thank you to Carrie Edelstein for giving me my first shot in print publishing and to Paul Hollis who spent awhile on the phone with me detailing the ropes.

I can't give thanks enough to the dyslexia community who has supported me, particularly Jayme Fingerman who continues to help me chart my course, and of course the teachers and staff at the wonderful Churchill School, who have given me hope for my child's future literacy after years of struggle. Thanks in particular to Dan Carney.

I'd like to thank Amy Wagner and Amanda Luft, who advised me and gave me that final push to actually do this. Also Jenny Kissel, Rekha Ramanuja, Jane Curry, Jessica Garnreiter,

Tim Gabrielle, Stephanie Dahl, the Hellmanns, Lori Siegel and Sarah Glasser for their support along the way.

And of course, my family – those who have read the book and those who have simply provided guidance, support and babysitting: Mom, Dad, Judy, Chris, Laura, all my in-laws, and of course those immediate family members who have to put up with me every day: Andrew, Ryan, Josh and of course my amazing and supportive husband Raphael. Thanks to all of you.

Made in USA - Crawfordsville, IN
30731_9781986534697
09.02.2021 1426